Abducted by the Highlander

Daughters of the Isle
Book 3

Christina Phillips

DRAGONBLADE PUBLISHING, INC.

ARE YOU SIGNED UP FOR DRAGONBLADE'S BLOG?

You'll get the latest news and information on exclusive giveaways, exclusive excerpts, coming releases, sales, free books, cover reveals and more.

Check out our complete list of authors, too!

No spam, no junk. That's a promise!

Sign Up Here

www.dragonbladepublishing.com

⟁

Dearest Reader;

Thank you for your support of a small press. At Dragonblade Publishing, we strive to bring you the highest quality Historical Romance from some of the best authors in the business. Without your support, there is no 'us', so we sincerely hope you adore these stories and find some new favorite authors along the way.

Happy Reading!

CEO, Dragonblade Publishing

Additional Dragonblade books by Author Christina Phillips

Daughters of the Isle
Beguiled by the Highlander (Book 1)
Deceived by the Highlander (Book 2)
Abducted by the Highlander (Book 3)

Dedication

With all my love to
Vincent, Jack, Tommy, Harry & Cooper
Grandbabies are the best invention ever!

PROLOGUE

Isle of Eigg, December 1565

"I S IT ANOTHER walk ye want, my darling lad?" Roisin MacDonald smiled indulgently at her beloved terrier, who panted excitedly at the prospect of a third escape from the castle today. In truth, she was as eager as her sweet Ecne to take advantage of the break in the weather. The storms that had buffeted the Isle of Eigg over the last few days had finally blown themselves out over the sea, leaving the air bright and crisp.

No wonder her eldest sister, Isolde, hadn't wasted any time in taking her mysterious stranger from the sea, Njord, up to the peak of An Sgurr, the magnificent ridge that defined Eigg, in the shadow of which Sgur Castle nestled.

Their young maid, Grear, handed her gloves to her. Roisin smiled in gratitude as they left the castle and entered the courtyard. Isolde had discovered an unconscious Njord on their beach a week ago. Although the poor man had no memory of who he was, Roisin knew in her heart that it didn't matter, for anyone could see he and her sister belonged together.

Ecne raced towards the stables, barking madly at his freedom. After a glance at Grear, Roisin laughed, picked up her skirts, and they both chased after him. It wasn't until she'd caught up with him and had scooped him into her arms that she realized she and Grear were no longer alone in the courtyard.

A dozen unknown men, leading their horses, were following

Sgur's formidable warrior, Patric, as he led them to the stables. To *her*.

Frozen to the spot, Roisin clutched Ecne to her breast as the humiliating realization hit her that these strangers had just witnessed her unseemly behavior. And worse than that, she had nowhere to hide.

As he approached, Patric gave her a kindly smile but for once his familiar fatherly presence didn't ease her disquiet. How could it, when she was the focus of twelve strange men who eyed her with varying degrees of interest?

"Lady Roisin, may I present Hugh Campbell. Hugh Campbell, ye have the honor of greeting Lady Roisin MacDonald, youngest granddaughter of Lady Helga of Sgur Castle. Lady Roisin, Hugh is searching for his missing cousin, William Campbell."

Roisin barely heard Patric's explanation over the thunder of her heart that echoed in her ears and made her feel faint with nerves. How could he put her in this situation? She never welcomed anyone to the castle. If her grandmother wasn't available, either Isolde or her other sister, Freyja, did the honors. No one ever noticed her, let alone expected her to assume any responsibility for greeting visitors.

Ecne wriggled in her arms and with deep reluctance she placed him on the ground. To her consternation, he instantly trotted up to the man who stood next to Patric and gave a welcoming bark. Before she could find her voice to admonish him, the man crouched and gave her dog a good scratch behind his ears before he stood and his gaze caught hers.

Eyes so blue they reminded her of a perfect summer sky ensnared her senses, and a delightful shimmer of warmth danced through her blood. Her breath stalled in her throat and her heart slammed against her ribs, but for a reason she couldn't fathom, she no longer wanted to sink through the ground and disappear.

Hugh Campbell gave an enchanting bow, before once again his gaze meshed with hers. "My lady, it's an honor indeed to meet ye. May I apologize for disturbing ye at this late hour."

There was no need for her to answer him. A polite smile would suffice and already Patric was moving forward with the clear intention of saving her from any awkward exchange. And yet, before she quite realized her intention, she spoke.

"There's no need to apologize, Hugh Campbell. May I welcome ye to Sgur Castle, on behalf of Lady Helga."

Patric shot her a startled glance, but she ignored him. The truth was, she could not seem to drag her bedazzled gaze from Hugh's compelling blue eyes and when he smiled at her, she entirely forgot how to breathe.

"Thank ye, Lady Roisin. Yer kindness is much appreciated."

It was a novel experience to be thanked for her kindness in welcoming a stranger to her home. Those words were always addressed to her grandmother or one of her sisters, but she had to confess it felt immeasurably wonderful to hear them directed her way from Hugh Campbell.

Ecne was still standing by Hugh's side which was extraordinary, since although her sweet lad was a friendly soul, he wasn't in the habit of taking such a sudden liking to a complete stranger. But if Ecne put such faith in Hugh, it had to be a sign that this Campbell was a trustworthy man.

She should really return to the castle. It wasn't her place to question Hugh and yet she couldn't help herself. "Ye are searching for yer cousin, William Campbell?"

"Aye. He went missing in the storm as we were returning from Skye to Oban, and we fear the worst, yet hope for a miracle that we shall find him safe and well."

Was it possible that Njord was Hugh's missing cousin? Certainly, the poor man had been half drowned when Isolde had found him upon the beach, and they all believed he had fallen overboard during the storm. And then the significance of the name occurred to her, and she gave a soft gasp.

"William Campbell, the man who is betrothed to my sister, Lady Isolde?"

"Indeed, my lady. Patric tells me there is a man with no memory of who he is staying at the castle. It is perhaps too much to hope he is my cousin, but it's possible."

"Oh, I do hope he is." She clasped her hands together at how perfect that would be. Isolde cared deeply for Njord, and she had never wanted to wed the unknown William Campbell. But if they were the one and the same man, then surely Isolde would be thrilled by how destiny had delivered her intended husband to her very feet.

"I hope so too." Hugh smiled again, and her insides melted at the sight.

"Ye and yer men must certainly stay for supper," she said before she could think better of it. What on earth had come over her, inviting strangers to stay for supper in the castle? And yet it was only something her grandmother would say, for whether or not Hugh found his cousin at Sgur, he and his men would still require hospitality.

It was simply that she had never said such a thing to anyone before.

"We should be most gratified, my lady."

Patric cleared his throat. Loudly. And she realized she was smiling at Hugh in a completely besotted manner. Heat flooded her cheeks, and she quickly inclined her head in the faint hope he might not notice. "Ye are most welcome."

Hugh bowed his head, but as he passed by her, following in Patric's wake, he turned his head her way. "I hope I'll see ye again." His voice was low, meant only for her ears, and there was no time to respond, even if she had thought of something to say. Instead, she silently admired him as he strode after Patric, leading his horse.

His midnight black hair was pulled back with a length of velvet, and surely she had never witnessed such fine, broad shoulders before on a man. As the rest of his men followed him, she hastily made her way back to the castle, and as she and Grear entered the great hall, her grandmother and Freyja greeted her.

"Campbells from Argyle," Freyja remarked. Clearly, Patric had sent a message to them before he had led the men to the stables. "Let us hope they recognize Njord and can return him to his kin."

Roisin pulled off her gloves before catching her grandmother's eye. She supposed she'd better let her know what she had done. "Amma, I invited Hugh Campbell and his men to stay for supper."

"Ye did what?" Freyja sounded astonished. Not that Roisin could blame her. "Ye spoke to them?"

"'Twas hard to avoid them." She busied herself by taking off her surcoat and handing it to Grear, so she wouldn't need to look at her sister. "I only did what Amma would have done herself."

"Ye did the right thing." Amma gave her an approving smile before turning to Grear. "Let the cook know, Grear, and see that more places are set for our guests."

Grear bobbed a curtsey before leaving the hall and Roisin went over to the hearth to warm her hands. As Amma and Freyja pondered the likelihood of whether Njord might be the missing William Campbell that Hugh sought, and Isolde's intended, no less, Roisin gazed into the flames of the fire, but all she could see in her mind's eye was Hugh's captivating smile. She dearly hoped she had the chance to talk with him again before he left Eigg.

Her daydreams were interrupted as Patric strode into the hall with Hugh and his men, and Roisin spun around from the fire as her grandmother welcomed them to the castle. Servants brought out jugs of warm mead for their guests and after giving Amma an elegant bow, Hugh came over to her.

"We meet again, my lady." His voice was low, his gaze focused entirely on her, and her cheeks heated. No man had ever sought out her company before, although to be fair she had never wanted a man's attention before. But there was something irresistible about Hugh and she had no wish to melt into the shadows the way she usually did when strangers invaded her peace.

"'Twas inevitable." Good Lord, had she really said that out loud? She had never made a teasing remark to anyone she hadn't known all her life. But it came so naturally when Hugh was standing in front of her.

Ecne pawed Hugh's boot, and he grinned before giving her dog a friendly pat. "There's a good lad." He glanced at her. "What's his name?"

"Ecne." She was inordinately thrilled Hugh paid such kind attention to her sweet lad.

Hugh cocked his head. "'Tis an unusual name."

"I named him after the god of wisdom from the Tuatha De Danann." How she loved those myths from Eire. But not everyone was aware of them. "Do ye know of the legends from Eire?"

"Not well, but I should like to learn if ye'd be willing to share them with me."

He was interested in something that fascinated her beyond reason. Could he be any more perfect?

"I would be happy to." How formal she sounded, but luckily Hugh didn't appear to notice. Encouraged by his easy charm, she added, "If ye wish, I could show ye my illuminated manuscripts of the myths."

There was no mistaking the admiration in his eyes. "Ye illuminate manuscripts? That is an impressive accomplishment, indeed."

His compliment warmed her down to her toes, and he hadn't even seen any of her work yet. Before she could think better of it, the words spilled unhindered from her lips. "Ye had best save yer kind words until I've shared them with ye."

Before he could answer, the castle doors swung open and Isolde and Njord entered. Hugh gave her a smile and bowed his head before turning around. And then he gave a sharp inhale of breath. "God's bones, William."

As Hugh strode across the hall, warmth flooded through her. Njord really was William, Isolde's betrothed, and she looked at her sister, expecting to see her own happiness at how destiny had entwined them together reflected on Isolde's face.

Her sister appeared to be stunned into silence, and a ribbon of concern flickered through Roisin. Hugh and his cousin spoke for a while and then, without warning, Isolde spun on her heel and stalked out of the castle.

That was unexpected. But she supposed it was a shock and Isolde simply needed a few moments to herself. As Njord, or, rather, William, strode after her, Amma called her personal guard over, but Roisin's attention was fixed on Hugh, who now stood alone.

She glanced at her grandmother, who was deep in conversation with both Freyja and her guard, before returning her attention to Hugh. Was she truly contemplating going to his side and striking up another conversation?

Before she could change her mind, she slowly made her way in his direction. She was still some distance from him when he turned to face her, almost as though he'd been aware of her stealthy approach and she came to an abrupt halt at the harsh expression on his face. Trepidation inched through her. What if he wanted to be alone?

But when he caught sight of her, he smiled, and her apprehension dissolved.

"I am so thankful yer cousin is safe and well," she said.

"Aye, 'tis a great relief." For a fleeting moment, his features hardened but then vanished so quickly she half-wondered if she had imagined it. "We shall forever be indebted to the ladies of Sgur Castle."

Her grandmother came to her side and gave her a curious glance, although she did not say anything. Flanked by Freyja and her guard, and with a great many warriors following her, she made her way to the castle doors.

"Lady Roisin," Hugh said. "I believe I should accompany Lady Helga."

"Oh, aye, indeed." She hastened after Amma although she couldn't imagine why her grandmother felt the need to take a small contingent with her, if all she was doing was following Isolde. As they braved the frigid weather, and she took her place beside her sister, Grear hurried up to them with their surcoats and gloves.

They found Isolde with Njord outside the armory and after Amma issued a few cold words to him, she beckoned Isolde to join them.

She and Freyja linked their arms through hers.

"Is this not the most romantic thing?" Roisin whispered. "To think, the man ye care for is none other than the man ye're destined to wed."

Instead of agreeing, Isolde merely pressed her lips together. With a start, Roisin realized her sister was furious.

"Romantic?" Freyja whispered, as though she thought Roisin had lost her mind. "That's not the word I would call this, and that's for sure."

"What do ye mean?" Anxiety twisted through Roisin's stomach at how everything had suddenly gone so wrong. "Njord cares for Izzie, I know it."

"He's not Njord," Isolde hissed, and Roisin flinched at the venom in her sister's tone. "His name is William Campbell."

Freyja was fierce as she berated herself for not having seen the truth of who Njord truly was, but Roisin wouldn't be swayed in her conviction that, however it had come about, Isolde and Njord—William—belonged together.

"Well," she said, when Freyja paused for breath. "I think ye both are wrong."

THE FOLLOWING MORNING, Hugh led the men into the great hall to break their fast, a gracious invitation Lady Helga had extended after supper last night, although William had left earlier for the kirk, as he wanted to arrange his marriage with Lady Isolde as soon as possible.

Hugh was relieved his cousin was well, although the knowledge William had shared that one of their own men had attacked him and thrown him overboard during the storm was a harrowing prospect. It was a pity William hadn't seen who had hit him over the head, but he had no doubt they would discover the traitor. They simply needed to remain vigilant.

And yet it wasn't the danger William faced that had kept him awake half the night. It was the vision of Lady Roisin, with her dark auburn hair that framed the delicate features of her face, and her breathtaking emerald eyes. God knew he wasn't one to believe in strange fancies, but he could almost imagine how easy it would be to lose his soul in those fathomless depths. But more than that, her soft voice had echoed in his mind as he'd futilely tried to fall asleep, and he found himself hoping she hadn't merely been polite when she had offered to show him her illuminated manuscripts.

Lady Roisin and her sisters were already at the table, although there was no sign of Lady Helga. He bowed in greeting. "Good morn, Lady Isolde."

"Is it?" She gave him a frosty smile, and he had to concede that after the way she'd reacted to the shock of discovering who William was last night, he could have chosen his greeting more carefully. "Well, if ye say so. Good morn to ye, too, Hugh Campbell. Now, ye must excuse me, I need some air."

With that, she inclined her head at him before leaving the hall.

"Lady Freyja." He bowed his head at her, relieved Lady Roisin had only two older sisters since if she had five or so, he wasn't certain he would survive the experience.

"Hugh Campbell," she responded. "There are a great many things I should like to say to yer cousin but only one thing I have to say to ye.

Did ye know William Campbell was on Eigg before ye arrived?"

Bemused, he stared at her. "No, my lady. How could we know that? We didn't even know he was missing from the ship until we arrived back at Oban. He could have gone overboard near any of the Small Isles for all we knew."

"Hmm." Freyja contemplated him as though she wasn't sure whether to believe him or not. He was tempted to tell her William had been attacked, but he and his cousin had decided discretion was the best course of action and the fewer people who knew the truth the better. When it became clear Lady Freyja had nothing more to say to him, he turned his attention to Lady Roisin.

She gave him a gentle smile that was already becoming achingly familiar, and he could not help but return it. "Good morn, Lady Roisin."

"'Tis another fine day," she said. "I hope ye rested well, Hugh." From the corner of his eye, he saw her sister send her a sharp glance, but Lady Roisin didn't appear to notice.

"'Tis a fine day, indeed." All the more for seeing her. Thank God he managed to keep that thought to himself. "And I slept well, thank ye."

It wasn't the truth, but he'd rip out his tongue before confessing he'd spent half the night with a rock-hard erection and frenzied fantasies of making her his.

He took his place on the opposite side of the table and the conversation flowed between his men and Lady Freyja, although he got the impression she was trying to trip one of them up about the real reason they had come to Eigg. He still couldn't fathom why she would imagine they had abandoned William for a week before rescuing him, but the truth was, he was only half-listening to the discussion. Mostly, he was trying not to stare at Lady Roisin, who hadn't said a word after he'd sat down.

When they finished, Lady Roisin and her sister stood. He and his men leaped to their feet in response. After a civil farewell, the ladies departed and servants cleared the table, and he and his men prepared to leave the castle and tend to their horses.

As they strode across the hall, he caught sight of Lady Roisin by the hearth, and he couldn't resist making his way to her. "My lady, I trust I am not imposing."

"Not at all." She smiled at him and her becoming blush all but paralyzed him. "If ye are not busy, I wonder if ye would like to see my illuminated texts of the Tuatha De Danann?"

"I should be honored to see them, my lady."

Before Lady Roisin could respond, Lady Isolde's voice cut through the air behind him.

"There ye are. Where's Grear?"

"She's here." Roisin shot her sister a bemused glance, and no wonder. Her maid was standing right behind her. "Why do ye want me?"

Lady Isolde didn't answer but she gave him another one of her frosty smiles and belatedly, realization struck. It wasn't Lady Roisin she wanted. She wanted him to leave her sister alone.

"Lady Isolde," he said, with a hasty bow before glancing at Lady Roisin. She didn't press her sister for an answer, probably because she knew as well as he did why Lady Isolde had interrupted them. But when he saw a flicker of anxiety in her beautiful eyes, he knew there was only one thing he could do. With a bow of his head, he retreated.

As he strode to the door, the encounter played on his mind. Lady Roisin was so gentle. Did her two sisters take advantage of her sweet nature? The possibility irked him, and the frigid chill as he stepped outside did little to cool his annoyance.

It wasn't his place, he knew that. And yet the urge to defend her, even against her own sisters, shifted deep in his chest.

"Hugh." Her breathless voice behind him had him swinging about. She stood clutching her shawl, her hair dancing around her face in the fresh breeze and he had never seen a more mesmerizing sight. "I'm sorry my sister interrupted us."

"I trust I didn't cause any problems between ye and Lady Isolde."

Lady Roisin looked surprised. "Of course not. Ye mustn't mind Isolde, she is still," she hesitated as though she were trying to find the right words. "Well, she is still trying to fathom that Njord is truly William. But I am certain all will be well once she's had time to mull it over."

Roisin shivered and he silently cursed at keeping her out here in the cold when she wasn't dressed for it. He indicated they should return to the castle, and it was a struggle not to wrap his arm around her shoulders to share his body heat.

Aye, his body heat. It had nothing to do with wanting to feel her melt against him, did it?

"Ye are close to yer sisters?"

"I am." Warmth filled her voice, but then she sighed. "I confess I'm not looking forward to Isolde leaving the isle."

Damn, he hadn't meant to upset her. "I'm sorry," he said inadequately.

She shook her head as she led him across the hall, Grear following them and Ecne at Lady Roisin's heels. "Do ye have any siblings, Hugh?"

"I've two younger sisters." Affection flickered through him as he thought of them. His sense of tranquility fled as his brother Douglas invaded his mind. "And an older brother, but I rarely see him."

Lady Roisin nodded before she opened a door and led him into the solar. Grear handed her a writing case she had brought with her, and he watched as Roisin went to the desk and opened the writing case before sorting through sheafs of paper.

"My favorite myth is *The Wooing of Etain*." She glanced up at him and he went to her side. Her elusive scent of rose petals swirled in the air and he swallowed, fixing his gaze on the manuscripts in the hope it might quell the fire in his blood.

And then he saw what she was showing him and admiration blazed through him. He had imagined something akin to religious texts, where the first character of the page was highly embellished. But instead, the image of a young woman with flowing fire-gold hair standing in a forest took up a quarter of the page and the details in the beautifully illuminated scene left him reeling.

"'Tis beautiful." His voice was hushed and when he glanced at Roisin, a rosy blush heated her cheeks, and she favored him with a smile that took his breath away. "I've never seen anything like this," he added, truthfully. "What is her legend?"

"The warrior, Midir, of the Tuatha De Danann, fell in love with Etain, a mortal woman, and took her with him to live with the sidhe. But his first wife was jealous and cast many spells on Etain." Roisin showed him another page, where a vibrant butterfly lit up the corner. "Etain was transformed into a butterfly, and after many adventures, she was swallowed by the queen of Ulster who promptly became pregnant and gave birth to Etain, one thousand years after she had first been born."

"A fantastical tale, indeed."

"Aye. But there is more to it than that. For when she grew to womanhood, Midir found her once again and after many trials he won her heart for a second time."

As she wove the myths around him he listened, spellbound by the way her eyes sparkled and how her soft voice was filled with wonder as she shared the ancient stories. He had never contemplated his future before. For sure, he would one day wed, as all men did, but he'd not met a lass who had ever made him think of such things.

But he thought of it now. A future with Lady Roisin.

☙

IT HAD BEEN five days since Hugh had landed on the Isle of Eigg and first set eyes on Lady Roisin, and yet in an inexplicable way, it sometimes seemed he had known her for much longer.

It wasn't even as though they spent much time together. She was invariably surrounded by her sisters, or with Lady Helga, but whenever their gazes meshed across the great hall or in the courtyard, the fierce certainty consumed him that she belonged with him.

God only knew how he'd win her. She was a noblewoman, and he was merely the second son of a laird, but he was determined to make his mark and prove himself worthy of seeking her hand.

On the rare occasions she escaped her relatives, and they spent some cherished moments together amidst the bustling hall or in the courtyard, his conviction strengthened. He would return to Eigg and make her his, if it was the last thing he did.

The wedding went without a hitch and as William and his bride made their farewells to her kin, he and Lady Roisin retreated to a shadowed corner of the great hall.

"I'm sorry we are leaving so soon." He doubted she would ever understand how sincerely he meant those words.

"As am I," she whispered, and she gazed at him so tenderly, it took every shred of willpower he possessed not to cradle her face and kiss her until the madness within him was quenched. Except he knew full well a kiss would never be enough and would merely stoke the flames that tortured him night and day whenever he thought of her.

Belatedly, he realized she was offering him something and he glanced at her hand where she held an exquisitely embroidered handkerchief.

"For me?" A note of awe threaded through his voice. No one had ever offered him such a precious gift before.

"Aye." Her shy response touched something deep inside, and primal protectiveness surged through him. "To remember me by."

As he took her handkerchief their fingertips touched, a fleeting, feather-light touch that seared his veins and thickened his cock.

14

Somehow, he kept his frustrated groan locked in his throat.

"I shall treasure it always." He pressed his lips against the lace. Lady Roisin's delicate fragrance of crushed rose petals spiced the air and sank into his blood more potent than any aphrodisiac. "And I shall never forget ye. We will see each other again, my lady." It was an unspoken pledge that he would one day return.

And claim her for his bride.

CHAPTER ONE

Eire, December 1566

HUGH CAMPBELL GRASPED the lantern as he strode across the dark courtyard of O'Grady's manor towards the stables. The rain lashed at him, chilling him to the very marrow of his bones, but he scarcely felt the discomfort anymore.

It was hard to recall how life had once been, a mere eight months ago, before the Earl of Argyll had ordered him to join the redshanks assigned to defend the chieftain O'Grady's land against the damn sassenach.

It had been eight months since he'd last set foot on his homeland or heard from any of his friends. But the earl's order had been absolute.

Hugh needed to forsake his former life, inveigle himself with MacGregor redshanks, and discover what the hell his missing older brother Douglas was planning.

He wiped his drenched hair from his eyes as he reached the stables and pushed open the door. The familiar scent of horse and hay eased his weary senses and for a few precious moments he imagined he was back at Balfour Castle, his childhood home. With the horses at least he didn't need to keep up any pretense of having turned his back on his own kinsmen or feign loyalty to Clan MacGregor.

Sometimes he wondered if he'd ever be able to wipe the stain from the last eight months of pretending to be someone he wasn't from his soul.

And sometimes the fear gripped him that he'd never be permitted to return to his former life at all.

"Hugh." Symon MacGregor emerged from the shadows, and Hugh's anticipation of a welcome respite fled. He forced a smile. Symon was barely a year younger than himself, and the two of them had arrived at O'Grady's the same day. It was hardly a recommendation to become friends, but Symon apparently believed it was and so here he was, reluctantly forging a friendship with a man from Clan MacGregor, the Campbells' sworn enemies.

"I thought ye'd turned in for the night." Hugh hung the lantern on a hook and shook his head in a vain effort to dry his hair.

"No, man. The manor walls stifle me." With a grin, Symon produced a jug of ale and two tankards. "I've been waiting here for ye to celebrate yer promotion. Sergeant."

Hugh grunted, and despite himself a flicker of pride heated him. He'd not expected the promotion. The life of a mercenary wasn't, after all, one he'd chosen for himself. But it was gratifying that their captain had acknowledged his efforts.

He took a tankard, and Symon filled it with ale. "Don't let it go to yer head, Hugh," he said. "I'd still best ye in a fight."

"The hell ye would." Hugh downed the ale and for a fleeting moment peace flowed through him, as though he shared a drink with a real friend, and not one in whom he could never confide the truth. The sense of peace shattered, and he exhaled a long sigh.

"The extra coin will come in handy," Symon remarked as he refilled their tankards. "See, I told ye 'twas in our best interests to stay with O'Grady throughout the winter."

Hugh eyed him. "I believe I told ye that."

Since he'd received no word from the earl to return to Argyll after his three-month contract in Eire had ended, he'd remained with O'Grady, and the chieftain had been appreciative. Extra men were always needed to defend against the intermittent raids of the sassenach queen's men. Three months had turned into six, and when winter approached, he'd been glad to accept the chieftain's invitation to remain until the following spring.

After all, what awaited him if he returned to Argyll? Although he'd sent regular reports to the earl, he'd been unable to discover the whereabouts of Douglas, and without a direct order to return home, he doubted the earl would be pleased to see him.

"Aye," Symon said agreeably. "Maybe ye did. I'll drink to it either way. And since ye're set for a handsome pay rise, ye can buy us another jug of ale."

"I'm not going out in this weather to get more ale."

"Tomorrow, then."

Hugh shook his head but couldn't help laughing before a thread of regret inched through him. If only Symon wasn't a MacGregor, there could be true camaraderie between them instead of this uneasy twilight alliance. Yet if the other man ever discovered he wasn't merely a Campbell, but one from a high-ranking family, even that would shatter.

"All right," he conceded.

"And now ye can write to yer lady love and let her know when ye return, ye'll be able to afford a wife."

And just like that, his laughter died. What a damn fool he'd been, within weeks of arriving in Eire, to make the mistake of telling Symon there was a lass back home waiting for him.

There was no lass waiting for him in Argyll. Or anywhere else.

But Symon and the other redshanks had been talking about their families and their sweethearts, and when Symon had turned to him and asked him outright, his heart, aided no doubt by the ale they'd all consumed, had overruled his head. And his deeply buried dream had found a voice.

"There's a bonny lass at home waiting. One day I hope to make her mine."

But Lady Roisin MacDonald of Sgur Castle on the Isle of Eigg wasn't his lass, and she wasn't waiting for him. For all he knew, she could be wed by now.

A dull ache wrapped around his heart, and he finished his ale in one long swallow as Symon ambled on about his own sweetheart who waited for his return.

It wasn't until much later, when he and Symon had returned to the manor and were in the small chamber the chieftain had allocated to them for the harsh winter months, that he allowed his mind to once again recall Lady Roisin's gentle smile when they had talked together at Sgur.

A year ago, this week.

The sound of Symon's snores filled the chamber, and in the soft glow from the lantern that stood upon a stool between their pallets, Hugh opened a leather pouch that hung from his belt and pulled out its precious contents.

Tenderly, he traced the delicate square of lace where she had embroidered *Roisin MacDonald* in the corner, encircling a tiny, exquisite rose. She'd given him her handkerchief the day they'd sailed from Eigg and he'd all but promised that one day soon he'd return.

God, how he wanted to. But even if he earned a small fortune from his time in Eire, unless the earl called him back, he was little more than an outcast from his clan and no noblewoman of Lady Roisin's impeccable lineage would wish to associate herself with such a dubious character.

It didn't matter that it was Douglas who'd somehow offended the earl. Douglas was his brother, and it was only the earl's sense of honor that had prevented him from venting his displeasure upon all of Hugh's family.

In return for finding Douglas and befriending men of Clan MacGregor, the earl would ensure Hugh's frail father and his two young sisters were taken care of.

The earl had framed Hugh's assistance as a request, but in truth there had been no choice. Because the alternative to taking up arms for O'Grady had been the loss of his sisters' future security. When they came of age, they deserved good men and advantageous marriages, but that could only happen if the earl looked favorably upon the Campbells of Balfour Castle.

He pressed the lace that Lady Roisin had spent untold hours creating against his lips and inhaled deeply. But although the last lingering hints of her scent had long since faded, the ethereal aroma of crushed rose petals still filled his mind with a bittersweet longing for what once might have been.

Chapter Two

Isle of Eigg, June 1567

ROISIN MACDONALD CLUTCHED the bedcovers and gazed up at the ceiling in her bedchamber, her heart pounding in her chest. Dawn had scarcely broken, and pale shards of light glowed through the cracks in the window shutters as sweet Ecne, her beloved terrier, pushed his wet nose against her chin in a gesture of comfort.

Slowly, she loosened her grip on the covers and buried her fingers in his fur.

'Twas just a dream.

Like the other dreams that had plagued her since the day her elder sister, Freyja, had wed Alasdair Campbell and left the isle. Strange, fragmented dreams, of unfamiliar landscapes and shifting perspectives, and threaded throughout, a pervading dread that something dark lurked just beyond the far horizon.

She glanced beside her, where her maid, Grear, still slept soundly. Thank goodness her troubled dreams hadn't disturbed her as they sometimes did. Grear thought she should confide in her grandmother, but there was a good reason why she didn't want to.

It was because in her dreams she'd left her beloved Sgur Castle for the Highlands. And as the last remaining daughter, that was something she could never do.

When Freyja had wed Alasdair just over a year ago, her sister had been concerned that the burden of their legacy would now fall squarely upon Roisin's shoulders. She'd assured Freyja all was well, that she was prepared for the responsibility of remaining on Eigg to ensure the decree of their ancient foremother was fulfilled.

The bloodline of the Isle must prevail beyond quietus.

The Deep Knowing was a sacred edict from their Pict queen foremother and had been handed down from mother to daughter for nine hundred years. Both Freyja and their eldest sister, Isolde, believed it meant if they left the isle, their bloodline would die.

Yet both of them had left, to be with the men they loved.

Stealthily, Roisin eased out of the bed so as not to wake Grear, and hastily washed before the banked fire. Neither of her sisters had made the decision to leave Eigg easily. All of their lives, they had been taught that their destiny was to protect their beloved isle and that their futures were irrevocably entwined with the land of their birth.

Their formidable Pict queen ancestor, who had commanded a fearsome band of women warriors to defend Eigg against her enemies, had entrusted the edict to her own daughter and so the legacy had been passed down through the ages.

But only through the female line, from mother to daughter. And in all that time, only one daughter of Sgur had been born in each generation.

Until now.

And so, despite their misgivings about going against the Deep Knowing, ultimately Isolde and Freyja had been free to leave Sgur because Roisin could continue the legacy by remaining on the isle and, in time, passing the history of their fierce Pict queen ancestor down to her own daughter.

Except the dark truth was, she'd never believed in the Deep Knowing the way her sisters, her grandmother, and her own mother had.

'Twas as unthinkable as blasphemy to ever breathe such a belief aloud, and she'd keep her secret until her dying breath. But just because she didn't believe in the same way as her sisters and foremothers, it didn't mean she wanted to leave Sgur Castle.

She smothered a sigh as she wrapped her shawl about her shoulders and left the bedchamber, Ecne at her heels. Before her sisters had married, her own questioning of the Deep Knowing hadn't worried her. After all, it changed nothing since the three of them were destined to remain on the Isle of Eigg forever. And as the youngest sister, no one had ever asked her opinion on it, anyway.

But now she couldn't stop fretting about it, and it made no sense. It wasn't as though, given the choice, she'd follow her sisters to the Highlands.

As she went down the stairs and into the great hall, her mind lingered on that notion and no matter how hard she tried to stop it, the image of Hugh Campbell and his incomparable blue eyes filled her thoughts.

Why did he haunt her so? It had been eighteen months since she'd last seen him, when he had all but promised to return. She should've known he was only spinning her a pretty line but how truly she'd believed him.

How dearly she still wished to believe him. He'd been so easy to talk to, and she hadn't wanted to disappear into a nearby tapestry the way she usually did when confronted by a strange man.

She'd even shown him some of her illuminated manuscripts and he'd been gratifyingly impressed. His manners were impeccable, his conversation delightful, and when his fingers brushed hers, fire forged by the fae themselves had blazed through her.

But neither Isolde nor Freyja had seen or heard any news about him, and it appeared he had vanished as completely as mountain mist on a fine summer's morn.

If only she could forget about him as easily as he, quite obviously, had forgotten about her. And yet the sad truth remained. If Hugh Campbell arrived on Eigg this day and asked for her hand, she'd gladly accept.

Shaking her head at her folly, she left the castle and took the path across the bracken moorlands to the beach, as Ecne followed his nose into every nook and cranny he could find. The sound of the sea lapping onto the sand soothed her and she breathed in deep, the salty air a familiar balm to her soul.

And then she saw her grandmother walking along the shore towards her.

What was Amma doing out so early? She usually liked to see to the affairs of the castle first thing, and a flicker of unease stirred. Was something amiss?

She hurried over to her and Amma took her hand. She seemed perfectly fine and smiled, and Roisin's fears faded.

"Ye're up early this morn," Amma said, before she glanced at her serving woman, who immediately took a few steps back, along with Amma's personal guard, so she and her grandmother could enjoy some privacy. "Are ye all right?"

"I was about to ask the same of ye." They linked arms and continued along the beach, as Ecne darted into the gently lapping waves beside them.

"I had strange dreams and needed to clear my mind."

Roisin glanced at her. It was uncanny how often she and her grandmother seemed to experience strange dreams or inexplicable feelings at the same time as each other. She also knew neither of her sisters had any idea about Amma's less practical side. Lady Helga was a force to be reckoned with among the people of the Western Isles, and her reputation would suffer if a whisper emerged that she'd inherited more than Sgur Castle from their formidable foremothers.

They didn't even discuss it between themselves. It was simply something she'd become aware of over the years and, truth be told, the unspoken understanding was more real to her than their revered Deep Knowing ever had been.

"What did ye dream?" She hoped she sounded casual. And she dearly hoped Amma hadn't dreamed of Roisin in the Highlands.

Amma sighed and they came to a halt as her grandmother gazed out to sea. The only sounds that filled the air were the call of the gulls and the waves breaking on the beach, but in her mind's eye all she saw were the unfamiliar mountains and glens that had pervaded her dreams.

Finally, Amma spoke. "Do ye not feel it also, my bairn?" Her voice was hushed and a shiver of apprehension raced along Roisin's arms. "Of all my girls, ye're the one I believe inherited the same gift as I. Do ye not dream that ye must travel to the Highlands to discover yer destiny?"

Despite her earlier tangled thoughts, and shock that Amma had finally voiced something she'd always wondered about, her response was instant. "I'll never leave ye, Amma. Ye must know that."

Amma patted her hand and gave a sad smile. "Tell me why ye're on the beach at dawn, without Grear accompanying ye."

Grear accompanied her everywhere. And to be sure, that was her duty, but it was more than that. She considered her maid her friend and, since both her sisters had left the isle, her only confidante.

It was the reason why Grear now slept beside her in bed, instead of at the foot, where maids usually spent their nights. But after Freyja had wed, the bed had been too big, too lonely, and honestly, 'twas foolish for Grear not to share the comfort of pillows and covers, rather than wrapping herself in a sheepskin to stave off the chill.

Yet this morning she'd needed to be alone. And Amma wanted to know why. Maybe Grear had been right, and she should've confided in her grandmother weeks ago.

"My nights have been restless since Freyja left Sgur. 'Tis as though an invisible thread pulls me to the mainland, and I cannot understand why."

Except that wasn't quite the truth. For why else would she dream of the Highlands, other than it was the land of Hugh's birth?

But although she might harbor the foolish wish that she had a future with Hugh Campbell, she wasn't reckless enough to let a misguided hope rule her life. Her sisters were convinced her head resided in the clouds, but she would never leave the safety of Sgur to chase an illusory fantasy.

Amma sighed. "I wish I could enlighten ye, Roisin, but I've no wisdom to share with ye about this. I see no man in yer future, the way I could when I had visions of Freyja meeting Alasdair Campbell before he arrived on the Small Isles. All I know is the Highlands awaits ye."

"Ye saw Alasdair in a vision?" How had she not been aware of that? Did Freyja know? Somehow, she doubted it. Her sister was the most practical person ever and didn't believe in anything she couldn't see or prove for herself.

"No, lass. I only knew she would meet a Highlander and that she would leave Sgur. Yet when I first saw him, I knew he was the one."

Another shiver raced through her. Although last summer she'd not had any inkling that Freyja would soon meet her soulmate, once Alasdair had arrived on the Small Isles, she'd instantly noticed a difference in her sister. When Freyja had talked of him, there had been warmth in her voice and a smile on her lips, and when Alasdair was near, her sister fairly glowed.

She'd thought it was obvious to anyone with a grain of sense that Alasdair was Freyja's destiny. But maybe the only reason she'd noticed was because of this strange gift she shared with Amma.

It was most disconcerting.

Before she could think better of it, her tongue ran away with her reason. "Did ye not sense anything about Hugh Campbell?"

Ah, curses. She hadn't even mentioned his name to Grear in the year since Freyja had left, but it wasn't as though Amma was unaware of how she'd fallen for him. Amma saw everything.

Concern wreathed her grandmother's face, which was all the answer Roisin needed. What else had she expected?

"No, my bairn." Sympathy threaded through each word and mortification slithered through her like a malignant serpent. She really should have kept her mouth shut. "All I know is that the Highlands are in yer immediate future."

"Aye, well of course they are." She kept her voice light, in the hope Amma wouldn't guess the depth of her disappointment. Her unrequited obsession with Hugh was truly getting a little irksome. It was time to push his memory into a dark corner of her mind and leave it there. "We're visiting Isolde in two months, after all. Maybe that is all these strange dreams are about."

It was possible, after all. She was excited about seeing both her sisters again, and the prospect of welcoming her newborn niece or nephew was frankly thrilling. But if that was the case, why did an undertow of apprehension permeate her every dream?

Surely it wasn't the danger of childbirth. Freyja would be there, and she was not only a healer of exceptional skill but also an experienced midwife.

Besides, these dreams had started before Isolde had told them of her pregnancy.

"Do ye truly think that?" There was a musing note in Amma's voice and Roisin heaved a ragged sigh. She could try to fool herself but clearly she couldn't fool her grandmother.

"I don't know what else it could be." Because nothing would induce her to bring Hugh Campbell's name into the conversation again.

Amma was silent for so long, Roisin half wondered if this uneasy conversation was over. But she should have known better. When Amma turned to her, she recognized the keen gleam in her eyes and knew her grandmother had reached a decision.

But a decision on what, exactly?

"Isolde is safe," Amma said, and Roisin stared at her, uncomprehending. Before she could ask what her grandmother meant, she continued. "And so is Freyja. I fear these visions will never cease until ye, also, find yer path away from our beloved Sgur."

Alarm spiked through her. "Are ye saying we're not safe at Sgur? But how can that be? 'Tis the home of our foremothers. Surely no harm can befall us here."

Amma shook her head and once again they resumed walking along the beach, heading towards the castle that stood high on the hill and yet still remained in the shadow of An Sgurr, the mighty ridge that defined Eigg and could be seen from the neighboring isles.

"The Deep Knowing has protected the daughters of the isle for almost a thousand years and will not fail us now."

Roisin held her tongue, and yet her mind asked the question, regardless.

How has the Deep Knowing protected us?

"But this strange compulsion consumes me, Roisin. Ye must leave Eigg and travel to Isolde at Creagdoun before the week is out. I shall meet ye there in two months, as we have already arranged, and only then can ye return home."

"So I shall return to Sgur, then?" This wasn't something she'd felt in her dreams, but there was a certain relief in knowing her grandmother had.

"Of course ye must. Whatever reasons the Deep Knowing has for sending the three of ye away, it is certain ye alone must return. For how else will our legacy continue? But first, there is a path ye must find and follow until its end, and that path is not on the Western Isles."

Chapter Three

Argyll, The Highlands, June1567

HUGH STRODE THROUGH the campsite that lay scattered on a small plateau halfway up an imposing mountain and returned the greetings hailed his way from its itinerant inhabitants. It had been more than six weeks since he and Symon had left Eire and returned to Symon's displaced clan, just days before they'd left their previous site to travel here. Six weeks since the MacGregors had, if not exactly welcomed him, at least allowed him to stay, after hearing from Symon of Hugh's tireless exploits against the damn sassenachs.

Six weeks, during which he'd felt like the worst kind of betrayer.

It couldn't be helped. Three months ago, he'd heard rumors that Douglas was back in Argyll and had sent word to the earl through his network of spies. A network that hid in plain sight, of messengers and couriers, and seemingly innocuous missives that were shrouded with secret codes. For the sake of security, he never knew for sure which ones were working for the earl or not, but the system worked and, by whatever means were employed, the messages reached their destination.

The earl had commanded him to return to Eire and maintain his subterfuge, in the heart of the rebel MacGregors' outposts, and to continue to keep him informed of anything he unearthed.

Was it treacherous of him to be thankful he'd yet to uncover plans of rebellion against the Earl of Argyll?

It was. If he did discover any such plans, he knew his duty and he'd inform the earl. In the meantime, he merely relayed whatever he heard regarding Clan MacGregor.

The only thing he didn't divulge was his exact location. There were women and bairns in the camp and while he doubted the earl was interested in launching an attack, since it would shut down his line of communication, Hugh wasn't prepared to risk it.

Symon emerged from a nearby tent and raised his hand in greeting. His exuberant nature had faltered when they'd joined the camp and he'd discovered his sweetheart had wed another and moved south in his absence, but lately he appeared to have recovered from his loss. At least he no longer made mocking references to Hugh's elusive lady love, for which he was thankful, since any chance he'd once had of winning Lady Roisin's favor had well and truly perished.

"Are ye up for hunting?" Symon asked as he fell into step beside him.

"Aye." He often went on hunting trips. They were dangerous, since it necessitated riding deep into Campbell-held territory with the risk of being recognized. But he'd only be recognized if he were caught, and he had no intention of that happening.

But that wasn't the only danger. Clan MacGregor had been outlawed, and poaching was the only way they could now survive. And MacGregor poachers ran the risk of being killed on sight.

He went to get his horse, a fine stallion he'd acquired in Eire as part payment for his services. How he wished the beautiful creature he'd named Deagh Fhortan had the comfort of a stable instead of facing the elements every night, but it couldn't be helped. Maybe one day he would, if Hugh ever returned home.

Good fortune. It seemed a fanciful name to call his horse considering his current circumstances, but it wasn't only because of the stallion's outstanding performance in battle. It was a promise to them both that this life wouldn't be their fate forever.

He and Symon rode away from the camp. They never hunted

locally, despite the nearby forest and loch, since the less attention they drew to themselves the better. And while it was uncomfortable hunting on the land of lairds he knew, he could scarcely object without raising suspicion.

A starving man didn't question where he found his food. And without these hunts, the MacGregors would starve.

He pulled his kerchief higher, so it covered his face more securely as ominous clouds rolled across the summer sky, obscuring the sun, and he and Symon went to work.

It was several hours later when, with their bags filled with small game, they were on their way back to the camp when the drizzle that had been their constant companion finally broke into a full-scale downpour. They urged their mounts forward, as thunder rumbled overhead, when through the slashing rain Hugh saw a commotion from the corner of his eye.

He frowned, squinting in the distance, cursing the mist that obscured his vision. But he could see enough, and it seemed the skirmish was not going well for the ones defending the wagon.

Symon pulled up beside him. "Bandits," he said. "Make haste, Hugh, before they see us."

It was good advice. It was foolhardy to get involved, but he didn't urge his horse on. Because two riders broke away from the melee and his heart smashed against his chest. "Christ, Symon. There are women. We can't leave them."

Not when it looked as though the bandits were winning and there was no prize for guessing what the bastards would do to the women once they caught them.

Symon cursed under his breath. "Aye, Sergeant."

They drew their swords and galloped over to the fray. Bodies were strewn across the ground and as the last defender fell, the two remaining bandits turned their attention to the fleeing women.

Their mistake. They hadn't noticed either him or Symon, and

Hugh had no compunction in using their negligence against them.

The element of surprise that they'd clearly used to slaughter their victims worked just as efficiently, and with brutal economy, Hugh dispatched his opponent to hell. Since Symon needed no help, he pulled his horse about and galloped in the direction he'd seen the women fleeing. God, he hoped they hadn't changed direction, or he might never find them in this forest.

A dark flash ahead alerted him and he charged forward, gaining on the riders with every passing moment. One lagged behind the other, and he focused on the one ahead. When he rescued her, the second rider would undoubtedly halt too.

He swerved into her, inching closer. A shawl covered her head, hiding her face, but it was the ungainly basket in front of her that momentarily distracted him. Whatever she'd salvaged from the wagon surely wasn't worth the inconvenience, when for all she knew she was fleeing for her life from the bandits.

In the end it didn't matter, since the bandits were dead. He lunged and grasped the reins. "Ye're safe," he yelled above the sound of the relentless rain and thudding hooves. "Slow down. 'Tis all right."

She ignored him, bending low over the basket, and with a muffled oath he tugged sharply on the reins, bringing both of their horses to a halt. Before he could regain his breath to reassure her once again there was no cause for alarm, she turned to him, and he saw her face.

The words lodged in his throat as the world plunged sideways and all he could hear was the sound of his heart thundering inside his head.

God's bones, she was Lady Roisin. Stupefied, he stared into her dark green eyes. Eyes that were filled with terror, and belatedly he realized the kerchief still hid his face.

Without releasing his grip on her mare's reins, he pushed the kerchief down and only when shock froze her features did it occur to him that he'd just made a fatal error.

Lady Roisin knew who he was. If she said anything to Symon

32

about him being a Balfour Castle Campbell, his cover was blown.

"Hugh." He scarcely heard her whisper, but his gaze fixed on her lips as though they were his only salvation. "What are ye doing?"

A section of his mind was aware that Symon had caught up with her companion and they were but a couple of horse lengths from him and Lady Roisin. He had to make her see it was safer for them both if she pretended not to know him and there was no time to lose.

"My lady." His voice was urgent. "Ye cannot know who I am, do ye understand? I cannot guarantee yer safety otherwise." Or his own, but that was of minor concern when Roisin gazed at him as though he were a demon from hell.

His grip on the reins tightened until his knuckles ached. All he wanted to do was pull her into his arms and reassure her she was in no danger, but that was the last thing he could risk with Symon so nearby.

He leaned in close until their breath mingled. God help him, but her elusive scent of crushed rose petals swirled about him like a tortured promise, and it was a struggle to recall that he needed her word.

"Promise me on yer honor." His whisper was harsh, and she flinched. She couldn't have wounded him more had she plunged a dagger through his heart.

"I promise."

He should be relieved, but only a dull sense of gloom-laden inevitability wrapped around him. He still needed to elicit another promise from her, and he had the certainty it would destroy any lingering fragment of tenderness she'd ever held for him.

"Ye can tell no one ye saw me. Do ye understand?"

She glared at him as though she'd like nothing better than to slap his face. Instead, her arm tightened around the basket before she drew in a ragged breath. "Ye have my word."

Goddamn it. In all the many wretched dreams he'd had of seeing her again, none had come close to this bitter nightmare. But no matter how dire the circumstances, he couldn't tear his gaze from her. Her dark auburn hair was drenched, and he had to fight the urge to push errant tendrils from her cheeks with his finger.

Symon came to his side, gripping the reins of the second horse. "Sergeant, we should retrieve the wagon. 'Tis sure to be loaded with goods we can use."

For a moment, Hugh stared at the other man, his words making no sense. The wagon belonged to Lady Roisin. And then a flicker of anger stirred as Symon's remark penetrated the fog clouding his mind.

They weren't going to damn well steal her goods. They needed to escort her to wherever she'd been heading, to ensure she arrived safely.

He glanced at her. She still glared at him, condemnation burning in her eyes. Only then did the harsh truth hit him.

If he escorted her—doubtless to her sister, Lady Isolde, who was wed to his cousin, William—there was no chance of keeping his identity hidden. Until he got word to the earl, explaining the situation and devising a safe way for Roisin to continue her journey, she needed to remain with him.

How many times had he wished they could be together? His wish had been granted, and it promised nothing but despair.

He tore his gaze from her and gave Symon a brusque nod. "We'll hitch the spare horses to the wagon." Horses were valuable and the MacGregors would find good use for them. He only hoped one day Roisin would understand. "Ye'll need to drive it, and have the lass sit beside ye."

As Symon rode off with Lady Roisin's companion to do his bidding, he once again turned to her. It wasn't right that he was about to take her into a rebel outpost, but he didn't have a choice. He exhaled a weary breath before attempting to smile.

"Lady Roisin, I'm sorry about this."

"I don't wish to hear yer apologies." Her voice wasn't gentle, the way he recalled when he dreamed of her. She sounded brittle, and he damned whatever cursed fate had led her to this road and into the clutches of those bandits. She didn't deserve to see this grim side of life, let alone be forced to endure it for who knew how many days before he managed to engineer her safe passage. "I demand ye take me to Creagdoun Castle this instant."

He'd been right. She had been on her way to visit her sister and William.

Sharp regret pierced his chest. For all he knew, his kin and friends might think he was dead. And then another thought struck him. Where was Lady Roisin's other sister, Lady Freyja? Surely Roisin hadn't made this journey from the Isle of Eigg on her own.

"I can't do that yet. It's not safe. But I swear on my life ye'll come to no harm."

She pressed her lips together and it couldn't be clearer that she didn't believe a word. He smothered a sigh and turned their horses around so he could return to the wagon and assist Symon. "Let me pack yer basket on the wagon, Lady Roisin. Ye'll be more comfortable."

"Certainly not." She clutched the basket harder and for the first time he realized exactly what she held.

"Is that yer wee dog?" He bent his head to get a closer look. The terrier had never left her side when he'd been in Sgur eighteen months ago. It seemed fitting the creature was here with her now.

"Leave him alone." A thread of panic edged her voice, and he hastily straightened. Christ, what did she imagine he was going to do to her dog?

Since there was no palatable answer to that, he refused to dwell on it. But the sting remained.

By the time they reached the wagon, Symon had rounded up the dead men's horses and hitched them to the wagon. Lady Roisin's companion sat on the wagon's seat, clutching her hands together on her lap, and he recognized her now as the young maid who had shadowed Lady Roisin on the Isle of Eigg.

She looked petrified.

He had no idea how to ease her fears, since his attempt to do so with Lady Roisin had been an abject failure, but he had to try. "Ye and yer mistress are under my protection. There's no need to fear."

She cast him a wide-eyed glance. It was obvious that, like Lady Roisin, she didn't believe a word.

Symon interrupted the excruciating silence that followed by striding to his side. "Ready, Sergeant?"

Lady Roisin drew in a shocked gasp. "Ye cannot mean to leave my men here like this."

He scanned the dozen or so bodies that lay scattered in the mud. It was impossible to tell who her men were and who were the bandits, but anger scorched through him. Why had she been so poorly protected that the ambush had put her in such danger?

Regardless, he understood her distress. It was an unspoken rule that, after a battle or skirmish, the victors ensured the vanquished were returned to their people for burial, and they never left their own dead behind.

But he'd never been in this situation before. There was nowhere to take the bandits, and they weren't equipped to take Lady Roisin's men with them to the camp. And even if there was room on the heavily laden wagon for the bodies, he could imagine the reception they'd receive if he and Symon returned with them.

It didn't sit right with him, but he had no choice but to leave them behind. And besides, he needed to get Lady Roisin and her maid back to the camp where at least they'd be safer than they were here.

"We must go, my lady. There's no telling if other bandits are lurking and my first priority must be ye."

Her bottom lip trembled as she cast her gaze over the fallen, and self-disgust ate into him. If they had time, the least he could do was bury the bodies beneath a cairn, but they didn't have that luxury. If, God forbid, they were attacked, the chances he and Symon could fight off half a dozen or more outlaws were slender.

He couldn't risk Lady Roisin being captured. The very thought of it turned his guts.

"Sergeant." There was a warning note in the other man's voice.

"Aye." He gave a sharp nod, and Symon took his place beside Lady Roisin's maid on the wagon, and they set off.

He eyed Lady Roisin, who sat stiff-backed on her mare beside him, clutching her terrier's basket as though it were her lifeline. They'd make better time if he released her reins, but first he had to elicit yet another pledge from her.

It burned his throat, but he pushed the words out, regardless. "Do ye promise not to escape if I release yer mare?"

The look she slung at him was so filled with contempt he all but reeled. "And leave Grear behind? What do ye take me for?"

He snatched his hand back and grimly glared ahead. He didn't dare glance at her again in case she saw something in his eyes he wasn't certain he could hide.

What did he take her for?

She was the woman he hadn't been able to forget these last eighteen months. The lass whose gentle voice and bewitching smile had been the only light in the darkness of his nights.

The one he'd woven impossible dreams around: of a future they could never share.

Chapter Four

ROISIN CLUTCHED ECNE'S basket close, even though her arm had gone numb long ago from its awkward position, but that was far better than the alternative of putting him back on the wagon where she couldn't be sure he was safe.

As safe as any of them were.

In her heart, she didn't believe they were safe at all.

Her stomach pitched and, against her better judgement, she cast the man at her side a quick glance. His profile was dark and proud, and his unsmiling face caused a dull ache deep inside her chest.

How could Hugh Campbell, the noble Highlander who had charmed her so, be nothing more than a fearful brigand?

A shudder wracked her, and it had nothing to do with the rain or the cold wind. It was because she'd been so terribly wrong about him.

Stealthily, she roamed her gaze over the path they took, but she didn't recognize anything. Certainly, they weren't traveling in the direction of Creagdoun.

Is this what her dream had been warning her of? That Hugh Campbell, of all the men in the world, would abduct her and take her deep into the unfamiliar Highlands?

No wonder Amma hadn't believed he was the man for her, the way she had with Alasdair for Freyja. For Hugh had forsaken everyone he'd ever known and become an outlaw.

She bent her head, blinking rapidly at the cursed rain that caused her eyes to sting. Eight brave warriors lay dead because they'd sworn to shield her from harm, and she hadn't even been able to give them the respect they deserved by protecting their bodies from the scavenging wildlife.

She swallowed around the lump in her throat. None of the men were strangers to her, and all of them were—had been—fierce warriors. But the attack had been so sudden, so violent, she'd scarcely had time to wrench Ecne's basket from the wagon and make good her and Grear's escape, in the hope they could hide from the attackers in the forest.

But Hugh Campbell had caught them. Had he known who she was before he and his men had attacked?

She tightened her grip on the reins. It didn't matter one way or another. The reason neither of her sisters knew where he'd been since leaving Eigg was because he'd turned rogue.

Did he mean to hold her for ransom? As despicable as that was, it was far better than the terrifying alternative of her and Grear being used for unspeakable purposes.

She glanced over her shoulder, where Grear sat huddled on the seat of the wagon beside a great hulk of a man. Her mare stumbled and she hastily returned her attention to where they were going.

Except she didn't know.

Every instinct screamed at her to remain silent and not anger this stranger who rode by her side. But even though Hugh Campbell wasn't the man she had once foolishly believed him to be, it seemed, just as when they'd been on Eigg, she wasn't afraid to speak to him.

It didn't make any sense since he clearly wasn't the man she remembered at all, but none of this made sense and the words were out before she could stop them.

"Where are ye taking us?"

He looked at her. The kerchief that had hidden his face was rumpled about his jaw and her stomach pitched as her mind replayed the moment he'd revealed himself.

The moment when all her witless daydreams about him had shattered.

"There's no need to be alarmed. 'Tis just a camp where ye can dry off and rest for a while."

"Rest?" she repeated. "Why should I wish to rest? My sister expects me to arrive at Creagdoun later today. Do ye think William will not try to find me?"

Hugh's jaw flexed. She'd clearly hit a nerve. "This will be much easier if ye just trust me to make arrangements for yer safe passage."

"I did have safe passage." She blinked rapidly. Damn the rain that kept getting in her eyes. Except it wasn't the rain, and well she knew it. "Ye're the one who took that from me."

"I couldn't leave ye there." He sounded affronted that she thought he should have. "'Tis not safe for women to travel alone."

What nonsense was he trying to trick her with? He'd not been dense when he'd been in Eigg, and she wasn't about to let him twist her words for his own purpose.

Don't say it.

Had he been anyone but Hugh, it wouldn't even have occurred to her to contradict him. In fact, she'd likely be too terrified to utter a word. But while fear still clawed through her, there was anger, too. Anger that Hugh, who had once treated her with such respect, had now shown his true colors, and he thought so little of her he imagined he could confuse what she knew to be the truth.

She leaned over the saddle and maybe he saw the outrage in her eyes as a frown flashed across his face.

"We weren't alone, Hugh Campbell, until ye and yer brigands slaughtered my men."

His confusion vanished, and disbelief glowed in his eyes. She was disgusted with herself by how fascinating she found the phenomenon.

"God's bones." He sounded shaken. She told herself she hadn't noticed. It was merely another trick to make her doubt her own mind.

"Lady Roisin, I swear on my honor I had nothing to do with that. Ye must believe me. The bandits were attacking yer party when we saw ye, and we came to yer aid."

Despite her best intentions, her conviction wavered. He appeared genuinely horrified by her accusation. Yet who was to say he wasn't lying? It was very likely he was lying. So why did she believe he spoke the truth?

Her head pounded and it was hard to straighten her muddled thoughts. If it was anyone but Hugh telling her this, would she take their word for it above the evidence of her own eyes?

That was an easy question to answer. She knew what she'd witnessed and Hugh, like the others, had hidden his face with a kerchief. But although it was clear she didn't know Hugh Campbell at all, she couldn't convince herself he was lying in this matter. After all, she hadn't seen him personally murder any of her men. And now she took a moment to think about it, neither he nor his compatriot had the savage, unkempt appearance of the others.

It was no small relief that he wasn't responsible for the death of her brave men, but it didn't explain why he now felt the need to spirit her away to this camp of his, instead of accompanying her to Creagdoun.

And if he wasn't associated with the brigands, why had he demanded she couldn't let anyone know who he was or tell anyone she had seen him?

Did his accomplice not know who he really was?

Once again, she glanced over her shoulder. Hugh's compatriot appeared to be attempting to engage Grear in conversation, but her maid gazed at her clasped hands in mute misery.

She returned her attention to Hugh, wishing she could somehow comfort poor Grear. "Ye speak of honor, so why delay my journey by taking me to this camp of yers? We can't be far from Creagdoun."

In truth, she wasn't at all sure how far they were from Isolde and William's castle, but she wasn't going to let Hugh know that.

He scanned the countryside, and she followed his glance, relieved the rain was finally easing. Not that she recognized any landmarks from the previous times she'd visited her sister.

Or from her dreams, either.

Finally, Hugh looked at her. "I can't take ye to Creagdoun yet. And Lady Roisin," he hesitated as though he weren't sure whether to continue, before he heaved a great sigh. "It might be wiser not to mention yer connection with William Campbell. Campbells aren't welcome where we're heading."

Speechless, she gazed at him. Where in the name of God was he taking her? "But we're in the heart of Campbell territory." She kept her voice low, although there was little chance of his compatriot overhearing them. "What are ye saying, Hugh? Have ye forsaken yer name?"

"No." He sounded reluctant to admit it. "But I'm trusting ye to keep yer promise to me. We've never met before today."

She shifted on the saddle, and Ecne gave a mournful whine at his enforced captivity. She didn't understand why Hugh had made her promise such a thing, but if it ensured her and Grear's safety, she was willing to go along with it.

"I'll keep my word, if ye keep yers."

He exhaled a harsh sigh and for a while they rode in silence. She tried to keep her eyes on the overgrown path, which although fine for riders was a challenge for a wagon, but she couldn't help surreptitious glances to the man by her side.

Now the rain had stopped, the sun broke through the clouds, dispersing them, and the surrounding forest looked less sinister. If only she could say the same about Hugh.

But astride the dark stallion, with his white shirt clinging to his broad shoulders like a second skin and his midnight hair plastered to his aristocratic cheekbones, Hugh emanated a nebulous menace that she'd never noticed when he'd been in Eigg. How easily she could imagine he was a mythical shapeshifting warrior from the mist-shrouded past when the fantastical Tuatha De Dannan had ruled Eire.

She shook her head and tore her gaze from his mesmeric profile. She had to stop thinking how different he'd been when they'd first met. This was the real Hugh, and the one who had captivated her in Eigg had been nothing more than an illusion.

It didn't stop the foolish pang of wishing what might have been.

"My lady."

His respectful tone and the way he used her title, when he was in the process of diverting her from seeing Isolde, was so surreal she had the alarming urge to laugh. She sucked in a deep breath to steady her nerves. It wouldn't do to lose her composure, and not just because it would upset Grear. "What?"

He shot her a glance as if her sharp tone surprised him. She was certain he'd be a lot more than merely surprised if she lost her tenuous grip on sanity and told him exactly what she thought of him.

"It occurs to me that ye were some distance from the road when I found ye." He eyed the wagon before looking back at her. "'Tis a straightforward journey from Oban to Creagdoun, even with a wagon. Did one of yer men suggest leaving the road?"

Was he implying one of her loyal men had ties to the brigands? It was a disgusting accusation. Besides, if there had been a traitor amongst them, surely he would have made provisions so he wasn't murdered along with everyone else?

"The road was blocked by a fallen tree." Her voice was icy, but she couldn't help it. "The choice was either to spend hours moving it or find an alternative route."

In hindsight, maybe it would have been better to clear the road before continuing, but then, hindsight was a marvelous thing. The expression on Hugh's face suggested he was thinking the same thing. Fortunately, he chose not to voice it.

"That road is frequently used. Seems odd a tree would fall across it, when there hasn't been a recent storm."

His implication was plain. And considering the treacherous route they'd needed to take to bypass the tree before they'd eventually arrive back on the road, she feared he could be right.

"Ye think we were targeted?"

It was bad enough to be attacked. But to suspect it might not have been random was infinitely worse.

"I don't wish to alarm ye, Lady Roisin."

This time she couldn't help an incredulous laugh from escaping. "Are ye serious, Hugh Campbell? I believe I have every right to be alarmed, and I don't need ye to tell me whether I should be or not, either."

"That's not what I meant." He shifted on his saddle, as if her retort had made him uncomfortable. *Well, good.* "I shouldn't have said anything."

For some reason, that remark stung far more than it should.

"Why not? Because ye think I shouldn't know of the dangers I might be facing?" And then she couldn't stop herself. "'Tis a little late for that, don't ye think?"

He heaved a great sigh. How irritating that she found it charming.

"I didn't plan this, Lady Roisin. But if I hadn't found ye, God only knows where ye might be by now."

A chilling shiver raced through her. She knew exactly what fate she and Grear would have suffered at the hands of the brigands. At least she had, when she'd tried to escape. But if the attack had been targeted, who knew what had really been on the outlaws' minds?

It was galling, but she had to concede that in this, at least, Hugh was right.

"I'm grateful for it." Especially since it appeared he and his compatriot had killed the remaining brigands. At least in that small way her brave warriors had been avenged. "Don't think I'm not. But ye cannot expect me to be happy ye're not taking me to Creagdoun."

"I will arrange for ye safe return to yer kin. I just cannot do it right this moment."

It was obvious he didn't intend to tell her why.

For a reason she couldn't fathom, after leaving Eigg, he'd abandoned his old life and, it appeared, his former friends. But what had happened to make him choose such a precarious path?

Whatever it was, neither of her sisters knew. Were their husbands also in the dark? Or had they just kept the truth from them?

They rode on in silence, for what seemed like hours, along nonexistent paths and keeping to the shadows of forests as they traveled higher into the mountains, and despite the rough terrain, the wagon didn't get stuck.

The edges of the basket dug into her thighs and Ecne grew heavier by the moment, but she'd sooner cut out her tongue than admit it. But how she hoped there wasn't much farther to go.

The sun was dipping low in the sky when Hugh came to her side and after an apologetic glance, once again grasped her reins.

It could mean only one thing. They had arrived, and her stomach pitched with nerves at what that might mean. Hugh might be the leader of the camp he'd mentioned, but did he truly possess the power to keep her and Grear safe from his men?

They emerged from the cover of the forest onto a mountainside. To their left, the impenetrable mountain descended into a steep glen, but Hugh led them along a secure path, wide enough for the wagon, before rounding a corner onto a small, secluded plateau.

Roisin sucked in a shocked breath. When Hugh had spoken of his camp, she'd had a vague idea of a small band of outlaws sleeping rough. But nestled against the rocky cliffs that surrounded the plateau on three sides, and undoubtedly gave protection from the elements, were a dozen or more tents in varying states of deterioration.

It wasn't the tents that unsettled her so. It was the bairns who ran over to them, before standing in a silent huddle, and the women who stood and stared at her with sullen, suspicious eyes.

This wasn't a camp of lawless men banding together to take what they could from unfortunate travelers. These were displaced families, barely scratching out an existence on the side of a mountain.

The knot of dread in the pit of her stomach that had temporarily eased while riding beside Hugh tightened, spreading tentacles of alarm throughout her blood. As Hugh dismounted, several men appeared from hidden crannies in the surrounding cliffs, where they'd doubtless been keeping a lookout, and one of them, an older man with a patch over one eye and a badly scarred face, came over to them.

"A good day's hunting." He cast his good eye over her, and she tried to suppress a shiver of fear, before his gaze fixed on the wagon behind her and the horses they'd brought with them. "Unexpected."

Hugh handed a couple of bulging sacks to a nearby woman, who pulled open the ties and peered inside. Apparently satisfied by the contents she gave a sharp nod before handing the sacks to a younger woman.

"Aye," Hugh responded to the other man's remark. "As we were returning, we crossed paths with bandits attacking this lady's escort. There was no choice but to bring her with us."

Hugh's compatriot—Symon—appeared, with Grear by his side, and Roisin grasped her hand as Symon, also, handed a couple of sacks to the woman. Belatedly, it occurred to her what the bulges in all those sacks were.

Hugh had been poaching.

The older man smiled, and it was a chilling thing to witness. "Ye didn't strike me as the type, Hugh, but then we never really know our fellow man, do we."

Her grip tightened around Grear's fingers, who was shaking so badly Roisin feared she might collapse. But then, she wasn't feeling so fine herself, either, although she was certain Hugh hadn't brought her here for the purpose the other man was slyly implying.

"The lady and her maid are under my protection, Darragh." Hugh didn't raise his voice but there was a note of pure steel in his it, and Darragh inclined his head, although a mocking smile remained on his face. "Selling the horses will bring in much needed supplies, and the goods in her wagon will cover any inconvenience until I can arrange to return her to her people."

She shot him a startled glance. Had she misunderstood? Was Hugh going to give these people everything she'd brought with her?

"A fair enough exchange." Darragh turned his attention to her, and she wanted to sink through the saddle and disappear from the malevolent gleam in his eye. "And who might ye be, then?"

Her voice locked in her throat and her heart thundered so loudly she feared everyone could hear it. Why couldn't she respond the way Isolde or Freyja would have when questioned by a fearsome stranger?

When it came to courage, no matter how hard she tried to be brave, her resolve always faltered.

"Too good to speak to the likes of us, then." There was more than a thread of contempt in Darragh's voice now. As though he could sense her terror, Ecne licked her gloved fingers through the gaps in his basket.

"No, Darragh, the lady is just recovering from her ordeal. Her name is Lady Roisin MacDonald of the Western Isles."

She didn't dare glance at Hugh. While she was falling apart, he was keeping his word to ensure her safety, by concealing her connection to William Campbell who, for whatever reason, these people despised.

"A MacDonald from the Isles, are ye?" Darragh's palpable distrust faded, and he gave a sharp nod. "I thought Hugh had picked up a damn Campbell. And where were ye heading, my lady?"

To visit my sister. But the words merely hammered inside her head, while she remained as mute as ever. Would this interrogation never end? Everyone was staring at her, as though she were a pitiable halfwit.

"Lady Roisin was on her way to Oban, to catch a ship back to the isles." Hugh offered her a tight smile that didn't reach his eyes, a silent warning not to contradict him.

As if she would.

"Can the lass not speak for herself?" Darragh hadn't taken his gaze from her, and she screwed up her nonexistent courage, and managed to force out a few words.

"I can speak for myself." Dear God, if only she'd never left Eigg, she wouldn't be here, needing to respond to a man who looked as if he'd not think twice about tossing her off the side of the mountain if the mood took him.

But if she hadn't traveled to the mainland, she wouldn't have met Hugh again and discovered the truth about his disappearance. It didn't make her feel better. At least if she'd stayed at home, she'd be able to remember him the way he'd been on Eigg, instead of having all those rose-hued memories shattered by this surreal reality.

"Good," Darragh said, "There's little in the way of hospitality we can offer ye, since the damn Campbells took everything we own, but ye'll be safe enough here for now. Maybe we'll even ransom ye. Are yer relatives rich, Lady Roisin?"

Appalled, she stared at him and after a heartbeat he laughed, as though he found it all a great jest. "I'll leave that to Hugh. He has a good head on his shoulders for such things. But for now, welcome to what remains of the grand bloodline of the MacGregors of Argyll."

The MacGregors? Hugh had brought her to a rebel outpost of the MacGregors?

But they were deadly enemies of Clan Campbell. And although the MacGregors hadn't personally offended the MacDonalds of the Isles, there was a tacit understanding between her clan and the Earl of Argyll. When it came to the feud between the Campbells and MacGregors, the MacDonalds were firmly behind the earl.

A new kind of terror clutched deep inside as the truth hit her.

She'd been wrong to think Hugh had forsaken his name. It was so much worse than that.

He had forsaken his clan.

CHAPTER FIVE

W ITH OBVIOUS RELUCTANCE, Lady Roisin handed Hugh her dog's basket before she hastily dismounted. Clearly, she didn't want his assistance. Her face was ashen, and she glanced around the camp in barely concealed despair.

Christ, what a mess. He needed to send an urgent message to the earl but that was a problem for tomorrow. Right now, he needed to make sure Roisin had some privacy, since everyone was staring at her as if she were an exotic, tasty morsel.

Luckily, privacy was something he could offer her.

"Lady Roisin, this way. I have my own tent where ye can be alone with yer maid."

"Is it safe for Ecne to stretch his legs?" She cast him an anxious glance.

"Aye. Of course." Carefully, he set the basket on the ground and watched as she opened it, and her wee dog went straight into her arms. He had the distinct feeling Darragh was judging him, and not favorably, but he wouldn't treat Roisin like a prisoner just to appease the older man's sense of justice.

The fact Darragh had lost his lands wasn't Roisin's fault. Hugh knew damn well it was only because she was a MacDonald, and not a Campbell, that Darragh had allowed her to stay, but it hadn't taken long for him to understand that at his core, Darragh despised everyone not of his own kin.

The older man only tolerated him because of Symon's high praise of when they'd fought side by side in Eire, and because he'd proven he was a good hunter during the last few weeks. He didn't fool himself that given the slightest cause, Darragh would kill him without a second thought.

Once the terrier had relieved himself against a rock, he led Roisin and Grear to his tent. It was one of the sturdier ones in the camp, as he'd brought it with him from Eire, and was pitched some distance from where most of the other tents huddled.

But it was still merely a tent.

He lifted the flap and Roisin stepped inside. Once, he'd imagined taking her back to Balfour Castle, despairing that it was in such a state of neglect. But at least Balfour possessed stone walls and a serviceable roof, and while its tapestries had seen better days, they still kept the chill at bay.

Here, the ground was damp, and the tent was empty, since he kept everything he owned secured upon his person, and when Grear took Roisin's hand and shivered, he silently cursed at his negligence. He needed to procure dry clothes at the very least for Roisin and her maid, but to smooth over the encounter with Darragh, he'd just handed over all of Roisin's possessions. He hoped it wasn't too late to salvage something before everything disappeared.

With an awkward grunt he bowed his head and hastily retreated. Darragh was supervising four other men who were removing a trunk from the back of the wagon and unhitching the string of horses they'd collected from both Roisin's men and the bandits.

Goddamn it. Logically he knew whether he'd offered or not, Darragh would have appropriated the wagon's contents, but he still felt responsible. There was no way Darragh would've only accepted the horses in exchange for Roisin's safety, even though such a windfall was nothing short of a miracle for the chieftain.

Since there was no other option but to brazen it out, he strode over to the other man.

"I'll take the lady's personal items before the rest is distributed."

"Will ye, now." Darragh didn't even bother to take his gaze from appraising the horses.

"Aye. There's plenty to go around."

Silence thudded in the air between them. Hugh kept his gaze fixed on the wagon, keeping a deliberately relaxed air about him, as though he had no qualms about his claim. Darragh would pick up on any sign that he wasn't certain of his stance and use it to crush him.

The men placed the trunk on the ground before Darragh, who eyed it speculatively. Then he looked at Hugh.

"Take what the lady needs and nothing more."

Hugh gave a sharp nod and opened the trunk.

Reams of fabric greeted him, and his heart sank. It appeared Roisin had packed a great many gowns and other feminine accessories. What the devil should he take back to her? He had no idea but, with a firm purpose he was far from feeling, he peeled away the top layer of material in the hope that might solve the problem.

Beneath the gown an assortment of exquisitely embroidered baby clothes confronted him, and heat crawled through him at the implication. Christ, were William and Isolde expecting a bairn?

Darragh gave a snort of amusement. "Maybe yer bonny lass is already wedded and bedded, Hugh. Ye had best hope she has no angry husband on her tail."

Hugh ignored the other man's jibe and grimly tossed a couple of gowns over his arm before retrieving a thick blanket. But the words burrowed deep into his brain, and he couldn't dislodge them.

Was Roisin married? Despite the notion crossing his mind during the last year or so, it hadn't occurred to him to ask her. He'd simply assumed she wasn't.

But for all he knew she might be meeting her husband at William's and that was why she was so eager to get to Creagdoun.

Several women joined him and started sorting through Roisin's possessions, and the baby clothes were snatched up in an instant. He stood back and glanced at the wagon.

The men had now turned their attention to the horses, leaving a smaller chest on the wagon and he went over and opened it. It was filled with what he presumed were feminine items, hidden in pouches, and small, dark bottles, along with rolls of ribbons and a comb and brush. Relieved he'd found something useful, he tucked the chest under his arm but as he passed by the now almost empty trunk, something caught his eye.

At the bottom of the trunk was a worn, black writing case. He knew that writing case. Roisin had carried it everywhere when he'd been at Sgur Castle. Swiftly, he crouched and grabbed it, avoiding the angry glare of a woman who'd obviously had her eye on it.

He returned to the tent and then hesitated. It felt wrong to simply enter, and so he cleared his throat and kicked the bottom of the flap a couple of times to let her know he was there. After a moment, Grear pulled open the flap and after a smile of thanks, he ducked his head and went inside.

Roisin turned to face him, and he caught his breath. She'd released her hair from its braids and the dark auburn tresses cascaded to her waist, and in the muted light her emerald eyes glittered.

For one paralyzing moment, he feared he'd fallen into one of his nighttime fantasies, except those despairing dreams had never come close to the vision who stood before him.

"Hugh?" There was a questioning note in her voice, and he brutally tore his besotted gaze from her and made much of placing the casket on the ground. Her wee dog came up to him and licked his hand, and he scratched the terrier's throat in greeting before once again catching her perplexed gaze.

"I managed to salvage a few things." He glanced around, but there was nowhere to put the gowns, so he continued to clutch them until Grear approached and tentatively took them from him. He thrust the writing case at Roisin. "I'm sorry I couldn't get more."

Her air of anxiety fled, and for a fleeting moment it seemed she'd forgotten where she was as she took the case from him and hugged it to her breast.

"Thank ye," she whispered, as though he'd handed her a precious gem. But then, he supposed he had. Her face had lit up as she'd shown him her manuscripts in the solar at Sgur and he could still recall, in fine detail, the wondrous illuminations she had shared with him. Illuminations she'd crafted herself to accompany the texts she'd written about ancient myths and folktales.

A shred of unease ate at him. The writing case was a good size, but it couldn't possibly have held even a fraction of the works she'd shared with him. "Did ye bring all yer manuscripts, my lady? I promise I'll find them, if so."

Even if he had to go tent to tent and barter what little he possessed in the process.

"No, I only brought my writing case. I fear I'd need an entire trunk to hold all my manuscripts. But thank ye for the thought."

He sighed, his unease sinking deeper into his chest by the notion she felt the need to thank him for acquiring something that was already hers. "Darragh considers anything brought into the camp his by rights. I didn't offer yer possessions lightly."

She shook her head. "I'm certain the brigands would have taken everything and not thought twice about it. At least ye've brought us dry clothes to change into."

Aye, and if he retained a scrap of honor, he'd leave instantly and let her tend to her needs. Yet the gnawing suspicion that Darragh had planted wouldn't rest and before he could stop himself, the words were out.

"Lady Roisin, are ye meeting yer husband at Creagdoun?"

She gazed at him as though he'd lost his mind, and then she blushed, the rosy hue highlighting her fine cheekbones and his worst fears were confirmed.

And then she spoke. "No. I'm not wed, Hugh. I told ye, I'm visiting my sister."

Relief washed through him, although God knew why. Her marital status changed nothing, when he had nothing to offer her, and his family's honor still hung in the balance.

The facts didn't change the way he felt.

"I trust Lady Isolde is well." It was as close as he could get to asking if her sister was with child.

"Her letters assure us she is very well and thriving in the foreign climes." Roisin gave a faint smile, and he grinned at her as he recalled how against the marriage with William Lady Isolde had initially been.

"I'm glad to hear it. William is a lucky man."

"Indeed." She hesitated. "Do ye know they are expecting their first bairn in two months?"

A pang assailed him, even though he'd guessed. Once, not so long ago, he would've learned of such news directly from his cousin.

"That's good news. William always wanted bairns." Even during the years before he'd met the elusive Lady Isolde, when he hadn't wanted to wed her, he'd always envisaged having a family to fill Creagdoun Castle.

Roisin gave him a curious look. "'Tis just as well Isolde wanted them too, then."

It was a cryptic remark. Bairns followed marriage the same way night followed day. But he wasn't about to argue with her, not when she appeared willing to forgive him for not immediately taking her to Creagdoun.

"I promise ye'll be with Lady Isolde for her confinement."

Once again, anxiety filled her beautiful emerald eyes. "Do ye think Darragh will let me go? Was he serious about holding me for ransom?"

"He'll let ye go. There's no reason for him to risk discovery by ransoming ye, my lady. The last thing Darragh wants is to draw attention to his clan."

"Do ye think ye'll be able to take us to Creagdoun on the morrow?"

Although the earl had a network of spies across Argyll, there was no way of knowing how long it would be before he received word on how to deliver Roisin to safety. But first he needed to send a message without rousing any suspicion.

None of which he could share with her.

"No," he admitted reluctantly, and watched the hope leach from her face. *Goddamn it.* He didn't want her to think he was keeping her from her kin for the hell of it. It was safer to remain silent, but he couldn't do it. "I can't risk Darragh suspecting ye're connected through marriage to a powerful Campbell, and he will guess if I push for yer release too soon. I'm only talking a matter of days, Lady Roisin. Once he sells the horses, his focus will shift from ye."

It wasn't a lie, but it wasn't the full truth, either. If he pushed Darragh too hard, too soon, it wouldn't be on Roisin that Darragh's suspicious eye would fall.

It would be him. And if Darragh acted on those suspicions, it would leave Roisin without protection.

"But what if Darragh hears rumors that Alasdair Campbell is searching for me? It won't take much for him to guess the truth, will it?"

"Alasdair?" He'd been referring to William, her brother-through-marriage. Although certainly Alasdair, as the earl's favored half-brother, was a force to be reckoned with, there was no reason for—

"Ye don't know, do ye?" There was a note of despair in Roisin's voice, and he had to battle the instinctive urge to take her hand in a fruitless attempt to comfort her. "My sister, Freyja, wed Alasdair a little over a year ago. Alasdair is now Baron of Glenchonnel."

An odd, echoey sensation filled his head, as though he were no longer connected to his body. For the last year, he'd done the earl's bidding, hoping that, in the end, he could return to his former life.

But his former life didn't exist anymore. He'd pushed through each day holding onto the memories of his friends and family to keep him from the edge of the abyss, but his two closest friends' lives had changed irrevocably, and he hadn't known a thing about it until now.

All the questions he'd forced to the back of his mind just so he could survive this cursed existence crawled to the surface. What else didn't he know? How did his sisters fare? Was his father even still alive?

Will I ever escape this hell?

"Hugh." Roisin's whisper dragged him back to the present, where her hand hovered a hairsbreadth from his chest. But she didn't touch him, and when he sucked in a harsh breath, she hastily wrapped her fingers around the writing case she still clutched against her breast. "Are ye all right?"

"Aye." He attempted a reassuring smile but wasn't sure he succeeded since Roisin still gazed at him as though she feared for his sanity. Brutally, he shoved his fractured thoughts into a dark corner of his mind where, with luck, they would wither and perish. "I didn't know."

Dammit, he hadn't meant to admit that, but the concern in her eyes had been his undoing. The last time he'd seen Alasdair was just over a year ago, on the day the earl had told him of his mission. Alasdair, he recalled, had appeared in fine spirits. And according to Roisin, Alasdair had wed her sister shortly afterwards.

By the command of his half-brother?

"They're very happy together."

Were they? Or was Roisin just saying that? He forced another smile to his face before she saw more in his eyes than he wanted her to. "That's good."

Except now she was related to two powerful Campbells, one of whom was blood-bound to the earl himself. If Darragh ever discovered Roisin's connections, Hugh was certain the older man would decide she was worth ransoming, no matter what objections Hugh might make.

"I don't understand." Once again, she raised her hand, and her fingers came perilously close to touching his chest before she appeared to realize what she was doing, and she snatched her hand back. "I thought ye were good friends with both William and Alasdair. What happened, Hugh? Why are ye living like this?"

If only he could tell her. Just so she knew he wasn't a traitor to his own clan, but it was a fool's dream. The truth would do nothing but put her in peril, for although he didn't know her well, he knew enough. Lady Roisin wasn't the type of woman who could lie without blinking in the face of danger. If Darragh, or anyone else in the camp questioned her, it was best she had nothing to hide.

Nothing but the fact her sister was married to the Earl of Argyll's half-brother.

He stifled a groan. There was nothing he could do about that, but the chances of anyone asking her directly about her sister's husband was remote.

And she still waited for his answer. An answer he could never share with her.

"I fought for a while in Eire." There was no harm in telling her that. Everyone in the camp was aware he'd met Symon when they'd both been redshanks. "And afterwards, Symon invited me to stay with his kin."

It was obvious she had more questions, especially since he'd completely sidestepped those she'd already asked him, and he hastily bowed his head. "I shan't keep ye any longer. I shouldn't wish ye to catch a chill."

With that inane comment, he backed out of the tent and exhaled a relieved breath, before casting a stealthy glance around the camp. Fortunately, Darragh was nowhere to be seen, and no one was paying him any attention to comment on how long he'd been inside the tent with Roisin.

He needed to be careful. He couldn't afford to draw any more unwanted attention to either himself or her, not when her freedom rested on him keeping on the right side of Darragh.

Chapter Six

I T WAS A relief to change into dry clothes and as Grear hung their
wet gowns over the wooden poles that supported the compact
leather tent, Roisin opened the casket Hugh had rescued. Of all the
possessions she'd brought with her, he had managed to save the two
most important.

Her beloved writing case and the contents of this casket.

It contained her personal medicinal supplies, essential at any time
but especially here, where there was little chance she'd be allowed to
forage in the nearby forest or glens for the necessary plants. Besides
which, most of them had been cultivated in the gardens at Sgur, under
the watchful eye of Freyja, who had ensured both of her sisters learned
the secrets that had been handed down from their ancient foremothers.

Neither she nor Isolde were as skilled as Freyja, but at least with
these supplies she wasn't completely defenseless against an unexpected
injury or malady.

There were also soaps and cleansers, and beneath several lengths
of linen, which she and Grear could use as a makeshift bed along with
the blanket Hugh had salvaged, was her trusty satchel. As she pulled it
out, Grear crouched down beside her.

"Should I see if I can find something to eat, milady?" Trepidation
shivered through every word and Roisin took her hand as they stood
up. Neither of them had eaten since they'd left Eigg at first light this
morning, but with everything that had happened, she hadn't realized

how hungry she was. And poor Ecne must be starving, too.

She glanced at her dog who gazed at her with trusting eyes, and she bit her lip. Although she'd much rather stay in Hugh's tent away from suspicious glances from Clan MacGregor, she and Grear needed to keep up their strength. And she certainly wouldn't send Grear out of the relative safety of the tent on her own.

"We'll go together." She hoped Grear didn't hear the quake of fear in her own voice. She pushed her writing case into her satchel and added as many of her medicinal herbs and soaps as she could, until the satchel bulged. There was no telling if her things would be safe in Hugh's tent once she left it, and at least this way she'd have a few essentials.

But it was more than that. If anyone discovered the sketches she'd done of Hugh during the last eighteen months, and which she'd kept hidden in her writing case, their story of never having met before would be exposed. She didn't know how Darragh would react to having been lied to but 'twas safe to assume her situation would become even more precarious than it was now.

That wasn't the main reason she was so relieved that Hugh had rescued her writing case, though. Even the prospect that he might see those sketches made her stomach cramp with nerves. Now they had met again, the last thing she wanted was for him to ever guess she had once harbored foolish romantic notions about him.

That was over. Now she had to be practical, like Freyja, and find a way to best survive this perilous interlude until Hugh found her safe passage to Creagdoun.

She just hoped the MacGregor women would be kind enough to share their food with her and Grear, considering they'd helped themselves to her belongings.

"Yer hair, milady."

"Oh." Self-consciously, she ran her fingers through the damp strands. She'd loosened her hair to help dry it but it wouldn't do to leave the tent looking like an unkempt forest fae. And then she remembered Hugh had seen her and heat streaked through her. What must he have thought?

She shook her head in disgust. What did it matter what he thought? The important thing was she had to maintain an appearance of calm, and no one would be fooled if she stepped outside in such utter disarray.

It took only a few moments for Grear to braid her hair, and once she was presentable, she slung her satchel over her shoulder and gathered her scattered courage. With a reassuring smile at her maid, she lifted the flap of the tent and stepped outside.

It was late afternoon, and the earthy aroma of roasting game wafted in the air, and her stomach growled in response. The horses and wagon had been moved to the far side of the camp, and there was no sign of her trunk. Hugh and the rest of the men were nowhere in sight, which was both a relief and a source of consternation. She'd secretly been hoping to find Hugh so he could procure some food.

But there was no help for it. She couldn't stand here dithering and hoping the MacGregor womenfolk would take pity on her and Grear and offer them some sustenance. She drew in a deep breath for courage, before she straightened her shoulders and headed to where the rest of the tents were pitched some distance from Hugh's. Small game, which she assumed Hugh and Symon had brought back with them, hung from a rope set up between two poles. A large fire pit had been dug in the middle of the semi-circle of tents. Once again, her stomach rumbled at the aroma emanating from it.

And then her burst of courage fizzled like a doused lantern, and she hesitated. Eight women, who appeared to range in age from herself to one in her early fifties, sat around the fire pit. Four of them were working on the various processes of tanning small animal skins while a fifth woman prepared wild plants for the meal. The remaining three were nursing their bairns.

They all ignored her, and she battled the overwhelming urge to slink back to Hugh's tent. But she couldn't let Grear and Ecne go hungry just because she wasn't brave enough to stand up for herself.

She stepped forward until she was within a horse length of the group but the only ones who glanced her way were two young lasses who were entertaining a wee bairn who was clearly just learning to walk. She smiled at them, and they stared at her as though she were a fascinating apparition.

It was obvious they had no intention of making this easy for her. She took a deep breath and aimed her question at the oldest woman. "May I help?"

"I don't know," the woman said, sparing her a fleeting glance before returning to her task of cleaning out the bloodied remains that clung to the inside of what looked like a rabbit. "Does a lady of the Western Isles know how to help?"

It was true she wasn't skilled in the tasks these women were undertaking. At Sgur, she hadn't needed to be. Amma had taught her and her sisters how to manage a grand stronghold and all that entailed, and while she could certainly cook, she had never needed to butcher the animal beforehand.

That was, after all, a task for servants. She'd cut her tongue out before she shared that with these women.

"I do," she said, before she could think better of it.

The older woman eyed her and for a terrible moment Roisin had the certainty she was going to tell her to skin one of the creatures currently hanging from the rope. But before she could say anything, one of the women nursing her bairn spoke.

"Let her do some mending, Elspeth." Then she looked at Roisin. "These grand ladies are good with their needles, so I've heard."

Mending was certainly preferable to butchering but she wasn't sure it would be a good thing to show her relief. "I can do that," she confirmed, then glanced at her maid before adding, "Grear and I can do that."

All the women were staring at her now. It was far worse being the focus of their attention than being ignored, but at least now they couldn't overlook her when they served the food.

She couldn't think about food, even though the aroma of roasting meat was all around her. She had to concentrate on showing these women she could be useful and not be distracted by her hungry stomach.

"All right then, Innis," Elspeth said. "Ye do as ye see fit."

"Rhona." Innis, the younger woman who had spoken earlier, nodded her head at the elder of the two girls. "Fetch the basket, there's a good lass."

Rhona ran off in the direction of the tents, and the wee lad she had been playing with toddled after her, his arms outstretched, before he tumbled at Roisin's feet. She smiled and crouched down, taking his hands to pull him upright, whereupon he instantly focused on Ecne.

Ecne was used to the bairns from the village in Eigg and didn't twitch so much as an ear as the wee lad gave him a hug. Gently, she extricated him before he fell onto Ecne and distracted him with a wooden ball the bairns had been playing with.

"Do ye have bairns?" Innis adjusted her shawl and put her bairn against her shoulder as she patted the babe's back. One of the other women soothed her fractious newborn, and it was only then Roisin noticed the wee thing was wearing one of the tiny outfits she had spent untold hours embroidering for Isolde.

She dragged her eyes away and caught Innis's steady gaze. Now was not the time to fret over such a thing. "No," she said in response to the other woman's question. "I'm not wed."

When the other women glanced at each other and smirked, heat rushed into her cheeks at her foolish remark. Why had she said such a thing? Now they would likely think she was so sheltered she believed one had to be wed before one could have a bairn.

Lord, maybe they thought she didn't know how bairns were made.

"'Tis fortunate Symon and Hugh rescued ye from the bandits," remarked one of the other women. "I doubt a lady such as yerself would've fared well among such barbarous men."

"Aye, 'tis a cruel world for an unprotected woman," Innis added. "We may have been brought low, but ye can be reassured our men won't take advantage of ye while ye're under the protection of Darragh MacGregor."

"Hugh Campbell is another matter." Elspeth cast her a calculating look and Roisin forced herself not to drop her gaze. She didn't know anything about these women, but something told her if she withered beneath Elspeth's scrutiny, she would lose all hope of gaining their respect. "Sleep with yer dagger handy if ye do not wish to end up..." The ghost of a smile hovered around her lips before she said, "wed."

The women smiled, as though they shared a secret jest as they glanced at each other. *Well, let them laugh at my expense.* She knew full well what Elspeth really meant and although Hugh wasn't the man she'd believed him to be, it still greatly irked her that Elspeth thought he was so lacking in honor that he'd resort to such contemptible behavior.

Still, it was good advice, for all of that. She'd be sure to sleep with a dagger in her hand for as long as she remained in this camp.

Rhona returned, dragging a large basket, and Roisin picked out the top garment. It was a man's shirt with a long rip along the sleeve. She handed it to Grear and pulled out another damaged shirt. Well, at least these tasks were simple enough. Then she settled herself next to Grear as they threaded their needles and the women, losing interest in them, returned to their own tasks.

Innis attempted to coax her bairn into another feed, but the babe, whom Roisin guessed to be maybe a year or so, fussed and his mother sighed heavily. "He's not taking enough."

Another woman glanced at her. "How often is he feeding?"

Innis pressed her lips together before exhaling another measured breath. "Not often enough, I am certain."

Roisin hastily tore her gaze from the women and concentrated on her work. She didn't want them to think she was eavesdropping, even though it was impossible not to hear their conversation. But still, it was obvious she wasn't included. They likely thought she wouldn't even understand the true nature of their concern, but Freyja was passionate about such things, and had ensured both her sisters were well versed in all the ways that lowered the chances of conception. And if Innis's babe was rejecting her milk, then all too soon her body would once again be receptive to a man's seed.

Elspeth's next words confirmed her suspicion. "Ye best start taking the tea again."

"The stocks are low." Frustration threaded through Innis's voice. "Goddamn this life. I cannot fall again, Elspeth."

She felt Elspeth's glance fall her way and kept her head lowered over her work. She understood the older woman's reluctance to speak with a stranger in their midst. Such things were women's knowledge, to be sure, but the ancient secrets were not shared with those who couldn't be trusted to keep their counsel.

After a heartbeat, it appeared Elspeth decided she posed no danger, likely because she believed Roisin had no idea how a bairn was even conceived, let alone the methods that had been used since the beginning of time to prevent such an occurrence. After all, how could one divulge a secret to a man if she didn't realize it was a secret in the first place?

"We'll forage farther afield tomorrow." Elspeth kept her voice low. "There are always herbs to be gathered, after all."

Silence hung in the air after her remark and Roisin chanced darting a swift glance around the women. There were, of course, another method of preventing pregnancy, but she hadn't needed Freyja's wisdom to learn that men did not take kindly to having their pleasure interrupted. There were enough women on the Small Isles who could testify to that.

As for the herbs, she had enough in her supplies that could be utilized in such a manner, but would the women take kindly to her offer? Or would they think she was pushing herself into business that had nothing to do with her?

She was still grappling with the conundrum of remaining silent or not when Elspeth stacked her work to the side and checked the food. "Call the men," she instructed, and one of the other women left her tasks and made her way to the other side of the camp, where the horses and her wagon were, and vanished around a rocky outcrop where, presumably, the men had gathered. As Roisin finished mending the shirt she was working on, one of the older bairns appeared with a stack of plates, and the men approached.

Hastily, she stood, folded the shirt, and placed it back in the basket. Elspeth distributed the food, Darragh first, and then the rest of the men, with Hugh bringing up the rear. For a moment, their gazes met and she fancied she saw a ghost of a smile touch his lips. But perhaps it was the fading light or simply her own foolish imagination since he didn't come over to her but turned away to sit with Symon.

She adjusted the satchel on her shoulder. It was heavy and her back ached, but it was a small price for the peace of mind of knowing at least a few of her possessions were safe.

Elspeth dished up the remainder of the food between the women and Roisin's mouth watered. She had never been so famished in her life. Finally, after the bairns had been served, the older woman handed plates to her and Grear, and Roisin's thanks stuck in her throat at the collection of small bones and the wee amount of meat without even a sliver of a vegetable.

But even she had been given more than poor Grear.

Face burning, she sat down, before pulling out her knife to cut the meat in half. She gave it to Ecne, who swallowed it in one gulp before gazing at her with sad brown eyes. But she couldn't give him the cooked bones and she needed a little sustenance for herself.

There was no help for it. She would have to speak to Elspeth. She waited until there was a lull in the conversation when the other woman caught her eye and she took a deep breath for courage. "Might I have a couple of raw bones for my dog?"

All the women and their menfolk who sat beside them for the meal stared at her as though she'd just committed an unspeakable act. Instead of wishing the ground would open and swallow her, a flicker of anger stirred. She'd seen with her own eyes that Hugh had brought back a sackful of game that now hung on the rope behind them, and considering it was Hugh who had brought her here against her will, she was certain they could spare her a couple of bones for Ecne.

She straightened her shoulders and stared right back at Elspeth. After a few moments, the older woman gave a slight nod in the direction of the carcasses. "Help yerself."

CHAPTER SEVEN

A S USUAL, HUGH didn't join the others when they gathered for the meal but instead sat some distance from the fire pit, with Symon. But it was hard to keep his gaze from straying to Roisin. It wounded him deep inside to see her mending clothes for Clan MacGregor men, when she was noble born and should spend her time on her exquisite embroidery or illuminated manuscripts.

He had to get her away from this life and back to her own as soon as possible.

After he had left her in his tent, he'd joined the men who'd taken the horses to the other side of the camp where they were examining them and discussing which ones to keep and which ones to sell. It was decided that the following day they'd take a couple of horses to a town some distance from the camp which, although they'd surveyed it when they first arrived five weeks ago, they'd yet to visit.

He planned on accompanying them. It was the best opportunity he'd have to find a messenger. It was always a risky undertaking whenever he sent dispatches to the earl, but he never took chances, and he wasn't going to start now. For should a MacGregor discover the truth about him, it would put Roisin in danger.

Since he had no intention of leaving her unprotected in the camp while he was gone, he planned on speaking with Darragh in the morning about taking Roisin and her maid—not to mention her wee dog—with him. He'd already worked out his strategy and was confident the chieftain would see the benefits of having two young women accompanying him and Symon.

He had half finished his meal when Roisin stood, her plate in her hand and dog at her heels and made her way around the fire pit towards him. His heart jackknifed and he forgot how to eat, but before he made a complete arse of himself, he realized she wasn't coming over to him at all. She avoided even glancing his way before crouching by the pile of carcasses and gingerly poking through them with her knife.

Something akin to horror assailed him that Lady Roisin was scavenging among discarded bones and without a thought as to what Symon might make of it, he shuffled closer to her.

"What are ye doing?" He kept his voice low, although nobody would hear above the murmur of conversation from the MacGregors.

She still didn't look at him. "Ecne needs to eat."

His gaze strayed to the plate she'd placed on the ground, the plate she'd been given just moments ago, and which now had only a few bones picked clean of whatever small amount of meat had once clung to them. His furtive glances her way, as he'd shoveled his own food into his mouth, gave him proof enough she'd scarcely eaten a morsel before coming over to pick at the few bones that hadn't been used, and a wave of anger burned through his chest.

He wasn't a MacGregor, and he wasn't on their side, but he'd never slacked when it came to ensuring the clan had enough to eat. It was, after all, the main reason why Darragh tolerated his presence. He knew damn well that until he and Symon had arrived, the clan had often gone without meat, relying on lichens to stave off hunger. And it wasn't conjecture on his part. He'd heard the whispered remarks between the women and, again, his ability to hunt was why the women welcomed him as readily as they did.

Aye, there had been unexpected extra mouths to feed, but the meal could have been stretched so as not to starve two young women, and he'd be damned if he'd let Roisin go hungry. Before he could stop himself, he flung an unwary glare in the direction of the clan, before scraping the remains of his meal onto Roisin's plate.

She gasped and glanced at her plate as though he'd just filled it with worms.

"I don't want yer food." Her voice was scarcely above a whisper, and she sounded mortified. That made two of them, although likely for different reasons, since he was mortified he'd dragged her into this mess in the first place. But what choice did he have?

"I'm full," he lied. "Share it with Grear and yer wee dog. I cannot have ye fainting from hunger, can I?"

His attempt at a jest fell flat as she didn't so much as give a glimmer of a smile, unlike when they'd been in Eigg, and her smile had lit up her whole face whenever he'd made a lighthearted comment. But then, in Eigg she hadn't been attacked or spirited away to an enemy campsite.

"I won't faint." There was a trace of affront in her voice, and she gripped her knife as though it were a weapon rather than an implement to eat with. "I'm not that fragile."

But she was fragile. From the first moment he'd caught sight of her after arriving on the Isle of Eigg last winter, her elusive air of ethereality had captivated him in ways he didn't even recognize. She wasn't fearless like her eldest sister, Lady Isolde, or straight-talking with whoever crossed her path like Lady Freyja. He found Roisin's gentle manner enchanting and when she had shared her art with him, her talent had stolen his breath.

As they had stood in a shadowed corner of Sgur Castle, on the morning of her sister and William's wedding, she had shyly offered him her beautifully embroidered handkerchief as a keepsake. And he had known, deep in his bones, that if she were ever in danger, he would protect her with his very life.

It was a noble thought, and it had kept him warm inside, like a glowing ember, on the journey back to Balfour Castle. An insubstantial pledge to himself that had little prospect of ever being discharged since Roisin wasn't in danger nor was she likely to be, on the isle where her foremothers had ruled for untold generations.

Yet here they were, in Argyll, the land of his birth, and the only way he could protect her was by ensuring he remained alive. Which meant not drawing any more unwanted attention to himself and Roisin, in case Darragh decided to look more deeply into her background.

He gazed into her emerald-green eyes that no longer glowed with warmth, the way they had on Eigg and in his countless dreams of her. The safest thing to do was to back away and return to Symon, but he couldn't do it. Not until he'd assured her that she would never again be overlooked when it came to dishing out the food he'd provided the clan.

"This oversight won't happen again, ye have my word. But ye must keep yer strength up, my lady. I vowed to look after ye, and I will, if it's the last thing I do."

She stared at him as though he'd lost his mind. "I don't know who ye made this vow to, Hugh Campbell, but if ye meant a word of it, ye would've taken me to my sister's instead of dragging me here, and well ye know it."

"'Tis not that simple." He thought she understood that from the last time they'd spoken of this, but how could he expect her to understand when he couldn't tell her the truth? He released a frustrated sigh and wished he could take her hands and reassure her all would be well. But although they were currently being ignored, he was certain if he crossed that boundary with Roisin, the entire clan would notice. "And I make the vow to ye, Roisin."

Her name slipped out, unguarded, but she didn't reprimand him for the lack of respect. By the way she was glaring at him, he suspected she hadn't even noticed.

"I don't need yer vow to look after me. Why would I?" She glared at her plate and pressed her lips together. It was obvious she was torn between rejecting the food he'd given her and putting her pride aside so her maid and dog, at least, wouldn't go hungry.

After a fraught silence, she gripped the plate and stood and he watched her walk back to her place on the far side of the fire pit, where she shared the food between Grear and her dog. The light was fading, and he narrowed his eyes, trying to see if she'd kept any for herself. Surely she had. She wasn't that stubborn, was she?

On Eigg, he hadn't considered she possessed a stubborn bone in her body.

With a disgruntled snort he returned to his original spot opposite Symon and finished the last gulp of his ale. Christ, what wouldn't he do for a good flagon of wine. He could scarcely recall the last time he'd drunk anything but bad ale.

"Careful, Sergeant." Symon regarded him over his own tankard of ale. "A man might think ye're sweet on her."

He flung the other man an irritated glance. "We're not barbarians, Symon." At least, Campbells weren't. And truth be told, neither were MacGregors, even if the earl had declared them Clan Campbell's sworn enemies. "The lady isn't our prisoner and shouldn't be treated as such."

Symon shrugged. "I'm not disagreeing. But ye look at her as though ye cannot bear to see her suffer. Does she remind ye of the bonny lass waiting for ye back home?"

Would his moment of madness when he'd confided in Symon forever come back to haunt him?

He decided to ignore the other man's remark. "I'll have a word with Elspeth on the morrow."

Symon grunted. Hugh couldn't fathom whether it was a grunt of warning or disbelief. He acknowledged it could likely be both. Elspeth was a formidable woman in her own right, without having the added benefit of being Darragh's sister. But if he wanted Roisin to be treated fairly, then he needed to speak to the older woman.

"I wouldn't advise it." Symon swallowed the last of his ale. "Elspeth doesn't take kindly to interference."

"I can be tactful." God knew, he learned that art years ago, when he'd mitigated disruptions caused by his brother's drunken ways.

"Don't say I didn't warn ye."

He knew he was glowering but couldn't seem to stop himself as he chanced another glance Roisin's way. At least she appeared to be eating, which was a relief. It was only when Symon kicked his boot and he dragged his besotted gaze from her that he realized several of the women, and one or two of their menfolk, were casting interested glances between him and Roisin.

Goddamn it. So much for not drawing any unwanted attention.

When a couple of the women stood and began gathering the plates he had to forcibly stop himself from leaping to his feet when Roisin and her maid joined them. He hadn't expected her to do that, especially considering how they'd disrespected her when it came to sharing the food. On the other hand, he had to admit that her gracious response was more diplomatic than his own feral reaction.

One of the women took his and Symon's plates and the knowing grin she leveled his way told him everything he needed to know.

He had failed to keep his interest in Roisin to himself. He could only hope no one guessed the true situation between them.

With difficulty, he relaxed his fists and took a deep breath. He had to mask his feelings. He'd spent the last year concealing his true thoughts. Why was it so hard when it concerned Roisin?

"Where are ye planning on sleeping tonight?"

Symon's question pulled him back to the present and he cast the other man a dark glare. He hadn't thought that far ahead but there was only one answer. "Outside my tent."

"Oh, aye." There was a mocking note in Symon's voice. "To protect the lady from roaming wolves, no doubt."

It wasn't wolves he'd been thinking of, but he wasn't about to contradict the other man. "That's right."

"I doubt she'll appreciate yer concern for her well-being."

He doubted it too, but he wasn't doing it to gain her favor. "I brought her here. I'm responsible for her."

"Maybe ye should ransom her. Her family will likely be grateful ye saved her from ruin."

No doubt Lady Helga and Roisin's sisters would be relieved he'd crossed her path before the bandits had dragged her to God knew where. But it reminded him of the possibility the attack hadn't been random. Who the hell would have targeted Lady Roisin?

The fact her sister was now wed to Alasdair Campbell, favored half-brother of the earl, certainly threw a new light on the likelihood it was one of the earl's enemies behind the attack. Lady Freyja was, after all, the earl's sister through marriage, and he would certainly take such an affront to his close kin's honor personally.

Considering Clan MacGregor had been on the receiving end of the earl's wrath for the last five years and their lands confiscated, it was certainly possible they might undertake such a risky venture as kidnapping a noblewoman for gain. The question was whether the earl would have paid whatever was demanded without dispute or instead hunted the perpetrators down and slaughtered them without mercy.

He was inclined to believe the latter. The earl didn't take kindly to threats. Although surely, had the bandits succeeded in their plan, he would have attempted to rescue Roisin first?

It was all conjecture at this point. At least he could be certain it wasn't Darragh MacGregor who had ordered the attack, and maybe the bandits had nothing to do with the MacGregors at all.

He had no way of knowing the truth. But one thing was certain.

Roisin's continuing safety was entirely in his hands.

CHAPTER EIGHT

ROISIN OPENED HER eyes as Grear left their makeshift bed and watched her open a tiny crack in the flap of the tent. Light flooded into the tent and with a sigh Roisin sat up and wrapped her arms around Ecne, who had spent the night snuggled between her and Grear.

Every part of her body hurt, but since she'd never slept on the ground before, with only a blanket and length of linen wrapped around her, it was only to be expected. She had a good supply of willow bark in her satchel, and she would make a soothing tea for them both as soon as she managed to find the clan's water supply.

And build a fire to boil the water. She doubted the women would offer her the use of their own fire and besides, she didn't want to ask them for anything else if she could possibly help it. It had been humiliating enough asking for a few bones for Ecne.

Although that was nothing compared to the aftermath, when Hugh Campbell had insisted she take the food from his plate.

Heat burned through her. She knew she shouldn't care what he thought of her. Not now when she had discovered he wasn't the man she'd always imagined he was. But it didn't matter how often she'd repeated that good advice to herself throughout the night, it didn't change the truth.

He'd felt sorry for her. And that was why he'd given her the remains of his meal. For a moment, she'd had the alarming urge to tip his offering over his head and stalk proudly away. Except she couldn't bear to see Ecne go hungry, and Grear certainly didn't deserve to suffer.

She'd fully intended to share it between Grear and Ecne, but in the end her growling stomach had overruled her pride. Even hours later, she was still irked by her lack of willpower.

Grear reached for something outside, before closing the tent flap. "A pot of water, milady," she said, placing it on the ground between them. "And there's a small fire just outside."

They stared at each other. It was obvious who had built the fire and left the water. Truly, she couldn't fathom Hugh Campbell at all. It was a thoughtful gesture, as was the fact he'd spent the night outside the tent. Although truth be told she'd been torn between relief by his implicit protection and chagrin that she needed his protection in the first place. Elspeth's mocking comment had echoed in her head, and feeling slightly foolish she had, indeed, slept with her knife beside her.

She wasn't going to fret about it. They needed water, and here it was. She rummaged in her casket before finding a small bowl and filled it with water for Ecne, and a second bowl so she and Grear could wash. But as she and her maid freshened themselves, she was reminded that, if not for Hugh's quick thinking in grabbing the casket that contained her personal items, she'd never be able to clean herself again until she returned to her kin.

It was galling, being grateful to him for something she had always taken for granted. But then, she'd always taken having a full stomach for granted, too, and it was only due to Hugh having shared his meal with her last night that she and Grear weren't suffering from hunger cramps this morning.

Was relying on Hugh for every drop of water and scrap of food the only way they were going to survive this ordeal? It was alarming to face the fact she was so utterly dependent on him. Even back on Eigg, when she'd woven fanciful daydreams of marrying him one day, she had never imagined being beholden to him for her literal existence.

She and her sisters, as the daughters of Sgur Castle with its formidable heritage, were wealthy heiresses who had been taught from an early age they did not need to marry to stave off destitution.

But here, deep in the Highlands, her heritage meant nothing.

She shook her head in an effort to clear her tangled thoughts. Worrying about something she couldn't change wouldn't help their predicament. And although, alas, there wasn't anything to eat hidden in the casket, she found the willow bark and various other herbs so they could, at least, have something to drink.

"Heat the water for our tea," she said to Grear who nodded. "I'll take Ecne out to stretch his legs."

She straightened her shawl and picked up her satchel, and Grear insisted on tidying her hair, but within a few moments they left the tent. As Grear heated the water, Roisin took Ecne towards the back of the plateau, away from the frightening drop to the glen that huddled between the surrounding mountains.

As Ecne sniffed the rocks and the mosses and lichens that covered most of the plateau, her gaze drifted to where the women had emerged from the far side of the plateau and were making their way through the campsite to her.

They weren't coming to see *her*, but they clearly wanted to get away from the men who gathered among the tents. Was Hugh there? She couldn't see him and apprehension flickered through her. But there was surely no need for alarm. He was likely simply beyond the rocky outcrop that lay behind the horses and her wagon.

It was too annoying that his absence made her anxious, but the stark truth was, whatever darkness consumed him and had led him to this existence, he was a slender thread to her past, and she clung onto the belief he spoke the truth when he promised he'd find a way to give her safe passage to Creagdoun.

The women stopped a short distance from her, and Roisin kept her gaze fixed on Ecne. Every fiber of her being wanted to return to

Hugh's tent to escape the women, but Ecne was enjoying himself and so she straightened her spine and gripped her wavering courage before it had the chance to flee into the mountains.

She wasn't doing anything wrong. She had the right to stand here. It wasn't her fault the women had decided to gather scarcely a stone's throw from her.

"He has no right to forbid us from leaving the camp." Innis sounded furious, and Roisin cast her an inadvertent glance. "Does he think we are foolish? We know how to forage without being caught by our enemies."

Hastily, Roisin refocused on Ecne. She didn't mean to eavesdrop, but she could scarcely block up her ears, could she? And she wasn't going to return to the tent just because the women were discussing something they obviously didn't want the men to overhear.

"Darragh is well aware we are not foolish." There was a hard note in Elspeth's voice, but Roisin had the strongest impression she was just as angry as the younger woman. "Something else is troubling him. I'll speak to him later. Let him know our medicinal stocks are running perilously low. Do not fret, Innis."

"Do not fret?" Innis practically spat the words at Elspeth. "I swear to God, if I—" She cut herself off and glared at Roisin, as if she'd only just become aware of her presence. "Aye," she said, even though Roisin hadn't said anything. "This is what our life is like on the run, unable to source our most basic needs."

"'Tis not the lass's fault." Elspeth drew in a deep breath. "'Tis rarely women's fault, after all."

Innis hiked her bairn more securely against her shoulder. "Yet we are the ones who suffer."

Roisin knew of the disputes between Clans Campbell and MacGregor, but the truth was it had scarcely touched anyone on the Western Isles. They backed the Campbells because it was politically astute to do so, but until her sister, Isolde, had been personally affected by the feud, she had scarcely given it further thought.

But Isolde, through her bravery, had survived an attack from a rebel MacGregor and the danger had passed. And once again life on Eigg had returned to its tranquil state.

Roisin had never wondered about the upheaval the MacGregors had endured after being driven from the land of their ancestors. And there was no need to wonder now, since the stark reality was here, in front of her eyes, with these displaced women and their bairns.

There was no doubt in her mind they were continuing the same conversation from the previous evening or that the herbs they so desperately needed were ones that men would never require for their medical uses.

If Freyja was here, she wouldn't hesitate to share her knowledge or her supplies. Her sister was a fierce advocate for women having the means to regulate their own fertility in a world ruled by men and their desires. She wouldn't care if there was a chance Innis would scorn her or Elspeth deride her for interfering. Freyja only cared about providing the best medicinal aid she could to anyone in need.

How she wished her sister were here with her now.

Her heart hammered and panic slithered through her chest like a greedy serpent, but she couldn't remain silent when she had the means to help Innis. Clutching the ends of her shawl for added courage, she faced the women.

"I'll be glad to share my herbs with ye."

Innis gave an impatient sigh. "I doubt ye have the ones we need."

It was a rebuff. Roisin licked her lips, gripped her shawl tighter, and pressed onwards. "I have juniper, rosemary, and sage."

Silence followed her comment. Certainly, all the herbs had culinary uses. It was also plain that the women understood what she had really just shared with them.

"Do ye now." Innis's voice was soft, but there was no hint of the antagonism that had heated her previous words. "And ye're willing to share with us?"

"Aye. They may help for a while, at least."

The women glanced at each other, but unlike the other times when they'd conversed, there were no half-hidden smirks or rolling of eyes. It seemed unspoken messages passed between them, and then Elspeth spoke to the little lass, Rhona.

"Fetch some bannocks for the lady and her maid."

⚛

IT WAS A torturous night. And Hugh wasn't thinking of the hard ground. He'd slept in worse places than on a damp pile of moss and at least it hadn't rained again for which he was thankful.

The reason for his discomfort was because just an arm's length from where he lay, was Roisin. He heard her whispered conversations with her maid, although he couldn't discern the words, and her dog's snuffling sounded strangely loud in the still night air.

Despite the long day, sleep eluded him as he stared into the dark sky, where stars glittered through the gaps in the clouds. Since the earl had banished him from his old life, it wasn't a rare thing for him to be awake at night where his thoughts invariably drifted to the brief, shining moments he'd spent with Roisin.

How many times had he fantasized about sharing his bed with her? Or imagined how she'd look, with her hair spread over his pillows? Even though the nightly visions had tormented him with their inevitable impossibility of ever coming true, in an odd way they'd also kept him sane.

'Twas never a good thing to tempt fate with deeply buried wishes and that was the truth. Roisin was, if ye counted his tent, all but in his bed, and God knew, that damn tent was nearly all he owned right now, and yet she had never been further away from him.

In the early hours of the morn, he undertook his usual two-hour watch, but he spent as much time scanning the camp to ensure no man went near his tent as he did on lookout for any suspicious activity in the surrounding area.

'Twas no good. He could scarcely concentrate on anything without weighing up how those actions affected Roisin's safety. The responsibility didn't simply lay across his shoulders like a mantle. From the moment he'd caught her in the forest, the knowledge that her very life depended upon whatever he said or did had consumed him like a veritable fever.

It was glaringly obvious that the longer Roisin remained under his protection, the harder it was to keep his hard-won façade as a redshank from cracking. They'd been in the camp for less than half a day and he wasn't sure how long it would be before Darragh guessed he had known Roisin before rescuing her from the bandits. And if the MacGregor chieftain suspected that truth, he'd soon conclude Hugh was no ordinary mercenary.

It was a relief when dawn broke across the mountains, and he could finally stop pretending to sleep. Except for a couple of the men who were finishing their night watch, no one stirred, and he took advantage of the silence to build a small fire and fetch some water for Roisin's and Grear's use.

Once that was done, he stood and glanced at the tent. It was still early, likely too early for a lady such as Roisin to rise, but already the MacGregors were stirring, leaving their tents and starting the day. *Should I wake Roisin?*

She slept in his tent, but it felt like a violation to enter it without being invited. Instead, he checked his horse that he kept tethered close by, and the familiar action of grooming the magnificent creature managed to release some of the tension that coiled through every muscle he possessed.

There was still no indication that Roisin and her maid had awoken, and so he took Deagh Fhortan across the plateau, beyond the rocky outcrop, where a river wound down the mountain, and while Fhortan drank from the fresh water, he inspected his sword and daggers.

It was a ritual he undertook every morning and usually it cleared his mind of any nighttime hauntings of what his future might entail should the earl never recall him home. But this morning he wasn't thinking of the life he'd once had. It was Roisin's plight that plagued him. How the devil he could return her to her kin if the earl didn't receive and act on his missive?

But first he had to send the damn missive.

He sheathed his weapons and took Fhortan's bridle. He needed to speak to Darragh about Roisin and her maid accompanying him to the town, and he also needed to have a word with Elspeth. He wasn't looking forward to that, but it couldn't be helped and the anger that had burned through him yesterday evening when he'd realized how poorly she'd been treated threatened to surface once again.

The alternative to speaking with Elspeth was to share his own meals with Roisin. Not that he minded. But he had the distinct feeling she had minded very much.

With a frustrated sigh he rounded the outcrop and spied Darragh talking to a couple of his men. He waited until they walked off before approaching the older man.

"Darragh, I've a suggestion." It was, he'd quickly discovered, always better to offer suggestions rather than a proposition to the chieftain, even if the outcome was the same.

"What's that, then?" Darragh spared him a fleeting glance.

"Two strangers wanting to sell horses in the town might cause questions to be asked. But if Symon and I are accompanied by Lady Roisin and her maid, we can pass more easily as travelers needing to fund our passage."

Darragh was silent for a moment, clearly contemplating the change of plan before he abruptly turned on his heel and strode across the plateau to where Hugh had pitched his tent.

Christ, what was Darragh going to do, rip open the tent flap and inform Roisin she was taking an unexpected ride? Irritated by the man's attitude, and alarmed that he'd further upset Roisin, Hugh hastened to his side. But Darragh didn't burst into his tent. He paused a short distance from it, and Hugh came to a halt as he took in the scene before him.

Roisin, the women, and their bairns were sitting around the fire he'd built, and they were all enjoying a breakfast of bannocks. Taken aback, he could only stare as Innis tore the last bannock in the basket in half and handed one piece to Roisin, who in turn pulled her share apart and gave some to Grear.

What in the name of God had happened since last night for the MacGregor women to change their stance regarding Roisin? Even Ecne had a large bone to chew on. It was uncanny, and while he was relieved for her sake, he couldn't help but feel he was missing something fundamental.

"My lady," Darragh said, addressing Roisin. There was a noticeable trace of disdain in his voice which set Hugh's hackles rising. "Ye'll be accompanying Hugh and Symon to the town this morning when they go to trade the horses, to alleviate suspicion that they're wanted outlaws."

Not the way he would have shared the news, but it was the truth nevertheless.

She shot him a startled glance and he offered her what he hoped was a reassuring smile. But before he had the chance to say anything, Darragh continued. "Before ye get any ideas in that pretty little head of yers, yer maid and dog will remain here in the camp to ensure ye behave yerself."

Goddamn it. That wasn't the plan. He shoved aside his ire at how Darragh had called Roisin's character into question, since there wasn't anything he could do about that, and focused on his original plan. "Less suspicion will fall our way if Symon also has a young woman by his side."

But that wasn't the only reason he'd suggested Grear accompany them. She was Roisin's personal maid and seemed to go everywhere with her mistress. Besides which, Roisin was of noble blood and noblewomen did not journey alone with two men.

Roisin pushed herself to her feet. The color had leached from her cheeks, and she gazed at Darragh as though he were the devil himself. "I'll not leave Grear and Ecne to fend for themselves."

Although her voice shook, she didn't drop her gaze from Darragh, and neither did she back down when he offered her an unfriendly smile. "Ye're our guest, and will be treated as such, but ye're in no position to make demands."

"Darragh, I can vouch for the lady's integrity. She'll not raise the alarm."

"Ye can vouch for her integrity, can ye, after knowing her for less than a day?"

Curse his unwary tongue. But there was no help for it but to brazen it out. "Aye. Ye have my word."

Finally, Darragh turned his attention to him. "The word of a Campbell means nothing to me. Ye've proved yer worth and that's the only reason ye're here. Do not test me, Hugh."

How the hell had this morning turned so quickly? He knew damn well he was barely tolerated by Darragh MacGregor, but until he'd brought Roisin into the camp, he'd managed to avoid antagonizing him. And he needed to continue to avoid doing so, if he wanted to protect Roisin until he returned her to her kin.

Innis stood and briefly touched Roisin's shoulder. "We will ensure Grear and yer dog are safe," she said, and he stared at her in growing incredulity. Innis, as Elspeth's niece, wielded almost as much power in the group as both her aunt and Darragh and if she'd decided to accept Roisin, he no longer had to fear she'd be overlooked or disrespected.

Yet yesterday Innis hadn't even tried to hide her contempt for Roisin.

"There ye are." There was a thread of amusement in Darragh's voice now. "No need to fret about yer maid or dog now." He turned to Hugh. "'Tis a fair plan to pose as a newlywed couple accompanied by yer brother. We'll use that trick again in the next town."

Hugh clamped his jaw shut to avoid any more incautious words from escaping as Darragh marched off, before he chanced looking at Roisin. At least she no longer looked as though she was about to faint, and he expelled a relieved breath.

"Ye needn't look so pleased with yerself, Hugh." Innis gave him a probing look which under the circumstances he felt was entirely unwarranted. "Ye can play make believe that Roisin is yer bride as much as yer like, but if ye lay one finger on her, ye'll have me to answer to."

Inordinately irked, he glared at her. He'd lost almost everything since he had first met Roisin, but by God he still had his integrity and Innis's unsubtle accusation, in front of Roisin, no less, cut deep. He sucked in a harsh breath and turned to Roisin, who was staring at him as though she expected him to grow horns and cloven feet at any moment.

"'Twas not my idea to pose as man and wife." No, because that elusive possibility was something too deeply buried inside his tattered soul to be so lightly exploited. Nothing more than a dream he'd once had and held onto through all the dark times. He forced those lost hopes back into the abyss and pushed out words that curdled his gut. "I shall present ye as my sister."

Innis actually laughed and he shot her another disgruntled glare. He didn't want an audience while he was trying to persuade Roisin of the merits of the plan, but he could scarcely tell Innis to leave. And not just because she was related to Darragh and Elspeth, but because, between last night and now, she had taken a shine to Roisin.

"Yer sister?" Innis cast a mocking glance between him and Roisin. "Trust me, that's a terrible idea and ye will never get away with such a story."

Heat scorched through him. This morning was going from bad to worse. He'd been so certain he had hidden how he felt about her. Christ, the last thing he wanted was for Roisin to guess that truth. It had been different on Eigg, when, even as the second son of his father, he'd had a future and a home to offer her and had promised himself that he'd one day return to Sgur Castle to ask for her hand.

But now he had nothing of value to offer her and he didn't want to risk seeing the shock, or worse, on her face if she guessed that he'd once harbored such intentions about her.

Far better to let her believe anything but that.

"We will pose as man and wife." Roisin tilted her head at him, as if daring him to contradict her. Relieved she appeared agreeable to the proposition, he kept his mouth shut and merely gave a sharp nod of agreement. "When do we leave?"

"As soon as ye are ready." As far as he was concerned, she looked ready to face the world with her dark blue, green and black plaid shawl around her shoulders, and a soft blue gown that clung to her curves as the highland breeze gusted across the plateau.

He swallowed, his mouth suddenly dry, but he couldn't tear his mesmerized gaze from her. As usual, her hair was in a loose plait that trailed over her shoulder, but all he could see in his mind's eye was how those auburn tresses had tumbled down her back when she had been in his tent yesterday afternoon.

"I'm ready now." Her gaze caught his, and for a heartbeat he was certain she was about to say more, but instead she shook her head, as if trying to dislodge unpleasant thoughts, before she turned to her maid and took her hand. "All will be well. I shall return shortly."

CHAPTER NINE

ROISIN RODE THE same mare she had hired when they'd docked at Oban. Was it really only the previous day? It seemed like a lifetime ago. And against all common sense, riding beside Hugh, as they made their way along a mountain pass, felt like the most natural thing in the world.

She exhaled a long breath and concentrated on the path ahead. She would die from mortification if Hugh caught the surreptitious glances she kept darting his way. With everything that had happened, she was certain she should remain infuriated with him, instead of this odd sense of calm that had descended as soon as they'd left the camp.

But then, Hugh had always made her feel ways she never had before. But back on Eigg, before he had left with Isolde and William, she'd never been conflicted about it. She had simply reveled in it.

Briefly, she squeezed her eyes shut. Not that it helped to center her. She fixed her gaze ahead, where Symon led the way with the horses he and Hugh were to sell in the town. She was also aware that two men from the camp followed them, keeping out of sight, as a surprise backup in case they were attacked.

A shiver wracked her, and she tightened her grip on the reins. She hoped the loyal men who had accompanied her from Eigg had been found by now and given the respect they deserved.

Before she could stop herself, she glanced at Hugh once again. His face was grim as he stared ahead, as though he weren't even aware of her presence. She bit her lip and tried not to notice how magnificent he looked astride the proud stallion but since that was impossible, she settled for admiring his captivating profile instead.

Without warning, he looked at her and heat washed through her, burning her cheeks. Curse it. Isolde and Freyja had never blushed like fools or become tongue-tied if a man so much as glanced sideways at them. Did Hugh think her as naïve as the MacGregor women had, until she'd offered to share her medicinal stocks with them?

It was bad enough knowing the women had thought her too sheltered to understand basic life skills, but it was far worse if Hugh thought the same. On Eigg he'd been gratifyingly admiring of her artwork and texts and certainly had appeared to be genuinely interested when she'd shared the myths behind them.

But what if he believed she possessed no practical competence at all? To be sure, until they had left the Isle both of her sisters were the practical ones, and she had merely done whatever was required of her. It was only during the last year after Freyja had wed Alasdair that their grandmother had started to include her in the castle's administrative decisions.

Amma hadn't really any choice, had she? Roisin was the only daughter of Sgur left.

It had never really troubled her before, but now the knowledge stung. She wasn't brave like her sisters, but that didn't mean she was incapable of strategic thought. And so, to prove it to Hugh, she said what had been playing on her mind ever since Darragh had informed her she was accompanying Hugh and Symon on their mission.

"When we reach the town, do ye think I might send a message to Isolde to let her know I'm still alive?"

"A message?" He sounded as though the concept was utterly foreign to him.

Somewhat aggrieved by his response, she said, "Why are ye so surprised? I only want to let her know there's no need to worry about me." She was certain her sisters and Amma would worry until she was safely reunited with them, but at least she could let them know she wasn't dead. "Isolde shouldn't have that burden. I'd never forgive myself if—" She sucked in a sharp breath.

She'd never forgive herself if the shock of thinking she had died in an ambush caused her sister to lose her longed-for bairn.

Understanding flickered over his face, although it was gone in an instant. "'Tis too dangerous." His voice was low and although he sounded sympathetic, it didn't make her feel any better about the fact he'd completely dismissed her concerns.

"Ye needn't worry I'll mention yer name." She couldn't quite hide her irritation, and he frowned, as though he thought she was being unreasonable. And that irked her even more. "Or that I'm in a rebel MacGregor camp. I just need them to know I wasn't taken by brigands."

Hugh glanced at Symon, as if to assure himself the other man was still too far ahead to overhear their conversation. Did he consider her completely irresponsible? She wouldn't have said anything if she suspected Symon was close enough to eavesdrop.

"I meant what I said, Roisin. I have a contact who knows both William and Alasdair who will let yer kin know ye're all right. I just need to wait for confirmation for when it's safe to return ye to them as soon as I can."

The intimate way he said her name was irresistibly distracting, and it wasn't the first time he'd omitted her title. Was it wrong of her to find it secretly thrilling? In Eigg he had been the model of chivalric propriety, and she'd found him charming. She'd gleaned from their conversations he was a second son, and his family were not vastly wealthy like Alasdair had proven to be, or even William with his own large estates. None of that mattered to her.

He was the first man she'd met who hadn't made her want to hide behind her sisters, the way she usually did when confronted by strangers or even those she didn't know well. He had been gentle, and kind, and she'd fooled herself into thinking that she knew his character well enough to daydream of a life together.

But she'd been wrong. She hadn't known him in the slightest and yet this other side of Hugh, this tough, dark side, which should have terrified her, merely left her feeling breathless with anticipation of the treacherous depths that swirled just below his deceptively civilized facade.

She might still find him irresistible, but it was plain Hugh Campbell considered her incapable of doing something as straightforward as sending a message to her kin.

And then, belatedly, something occurred to her. "Is this why Darragh is keeping Grear and Ecne hostage? So I don't try to send a message?"

Horror skated through her. She'd assumed Darragh had been warning her not to escape once they reached the town. As if she would. Where would she run to? She certainly didn't need his implicit threat that harm would befall Grear and Ecne if she attempted such a foolish thing.

"Aye." Hugh gave a heavy sigh, and she focused ahead, so he wouldn't guess that she'd only just reached that conclusion, when it should have been glaringly obvious from the start. "He cannot risk a messenger being traced back to the town, where questions would be asked and a search undertaken."

"Then how do ye propose to keep yer promise to me, and send a message to this mysterious contact of yers, when clearly ye cannot risk Darragh's wrath?"

He shifted on his saddle, as though her questions unsettled him. As they should. Did he think she should remain mute and simply accept everything that was happening?

The way I used to on Eigg?

But on Eigg she had been safe and protected, and the need had never arisen for her to ensure her concerns were heard. He would likely ignore her question since she doubted he had an answer for her.

And then he spoke. "A man will not raise the same interest as a lady would. There'll be enough raised eyebrows as it is with ye simply being in the town, but I couldn't leave ye behind at the camp."

"But ye didn't mind leaving poor Grear behind." Or Ecne, either.

"'Twas not my idea to do so." He sounded faintly insulted that she should think such a thing. "But Darragh would not be persuaded otherwise. He cares little for the word of anyone not of his blood kin."

That Hugh had planned on bringing her maid and, doubtless, Ecne with him, took the salt from her ire. She could scarcely blame him for something that wasn't his fault, but she still felt the need to defend her position even though Hugh wasn't accusing her of anything. "Then I shall write the missive, and ye can find the messenger."

For a moment, she had the impression he was about to argue. But then he gave a deep sigh and inclined his head. "Very well. But I must ask ye to keep yer counsel. It could go badly if Darragh gets wind of it."

"I've no intention of repeating our conversation, Hugh. I'm not ignorant of the danger, ye ken."

He shook his head. "I wasn't implying that ye were."

For a short while, they traveled in silence as they descended the mountain along nonexistent pathways. Hugh followed her as they navigated the way in single file. Sunlight dappled the forest undergrowth, and the scent of pine needles filled the air, giving a deceptive sense of tranquility. But nothing about this was normal. She couldn't quite understand why she wasn't quivering in terror at the reality she was alone with two men in the middle of the Highlands.

And yet the truth was, no matter how bizarre the circumstances, Hugh made her feel safe. She shouldn't trust him so completely, but the alternative was to think the worst of him and how would that make this better?

When the path widened, Hugh once again rode by her side, and she exhaled a long breath in the hope it would untangle her thoughts. Alas, it did not.

"I see ye have made friends with Innis." He shot her a smile, one that reminded her of when they'd shared clandestine conversations in Sgur Castle. Obviously, he didn't want to continue with the prickly topic of sending word to her kin and since she'd extracted a promise from him that he intended to find a messenger in the town, she supposed there was nothing further to say about it.

"I don't believe we're friends, but I think maybe we understand each other a little."

"'Tis a miracle ye wrought, make no mistake. After I arrived at camp it took Innis a fortnight before she'd even look at me without murder in her eyes."

Curious, she caught his warm blue gaze and despite her best intentions to remain calm and collected, a swarm of butterflies collided deep inside her chest as she returned his smile. But she wasn't going to be distracted. His confession was intriguing.

"How long have ye been staying with them?"

"About six weeks."

"Only six weeks?" she repeated before she could stop herself. She'd assumed he had been with the rebel MacGregors far longer. After all, Freyja had been wed for a year, and neither she nor Isolde had heard a whisper about him which was odd, considering William and Hugh were cousins, and they and Alasdair had, by all accounts, grown up together as close-knit as blood brothers.

"Aye."

She waited for him to elaborate, but it seemed that was all he had to say about the matter. And then she recalled he'd told her he had fought in Eire before accompanying Symon to the camp. "Why did ye go to Eire? I'm thinking that's where ye met Symon before he invited ye back to his camp."

He shrugged and narrowed his eyes, as though searching for something within the cover of the forest, but she recognized a diversionary tactic when she saw one. Since she was a small child, she'd witnessed how Amma used every strategy at her disposal when dealing with fellow clan chieftains. And before she'd wed William, Isolde had spent untold hours teaching her and Freyja of common attack strategies and how to recognize and deflect them.

Obviously, Hugh wasn't about to attack her, but he was certainly trying to divert her attention. But if there truly was danger lurking among the trees, she was certain he wouldn't be taking so long to do anything about it.

"Hugh?"

Finally, he caught her gaze. "I was a redshank." He sounded reluctant to admit it. "I had nowhere to go when we returned to the Highlands, so I took Symon up on his offer."

"But why didn't ye go back to yer own kin?"

He sucked in a shuddering breath. "I cannot share my reasons with ye. My only home is wherever I pitch my tent."

She contemplated that as they continued through the forest, her mind swirling with possibilities both practical and fantastical as to why he'd abandoned his former life for one, essentially, on the run. The most likely reason was he had done something terrible, and the Earl of Argyll had banished him from his lands, except she couldn't imagine Hugh capable of doing anything so bad as to merit such a harsh fate.

"Do ye think ye will ever return home?" Her voice was hushed, and her heart ached at how dreadful it would be to be banished from loved ones and friends. She had been torn from her kin for barely a day and felt as though her world had turned upside down, but at least she knew sooner or later she'd see them again.

"I don't know." His smile this time was sad, and the ache dug deeper into her heart at the sight. If only she had the nerve to reach over to him and take his hand, just to show him she understood.

She clutched the reins tighter, in reaction against her absurd thoughts. The truth was, she didn't understand. How could she, if he didn't confide in her? And she was only guessing the earl had banished him for something minor. Suppose the truth was he'd done something unforgivable? Did she really want to know the truth, if that was so?

Since it appeared unlikely Hugh would ever confide in her, it wasn't something she needed to fret about. But regardless, she would never believe he had done anything to merit exile from his clan.

"Maybe ye will, in time." When she next saw Freyja, she'd ask her to see if Alasdair could speak to the earl on Hugh's behalf. In fact, why hadn't Alasdair already done so? They were supposed to be great friends. Or didn't Hugh's blood brothers know what he had been accused of?

It was a mystery, for sure. And since her sisters' husbands seemed to share everything with them, she was certain either Isolde or Freyja would have told her had they been aware of Hugh's fall from grace.

Up ahead, Symon came to a halt, before he looked over his shoulder at Hugh. "We're leaving the forest now, Sergeant. The town is another hour eastwards, but there's not much cover."

He'd called Hugh Sergeant before. And while she knew redshanks were savage mercenaries who went wherever there was coin to be had, it hadn't occurred to her they used military rankings until now. A small pain pierced through her breast at the realization Hugh had been so successful as a mercenary that he'd been promoted. It was almost as though it was proof that he'd embraced this fugitive life and had no illusions he'd ever return to his former one.

But if only he would.

As they left the shelter of the forest and joined a well-worn path that presumably led to the town, she shook her head to disperse the foolish wish. Even if the earl issued a pardon and Hugh returned to Balfour Castle, he wouldn't necessarily want her to join him.

Why couldn't she stop imagining a future with him? Only yesterday she'd wanted to hate him. And now she was back to weaving romantic notions about him, as though they had never left Eigg.

She couldn't help the way her imagination always ran away with her. But at least she could control what she said and did when they were together. He'd never guess how she really felt about him.

It was a wise plan. She hoped he'd never see through it.

CHAPTER TEN

T HE TOWN WAS large, enclosed by a ditch and palisade fortifica-
tion, and as they approached the gates, where other travelers
they had seen on the road were also heading, Hugh glanced at Roisin.
When the town had come into view, she'd pulled a kerchief from her
satchel and covered her hair, as befit a married woman, and he'd only
just stopped a frustrated groan from escaping.

Damn the fates to hell. Pretending she was his bride, when there
was no chance of that ever coming true, was a new kind of torture
he'd never imagined. But there was no help for it but to play the part
of a devoted husband and hope neither Roisin—nor Symon—guessed
how wretchedly he wished it were true.

But that wasn't his main concern. No one with eyes in their head
could look at Roisin and think she came from a local village. It wasn't
merely the quality of her gown and shawl or the elegance of her
gloves. He was certain even if she were dressed in the meanest of rags,
her gentle demeanor and indefinable air of grace would ensure her
heritage was as plain as day.

And that was before she spoke and dispelled any lingering question
of her noble blood. But the likelihood of her speaking to any of the
townspeople was remote, so at least there was that. As for the rest, it
was his own shortsightedness in not suggesting she borrow her maid's
clothes.

They entered the town through the arched gateway and caught up
with Symon who had come to a halt on the side of the main road near

a farrier who, by the look of it, was enjoying a roaring trade.

Hugh eyed the bustling marketplace up ahead with approval. "'Tis busy. It means we can disappear into the crowd and be less likely to be remembered."

Symon's gaze strayed to Roisin. "Aye." He sounded doubtful as to the possibility that she could disappear into a crowd of townsfolk, and he had to agree. But there was one thing they could do to become less conspicuous.

He dismounted, and Symon followed suit. "My lady," he said to Roisin, who gave him such a sweet smile the breath lodged in his chest. He swallowed and tried to ignore how his cock thickened as lust seared his blood, but it appeared the power of speech had deserted him.

"We'll draw less attention if I walk, too," she said, anticipating what he'd intended to say to her. With another smile, she prepared to dismount. Before he could think better of it, or remember where they were, he caught her around her waist as she reached the ground in a gesture of misplaced gallantry.

Her gown was soft beneath his fingers, a fragile barrier that did nothing to disguise her enchanting curves or the warmth of her flesh. He felt as much as heard her soft gasp at his presumption. His fingers lingered, savoring the illicit touch. Even though he knew he should step back and release her, the stark truth was he might never have another chance to hold her. If this fleeting moment were to last him a lifetime, he had to make the most of it.

For endless moments, she remained motionless, but then she slowly turned to face him. He still couldn't pull back. Her eyes didn't blaze with anger, and she didn't slap his face for his impertinence. Instead, her lips parted, and her breath shortened. As an enchanting blush heated her cheeks and her eyes, God help him, her eyes were dark with something he dared not name.

Her ethereal scent of crushed rose petals swirled in the air, as insubstantial as a dream. And yet the fragrance sank into his blood as potent as the strongest French wine, forging a fiery trail through his very veins that caused his cock to throb with frustrated need. He didn't move, as he wasn't sure he was capable of such a thing, even if his life depended on it. When her gloved hands lightly clasped his biceps, he could barely keep his groan locked fast in his throat.

From a thousand miles away the snort of horses and the dull cacophony of the market square floated in the outer reaches of his mind like a nebulous fog. But the outside world scarcely mattered. Not when Roisin was in his arms, and she looked at him as though there was no other place she would rather be.

His heart thundered in his chest and echoed through his head like a primal drumbeat. Instinctively, his hands slid from her waist and palmed the small of her back, pressing her closer and she did not resist. With a tantalizing, breathy sigh, she tilted her head back, exposing her throat, and her desire-filled gaze never wavered from his.

Honor demanded he pull back instantly. But God help him, he was no saint, and his honor was no match for the innocent invitation glowing in her mesmeric eyes. He lowered his head, and his lips brushed hers in a featherlight touch, yet one that seared him like a branding iron. Her fingers tightened around his biceps, and he forgot where they were and why this was so wrong and roughly pulled her closer until she melted against him.

Her breath was intoxicatingly sweet and warm with a subtle hint of mint. Never had he tasted something so exotic. He traced the seam of her lips with the tip of his tongue, and she quivered in his arms before threading her fingers through his hair.

The last strands of reason unraveled, and he pushed his tongue inside her willing mouth. She tightened her grip on his hair as his hands roamed over her back, beneath her shawl, desperate to feel her naked flesh and make her his.

He cupped the back of her head, and her silken hair curled around his fingers in a gossamer caress. Need pounded through him. The only sound that filled his mind was the erratic thunder of his heart.

Imagining Roisin in his arms was the only thing that had kept him warm during the bitter winter nights in Eire, but nothing could compare to the reality.

She held him as though he was all she had ever wanted, her glove-clad fingers digging into his head, keeping him close, and the frantic beat of her heart against his chest scrambled his reason and inflamed his blood.

Only one frenzied truth resounded through his head.

Mine.

"No one will doubt ye're a newlywed couple, and that's a fact."

Symon's dry words slammed into him like a steel forged mace, and he broke the kiss, panting into Roisin's dazed face, as reality returned like a drunken slug.

Christ, what had he been thinking to kiss her so? Except he hadn't been thinking. He'd lost himself in a maelstrom of lust and desperate possibilities of what could never be. But it was far worse than that. For a few glorious moments, he'd forgotten his pledge to keep her safe at all costs. How could he protect her if he wasn't even aware of their surroundings? What if his lapse in judgment had caused unwelcome attention to be drawn their way?

God knew, if not for Symon, he would likely still be kissing Roisin. What wouldn't he do for the chance to keep her by his side? But it was a fool's dream, and one he couldn't afford to fall victim to. Not when his negligence could put her in danger.

His only task was to keep her safe until he could ensure her escape to her kin. There was no alternative future where she could stay with him, and he couldn't forget that again.

With more reluctance than he'd ever admit, he finally released her. But it was another heartbeat before Roisin dropped her hands from him, and he missed her touch far more than any rational man should.

He couldn't tear his wretched gaze from her, but he had to ensure that Symon, and Roisin herself, was convinced Hugh knew exactly what he was doing. If either of them suspected he'd temporarily lost his mind when he'd taken her in his arms, his credibility with Symon would vanish, and God only knew how Roisin would react.

"Thank ye for playing along, my lady." He kept his voice low, cursing the huskiness that betrayed the ravening lust that still burned through his blood. "'Tis imperative no one questions our story of being wed."

She blinked twice and something deep inside cracked at the knowledge she would now despise him more than ever. But it couldn't be helped. He'd much rather she believed this was a strategic ploy than guess he hadn't been able to help himself. At Sgur he'd wanted her, more than anything, but he'd kept his distance because she was a gently brought-up lady. No man worth his salt took advantage of an innocent lass.

Yet moments ago, that was exactly what he had done. He'd rip out his tongue before he admitted to such a despicable lack of honor.

"Of course." She inclined her head and avoided looking at him as she straightened her impeccable gloves. "I understand."

The fact she was being so agreeable should have been a relief. Yet for a reason he couldn't fathom, her complaisance rubbed him the wrong way. He fought the destructive urge to pull her back into his arms and assure her that he hadn't been playing at all.

He expelled a measured breath and faced Symon, who was eyeing him with an unreadable expression on his face. But since he didn't answer to Symon, he ignored the unspoken questions hanging between them and gave a brusque nod in the direction of the market. "We'll start there."

It was possible traders might be at the market looking for horses. If not, one of the town's inns would likely be interested in purchasing them. There was always a need for travelers to hire fresh horses on extended journeys.

They made their way along the road towards the market, with Roisin between himself and Symon. Rising above the milling crowds he spied the mercat cross, with its intricately carved column, that stood on an eight-stepped octagonal plinth in the heart of the market square. Myriad stalls were set up around the cross and the sound and smell of livestock permeated the warm summer breeze.

"Do ye want us to stay together or should I hunt down a purchaser alone?" Symon glanced at Roisin as he spoke before returning his attention to Hugh.

He'd assumed he and Symon would stay together in the market, but he instantly saw the benefits if they split up. Not least because it would be easier for him to find a messenger and send word to the earl, without needing to find an excuse to part company from Symon.

"Ye find a buyer. The lady and I will wait for ye in the inn." He indicated the closest inn. It was a substantial stone building set back from the market and he was hopeful it would have a private room where Roisin could have a drink and a bite to eat in relative comfort. "Then we'll purchase the goods Darragh requires."

Symon gave a sharp nod before leading the horses away, and Hugh turned to Roisin who was gazing at him with an unfathomable expression on her face. His heart sank. Had she been keeping her true feelings to herself while Symon was around? But now that they were alone, did she intend to let him know exactly what she thought of his unpardonable behavior?

CHAPTER ELEVEN

ROISIN TIGHTENED HER grip on her mare's reins before she did something ridiculous, such as trace her fingertips along Hugh's jaw. When he had kissed her, her good sense had fled and all the foolish dreams she'd woven around him had once again flooded her mind. Then he'd informed her it was nothing but a strategy, yet instead of wanting to sink through the ground with mortification...

She hadn't believed him.

She still didn't.

There was no logical reason for her certainty. She wasn't so sheltered that she believed a man's kiss meant anything deeper than a fleeting desire, however much she'd love to think so. Hugh had likely kissed many lasses in the past and there was no reason to think the one they had shared was anything special to him, even if it was to her.

But this certainty that shifted within her, like the fragile flicker of a candle's flame, would not be extinguished by rationality. It was the same way she'd felt, deep inside, that when William Campbell had washed up on Sgur beach he was Isolde's soulmate, and how, from the moment she'd met Alasdair, she'd known it was Freyja's destiny to wed him.

Whether he admitted it or not, Hugh had kissed her because he'd wanted to. Not because it would distract passersby into believing they were a married couple. And maybe he didn't want Symon to know, either, although she wasn't sure what difference that would make.

For an eternal moment, he simply gazed upon her with eyes as blue as the finest summer day. She had the surreal notion that if she didn't break this spell, she might lose her soul forevermore in those sapphire depths.

Would that truly be such a terrible thing?

Before she had time to berate herself for such a foolish thought, he spoke.

"We can wait for Symon in the inn. There's sure to be a private room I can hire and ye can have something hearty to eat."

She tore her besotted gaze from him and glanced at the market stalls that overflowed the square like unwrapped treasures. "I'd rather explore the market."

There was no mistaking the surprise on his face. "Ye would?"

"Ye mustn't laugh, but I so rarely have the chance to visit such a grand market. I should like to browse." Even though the coin she had brought with her, and secured in her trunk, had vanished along with most of her possessions, it would still be an intriguing expedition.

"Then we shall explore the market." He offered her a smile and the warmth in his eyes tugged at her heart, as though no time had passed since they'd first met at Sgur Castle. It wasn't that she ever forgot she had been spirited away to a rebel MacGregor camp, but the truth was whenever she was in Hugh's company, the danger she was in simply faded. "It didn't occur to me that ye'd enjoy such a thing."

"I went with Isolde and Freyja to a large market the last time Amma and I visited the Highlands." She didn't want him thinking she had never been to such an impressive market before, although admitting she had only visited one was likely quite tragic. Ah well, it was too late to regret that now. "'Twas rather thrilling to see so many different things for sale."

She'd certainly spent a good amount on beautiful new goose quills and had been unable to resist purchasing an elegant swan quill and a vibrant peacock quill, as well as colored inks and a new bronze inkwell, all of which she had left behind in the solar at Sgur.

"Then I'm glad ye have the chance to browse another."

"'Tis certainly more exciting than entertaining visiting merchants at the castle."

He laughed, as though she were jesting although she'd been serious. She had never enjoyed the enforced proximity that receiving merchants had entailed, despite whatever luxuries they had brought with them from across the sea.

"I doubt ye'll find the silks or fine jewelry here that a merchant could acquire."

"Then 'tis lucky I have little interest in silks and fine jewelry. And what would I do with such things here, anyway?"

He had the grace to wince. "Ye're right. Here, let me carry yer satchel for ye."

"Oh." Instinctively, she clutched the strap that was slung across her breasts, and the images that she had drawn of him flashed across her mind. Of course, he wouldn't see them if he carried her satchel, but inside she shuddered at the notion of having those portraits she'd sketched with so much tenderness merely inches from discovery by him. "Thank ye, but I can manage."

"Are ye certain? It looks mighty heavy." He gave her satchel a dubious glance and she couldn't blame him. It bulged in a most ungainly manner with everything she had stuffed into it yesterday afternoon. And now that he had drawn attention to it, the weight upon her shoulder magnified excessively.

She forced her fingers from the strap and rubbed her mare's neck to give her hand something useful to do so she wasn't tempted to reach out to Hugh instead. "'Tis fine. I'm simply glad I have it."

"So am I," he said, and he smiled at her again before offering her his arm. After a moment's hesitation, she looped her arm under his and rested her fingers just above his wrist. It was an intimate gesture and illicit thrills coursed through her, even though she was wearing gloves. "I shouldn't wish to lose ye in the crowd."

"I shouldn't wish to lose ye, either. I'm not certain how far from either of my sisters I am."

He sighed and as they headed further into the heart of the market, he moved closer to her side and, combined with his evocative scent of leather and wild Highland grasses, it was a struggle to breathe normally. She hoped he wouldn't notice. "We're a fair way from either of them." He sounded reluctant to admit it. "But don't worry, I'll find a messenger in town, I promise ye."

That reminded her. "Maybe we can stop at the inn after we've looked around the market so I can write a note to my sisters."

He didn't answer but he gave her a contemplative, sideways glance as though he wanted to say something but had thought better of it. She certainly hoped he'd thought better of it if he had intended to tell her he had changed his mind about sending a message from her to her sisters. Did he think she'd break her promise and tell them she was being held by rebel MacGregors?

To be sure, it would be a tricky message to write, and she hadn't yet worked out what she was going to say. But the most important thing was her sisters knew she was alive and well and would return to them as soon as she could. She could explain everything to them once they were together again.

Perhaps she wouldn't tell them everything. She was still trying to come to terms with that kiss and Hugh's reaction to it. But more than that, she harbored the hope that when she left the MacGregors, Hugh would accompany her. Surely the earl would look favorably upon him, if he realized Hugh was the reason she had escaped a fate involving the brigands?

They passed by several stalls selling grains, fruit and vegetables. On Eigg, they grew most of their own produce in the castle's kitchen gardens, and their meat was hunted on the Small Isles. There was a weekly market in the local village, of course, but it was a far cry from the wonders displayed here.

She lingered at a stall that displayed a vast array of dried herbs and spices, and while Sgur imported a great variety of exotic spices from foreign lands, they cultivated most of their own herbs. The castle's gardens had always provided these necessities, but ever since she was a child, she'd grown up with Freyja's passion for exploring every possible medicinal use for everything the gardens yielded and her sister's enthusiasm for ensuring whatever she used was exactly as she believed it to be, and it had inevitably affected her.

She picked up a glass jar and scrutinized the contents. Unless one grew the plants oneself, how was it possible to tell whether the herbs had been cut with a cheaper alternative to enhance profits? And if the product was compromised, how could anyone judge its effectiveness?

"Do ye want that?" Hugh glanced at the jar she held, and she heard the concern in his voice. Hastily, she returned it to the stall.

"No, I'm just looking."

He leaned closer so there was no chance of them being overheard, and she held her breath, so she wouldn't inadvertently succumb to the faint, tantalizing aroma that would forever remind her of him. Not that she succeeded, and her head spun as though she'd overindulged in the finest French wine.

"If there's anything ye need, let me know."

She tore her bewitched senses from his mesmeric gaze and cast another glance at the goods on display. If Innis had come to the market, would she have bought any of these offerings? Maybe she was being overcautious, but she couldn't risk giving the women anything if she wasn't absolutely certain of its origins.

Besides, she had no coin on her and the last thing she was going to do was ask Hugh to buy things for her. "I've everything I need in my satchel."

He glanced at a neighboring stall. "Then I'll get some apples for ye and yer maid. Be sure to keep them out of sight of the women." He flashed her a grin. "And don't worry, once Symon has sold the horses, we plan on taking back plenty of fresh fare for the bairns."

That was good news, and it made her feel better about accepting the gift of apples from Hugh. "Thank ye. Sweet Ecne has missed his daily treat of apple slices."

"Aye, well, I should be grieved if Ecne went without." His smile caused the breath to lodge in her chest. "And his mistress, too."

"The difference is I know we shall soon return home, but there's no way to make Ecne understand that."

As they moved on to the fruit stall, Hugh moved closer to her, so that her arm brushed against his body. The air evaporated and she was strangely lightheaded as her heartbeat echoed in her ears, but for all that she berated herself by reacting so to his touch, she wouldn't change it for anything.

"As long as he's with ye, I'm certain he is happy."

"I cannot imagine ever being without him." A shiver raced through her at the prospect, and with it a sliver of fear. "But he is eleven, and although he still runs around like a young pup, his years are catching up with him."

He flashed her a glance that was filled with concern and they came to a halt a short distance from the fruit stall. "Ye grew up together."

She sighed. "I was nine when he was born, along with his littermates Sjor and Dubh. Their dam was Amma's favorite, and she gifted the pups to my sisters and me. We had recently received word that our parents had died of the fever on the mainland and although, of course, nothing could ease our grief, having sweet Ecne by my side helped me get through the dark hours."

"I'm sorry." His voice was hushed, and she gave him a faint smile.

"I'm sorry too. I can scarcely remember them, and that breaks my heart."

"My lady mother also died of the fever eleven years ago."

"That is a sad coincidence, indeed."

"I'm fortunate that I had almost fourteen years with her. My wee sister was scarcely two years old when she died and cannot recall a thing about her."

Her heart tugged for the unknown young lass who had barely known her mother. "Ye have two sisters, do ye not?"

"Aye, Mary is my youngest sister, and Agnes will be sixteen next month."

She heard the anguish in his voice. It was clear he missed his sisters and again she couldn't fathom what terrible crime he could have committed that had condemned him to an existence as an outlaw. It was likely best to move the conversation on, but she couldn't help herself. "I'm sure they must miss ye."

He swallowed and looked away from her, focusing on the nearby stall and before she could think better of it, she threaded her fingers through his. Warmth suffused her when he fisted his hand, entrapping her fingers, as though in a small way her gesture had given him comfort.

"Aye." There was an undeniable catch in his voice, and any lingering reservations she'd harbored that maybe the earl had just reason for treating him so harshly dispersed like early morning mist on a summer's morn. "I should dearly like to know how they fare."

She recalled he'd once told her he was a second son. "What of yer older brother? Have ye no way to contact him, to find out how yer kin are?"

His mirthless laugh sent a shiver along her spine. "It's been well over a year since I last saw him and I've no way of contacting him. My brother—" He hesitated, as though he were unsure whether to continue, and then he shook his head and expelled a deep sigh. "I shouldn't speak of him to ye, Roisin. I don't know what he's doing."

If only there was something she could do to take away the pain that throbbed so clearly through every word Hugh said. And then something occurred to her that she could do, even if it meant visiting people she had never seen before.

"When I am reunited with my kin, I could give a message to yer sisters, if ye would like."

He stared at her as though he couldn't quite believe his ears. "Ye'd do that?"

She shoved the tendrils of anxiety that her rash offer had awoken to the back of her mind. It was, after all, such a small thing if it gave Hugh some peace of mind. In any case, she was more than hopeful that, when the time came, he would be able to give his sisters whatever messages he wished himself.

"I am. I'm certain it will greatly relieve them to know ye are alive and well." Even if he had taken refuge with the Campbells' bitterest enemy.

"That's kind of ye." There was a gruff note in his voice. "And make no mistake, I'm grateful for it. But 'tis best they know nothing about this life I'm leading. I shouldn't wish them to think ill of me when there's no way I can—" He clamped his jaw together, but she understood.

It didn't matter how circumspect the message was. His sisters were bound to ask questions, and what could she tell them? They would be sure to guess she was withholding something, and she wasn't certain she could make up a story if they put her on the spot.

But how dreadful it was that they—and Hugh's father—might think he was dead.

Her hope that he would turn his back on this life and confront the earl for his unjust banishment surged through her and she couldn't keep silent any longer. "Maybe when I leave, ye can join me. There must be a way ye can reclaim yer former life, Hugh. Surely the way ye rescued Grear and me from the brigands will stand ye in good stead with the earl."

His smile was sad, and it told her all she needed to know. He had no intention of leaving the rebels when he took her to Creagdoun.

Chapter Twelve

HUGH PURCHASED A dozen apples, despite Roisin's protest that she didn't need that many, and stowed them in her mare's saddlebags. She smiled in gratitude, and he tipped his head in acknowledgement, but he couldn't help comparing these practical market apples to the gifts he'd once imagined bestowing upon her.

Extravagant luxury gifts of jewelry, perfume, and exotic delicacies. Things he'd never considered purchasing before, until he'd met Roisin.

But even at Sgur, he'd known such fantasies were unlikely. He was the second son and while Balfour Castle wasn't steeped in debt or anywhere near the point of ruin, its income wasn't great enough to support such a lavish lifestyle for the wife of a son who wasn't even the heir.

'Twas ironic that, after his months as a redshank, he now possessed more ready coin than he ever had before that fateful meeting with the earl.

For all the good it would do him. He could possess a thousand gold pieces, and it wouldn't be enough to erase the stain on his soul and allow him to win Roisin's hand.

They moved on to the next stall and while he pretended to scrutinize a selection of pewter dishes engraved with intertwining plants, he surreptitiously watched Roisin as she examined an inkwell that had been exquisitely crafted in the shape of a woman in a flowing gown gripping the rim of a large pot.

"'Tis the finest quality bronze, mistress." The stall holder, a matronly woman, smiled encouragingly at Roisin, who hastily replaced the inkwell. "Imported from Florence."

"'Tis very beautiful." Roisin gave the piece another longing glance. "But alas, I am not looking to purchase anything today."

"Then maybe yer fine husband will buy it for ye." The woman smiled benignly at him. "'Tis a fitting gift for such a bonny bride."

It was very fitting, considering how dearly Roisin loved art, but she backed away from the stall, shaking her head, an enchanting blush heating her cheeks. "Thank ye, but I would never expect such an extravagant gift from—" She caught herself and looked at him, and for a timeless moment the world ceased to exist as he lost himself in the emerald mystique of her eyes. "From my Hugh."

Her last whispered words rippled through him, more potent than any fabled aphrodisiac from ancient tales. Her kerchief framed her face, but a few dark auburn tendrils had escaped their restraints, and he had never been so captivated in his life. Without thinking, he gently brushed an errant curl from her cheek and her skin was silken soft beneath his finger. His hot gaze dropped to her tempting lips and his blood thundered in his ears. Just one more kiss…

"Ah, young love." The words, with a hint of amusement, hauled him back to the present and he froze mere inches from Roisin's upturned face. She appeared as bemused as him, as she blinked twice before pressing her lips together and drawing herself back so her uneven breath no longer dusted his jaw.

From the corner of his eye, he saw the woman fold her arms and nod sagely, and in the back of his mind he knew this attention was the last thing he needed. If anyone came to the market asking questions about Roisin, or about rebel MacGregors, if it came to that, he didn't want to be memorable.

But God help him, it was hard to shatter this moment.

My Hugh. Roisin's soft words echoed around his head. If only that were true. But she was merely playing her part, the way he'd asked her to, and how well she played it, too. He'd be impressed if he didn't wish with every fiber of his being that she weren't playing at all.

With a nod of farewell to the woman, he took Roisin's hand, and they led the horses from the stall but the way she'd gazed at the bronze work tugged at him. "Was there something about the inkwell that ye recognized?"

"Oh." She shot him a glance, and a small smile played around her lips. It was only when his horse snorted and gave him a head-butt, that he realized he'd been gazing at Roisin like a bewitched fool and had almost collided into a group of townsfolk. Hastily, he corrected their course before he managed to create a fracas. "That was observant of ye."

For a second he thought she was teasing him about narrowly missing a collision, but when he caught her warm gaze again, he had the uncanny certainty she had no idea why he'd so swiftly changed direction. For which he was thankful. "Was it?"

"First, ye must understand that I realize the Florence artisans were thinking of something quite different when they crafted it, but she reminded me of Dunu, the Great Mother of the Tuatha De Danann with her cauldron of wisdom."

A cauldron. Of course. He could see it now. And although he knew little about the ancient, mythical race that had, once, supposedly ruled Eire, he remembered the tales Roisin had shared with him of those godlike beings when she'd shown him some of her artwork in Sgur Castle. "Ye never know. They might have been thinking of Danu."

"'Tis unlikely." She sounded amused. "But I shall think it nonetheless."

He glanced over his shoulder, but the stall had disappeared among the many others in the market. But he knew exactly where it was. And before they returned to the camp, he would purchase the inkwell. It was perfect for her. Maybe whenever she used it in the future, she would think kindly of him.

He didn't want to think of a future where he'd never see her again, but it was a stark reminder of what he needed to do. As much as he wanted this leisurely stroll to continue, he had to send the missive he'd written last night, before Symon returned from trading the horses, and the only way he could do that unobserved was by ensuring Roisin was safely ensconced in the nearby inn.

"We should go to the inn. They will have food there." And he'd purchase some extra pasties that Roisin could take back to the camp for her and her maid.

"And I'll write my letter to Isolde."

He grunted and avoided her eyes, instead leading them from the busy market to the inn he'd pointed out to Symon. He couldn't risk sending her letter. If it was intercepted, it didn't matter how inconsequential she managed to make her letter sound, its very existence, and the fact it was addressed to the wife of a Campbell of high rank, would put her in jeopardy.

But he didn't want to risk offending her again over the matter, so he kept his mouth shut. Letters, after all, went missing all the time. She'd never know it hadn't arrived at her sister's because he had failed to send it.

It didn't sit right with him, but there was nothing else he could do. It was far safer to keep to his usual methods of communicating with the earl.

He left their horses in the stable block next to the inn before pushing open the great oak door for Roisin to precede him into the inn itself. A large hearth took up one side of the grand hall, and there were fresh rushes on the flagstone floor with several long tables and benches for patrons. Although the place was busy, which helped to keep him and Roisin from attracting too much attention from the proprietor, at least they didn't need to push through crowds for which he was thankful on Roisin's behalf. He doubted she'd ever set foot inside an inn before and didn't want the experience to be more unpleasant than it had to be.

The innkeeper eyed him as Hugh, arm in arm with Roisin, strode towards him. "Good day," he said. "Do ye have a private room where my bride might take refreshment?"

"Aye." Despite the innkeeper's surly appearance, he sounded agreeable. "This way." He took them to a small room that led directly from the hall and glanced at Roisin. "Ye'll be comfortable enough here, mistress." Then he faced Hugh again. "What can I bring ye?"

Hugh glanced at Roisin, who was gazing around the small room in evident curiosity before returning his attention to the innkeeper. "We'll have cheese and bannocks and six of yer veal pasties. And a flagon of yer best wine."

The innkeeper nodded and headed to the rear of the inn where, by the smell of it, the kitchen was located. He closed the door, and Roisin went over to where a table and four chairs were placed before the window. She sat down, rested her satchel on her lap, and rummaged through it before pulling out her writing case.

He sat opposite her, and as she set a small inkwell on the table, he thought of the missive he had to send to the earl. At least now he wouldn't need to use subterfuge to distract her while he found a messenger since she would expect him to find one to send her own letter.

Silence fell between them, broken only by the scratching of her quill on the paper. He leaned back in the chair and exhaled a silent sigh, unable to tear his gaze from her bowed head. A small frown creased her brow, and she bit her lip, as though the words weren't coming easily to her, and fascinated, he watched her sketch a perfect rose in the top corner.

She looked up and caught him watching her. "I fear my sisters won't believe this odd letter is truly from me, unless they see evidence. They know I can never resist scribbling in the margins so hopefully, they'll understand I am quite well, and not under any duress."

"'Tis far from scribbling." He was compelled to defend her self-deprecating comment, but inside guilt stirred that whatever Roisin might say, she was under duress by the very fact he hadn't managed to already arrange her safe passage from the camp. "Yer talent is plain for anyone to see."

She gave a small smile as she signed her name around the rose. His chest dully ached at how similar her signature was to the exquisitely embroidered design on the handkerchief she had given him eighteen months ago, the one he still kept hidden in a pouch on his belt.

Finally, she finished and wrote her sister's name on the envelope before handing it to him. "Do ye think Isolde might receive my letter in a couple of days?" There was a hopeful note in her voice, and he hated that he was deceiving her, but it was the only way to keep her from harm.

Although he was confident of sending his own missive this day, he had no way of knowing at which manor or castle the earl was currently residing, which made taking a guess at how long it would be before his message was received unknowable.

He could hardly tell Roisin that and he didn't want to outright lie to her, either. Keeping the truth from her was bad enough. "It shouldn't be too long."

CHAPTER THIRTEEN

ROISIN WATCHED HUGH carefully place her letter into a pouch hanging from his belt, but the unease wouldn't leave her. She was certain her sisters would know the letter was from her, but she wasn't certain that receiving it would ease their minds. How could it, when she'd had no option but to leave out so many details that would explain her true situation?

And it wasn't just the details she'd omitted that would cause them distress. She hadn't been able to bring herself not to mention the terrible fate that had befallen the brave warriors of Eigg. They deserved to be found by those who had once known them, so they could be given a proper burial. She only hoped her directions on where the brigands had attacked were straightforward enough to follow.

"I don't like to leave ye, but will ye be all right in here for a few moments while I find a messenger?"

"Of course." She smiled at him, so he didn't guess anxiety knotted her stomach at the notion. If only Grear and Ecne were here. It was most unconventional that she should be left unattended in a strange inn, miles from home, but then, it was just as irregular she was spending so much time alone with Hugh and she didn't mind that, did she?

"I'll leave the door open so ye can keep an eye on me." He frowned. "Unless ye'd prefer the door shut? I know this isn't what ye are used to, but I cannot think how else to send the message. 'Tis imperative Symon knows nothing of it."

A new thread of anxiety attacked her at the thought of Symon catching Hugh in an act that, she was certain, Darragh would consider treachery. It hadn't occurred to her until now just how much danger Hugh was putting himself in so that she could get word to her sisters.

"Leave the door open," she said, even though a part of her wanted it shut, to hide her from any curious eyes. But the possibility of strangers casting a glance her way was a small consideration when it meant she would be able to keep Hugh in her line of sight.

He gave a brief nod and stood, and for a surreal heartbeat as she lost her senses in the blue of his eyes, she fancied he was about to kiss her. She tipped her head back, a blatant invitation, yet she couldn't help herself, and her breath caught in her throat as anticipation sparked through her.

But instead of leaning across the table and kissing her until she lost all sense of time or propriety, he merely brushed his fingers across the back of her hand before swinging on his heel and leaving the room.

She expelled a shaky breath, her gaze fixed on his back as he strode across the hall towards the bar. Her skin tingled where his fingers had trailed across her knuckles and it was both intoxicating and utterly foolish that such a brief touch could affect her so.

Within moments, he was in an animated conversation with a woman who was serving drinks to her customers. The innkeeper's wife, perhaps? Then she lost sight of him as he weaved his way through a throng of men. It didn't matter how she told herself to stay calm. Nerves spiked through her chest regardless.

This was madness. Hugh wasn't about to abandon her. She took a deep breath and forced herself to look out of the window, so it didn't appear as though she was desperate for his return. Not that the view of the stone wall of the stables was enticing, and she shook her head at her folly of being unable to get Hugh out of her mind and turned her attention to tidying away her ink and paper.

There was a sharp tap on the door, and she looked up, startled. The innkeeper Hugh had been talking with earlier stood there holding a tray with the food he'd ordered and an interested gleam in his eyes. Roisin's stomach churned.

As the youngest sister, whenever she'd been outside Sgur Castle it had never fallen to her to assume responsibility in any given situation, since she'd always been accompanied by Amma, Isolde or Freyja. Even though Hugh wasn't here, but before panic had a chance to lock her tongue, it occurred to her the innkeeper wasn't nearly as frightening as Darragh and she'd managed to speak to him, hadn't she?

She forced a smile and inclined her head. "Thank ye."

He entered the room and placed the platters and flagon of wine from the tray on the table. "I hope it's to yer liking, mistress."

"I'm sure it will be." Should she mention that Hugh—her husband—would be back at any moment? But maybe that would draw too much attention to the fact he wasn't here with her now. Before she could agonize on the wisdom of saying anything more, or not, Hugh returned, with Symon behind him.

Dismay streaked through her. Had Symon caught Hugh sending the message? Neither of them appeared to be spoiling for a fight, which was surely a good sign. As the innkeeper finally tore his attention from her to focus on Hugh, she slid her hands under the table before anyone noticed them shaking.

After a few inconsequential words between the three men, the innkeeper left. Hugh ignored his old seat and came to sit beside her. Before she could get too excited by that development, Symon kicked the door shut and then sat himself opposite them both.

"'Tis lucky ye saw me at the bar," Symon said. Then he placed a tankard of ale and a hearty bowl of stew on the table and dug in as though he were starving. He swallowed before continuing. "It wouldn't have occurred to me to start looking in private rooms for ye."

Hugh poured wine into the goblets and handed one to her. "I was keeping an eye out for ye."

Roisin kept her eyes on her goblet, but a shiver trickled over her arms at how easily Hugh had lied. But what else could he say? The truth?

The truth would put them both in danger. And since he was only doing this to help her, she'd tear out her tongue before she inadvertently gave him away.

Symon nodded, as though Hugh keeping an eye out for him was a commonplace thing. "Now we cannot be overheard, ye can ask me what ye want to know."

"There's no need. The satisfied look on yer face tells me ye got a good price."

"Aye, better than Darragh hoped. We'll be able to get all the supplies we need. And that was by selling only two of the horses." He glanced at Roisin and had the grace to look a little abashed. "With apologies, my lady, but 'tis no exaggeration to say finding ye was nothing short of a miracle for us."

She knew it wasn't his fault they had been attacked by brigands, but it was hard to keep her feelings to herself when his miracle had only been made possible by the deaths of the MacDonald warriors of Eigg. Irked with herself for not having the courage to respond, she picked up her goblet, and then it seemed her reticence fled. "'Tis a pity yer miracle is drenched in the blood of my countrymen."

Her rebuke rang in her ears and echoed around the suddenly silent room. Usually, her unwary thoughts remained locked tightly inside her head. Had she really spoken them aloud this time? A swift glance at Hugh's face assured her that she had. He looked mortified.

"Roisin, Symon didn't mean to offend ye. He doesn't always think things through."

"Aye, Hugh is right. I shouldn't wish to upset ye, and I'm sorry that I did. But when ye live life on the edge, ye must grab whatever advantage ye can."

She took a sip of wine, hating the way her face burned at being the center of such intense attention from both Hugh and Symon. But she couldn't take her words back and even if she could, she wouldn't.

No. She replaced the goblet on the table. She didn't regret her outburst. It was something that had to be said. The memory of her men demanded nothing less.

"I know 'tis not yer fault they were slaughtered. But their deaths grieve me, and I will not apologize for it."

"I only wish we'd arrived earlier, so we could have helped yer men fight off the bandits' attack." Hugh took her hand as he spoke, and his fierce blue gaze was spellbinding. "Then ye could have continued yer journey and never known—" He came to an abrupt halt before sucking in a ragged breath. "Any of this."

She knew what he really meant. She would never have discovered he'd become an outlaw with the rebel MacGregors.

His callused fingers tightened around hers as though, once again, he had forgotten they weren't alone. "But for all that, it's true. When ye have nothing, a miracle can be found in tragedy."

"'Tis a fearful way to live." Her voice was hushed. Although she thought of Hugh, she could neither forget the bairns in the camp nor the women who hadn't the means to grow essential herbs for their basic needs.

"Aye. Ye shouldn't be exposed to it, and that's a fact."

Despite how dearly she cherished these moments with Hugh, she suddenly bristled at his comment. Did he truly think her so shallow that he believed all she thought about was her own comfort? When, sooner or later, at least she was assured of returning to her former life, when the MacGregor women had no such certainty?

"What of the women and bairns, though? They shouldn't be exposed to this life either, just because the menfolk cannot keep their damn swords sheathed or their pride in check."

Hugh looked taken aback by her outburst, but he didn't release her hands. And she didn't have the overwhelming urge to sink through the floor the way she usually did when her words caused anyone to stare at her so.

Except she'd never said anything like this before, not even to her sisters. Because not only had she never faced such injustice before, but she had never taken the time to think about it, either.

"Men must protect their clan and their kin from their enemies." There was a tortured note in his voice and an eerie shiver chased through her. Was he speaking of the Earl of Argyll, who had banished the MacGregors from their land, or was he referring to the Mac-Gregors, who had first raised their swords against their earl?

In the end, did it even matter? The result was the same.

"'Tis a steep price to pay, Hugh," she whispered sorrowfully. Would those MacGregor bairns ever have a place to call home again? Her eyes stung at the question.

A dull clunk of a spoon against a bowl tore her back to the present and, as one, both she and Hugh looked across the table where Symon was slowly chewing, his eyes darting between her and Hugh. Shock stabbed through her. Yet again, she had forgotten about Symon's presence, and heat gushed through her, aye, and mortification too. She might not mind what she said to Hugh, but Symon was a different matter.

A small, unfamiliar voice drilled into the back of her mind.

I wouldn't take any of it back, even if I could.

With apparent reluctance, Hugh released her hand and for a heart-beat he appeared disconcerted. Then he drew in a deep breath and after a guarded glance in Symon's direction, once again caught her gaze.

"Forgive me." There was an oddly detached note in his voice and she shivered as though a draft had swept through the room. "This isn't a fit discussion for a lady." He picked up the platter with the food he'd ordered from the innkeeper and placed it closer to her. "Eat. Ye must keep yer strength up."

With as much dignity as she could muster, she picked up her goblet and took another sip. She was afraid if she didn't, her newfound courage might entice her to retort something unforgivable. And while Hugh certainly deserved it, she had no wish to continue the discussion while Symon eavesdropped.

Alas, it appeared her courage had no intention of retreating into its previous deep cave. She eyed him over the rim of her goblet and the words simply poured out. "Do not order me about, Hugh Campbell. We are only pretending to be man and wife. And please do not tell me what is or isn't fit for my discussion."

With that, she replaced her goblet on the table and bit into a pasty, ignoring both Hugh's wounded countenance and Symon's muffled snort of laughter. She wasn't sure if she was more irked by Hugh's order that she eat or his apparent belief she was incapable of serious discussion by virtue of her birth.

"That isn't what I meant." Hugh picked up a pasty and glowered at it as though it had personally offended him.

She didn't know if he was referring to their sham marital status or his presumption in deciding what topics of conversation were acceptable for her ears. Either way, it was disheartening to know her opinion scarcely mattered to him one way or another.

An uncomfortable silence fell. When Hugh finally sat back in his chair and tossed his napkin onto the table, Symon spoke. "We should buy our supplies now, Sergeant."

"Aye." He still sounded out of sorts, but she wasn't going to look at him since he might take that as a sign of apology. Instead, she wrapped the remaining food in one of the napkins. Too bad if the innkeeper charged Hugh for it.

"Let me take that for ye." He nodded at the napkin.

"Thank ye, but I'm quite capable of carrying it myself until I can stow it in the saddlebags."

He didn't argue with her, which was a relief, since it was such a foolish thing to disagree over, but nevertheless, it was simply a point of principle. Hugh Campbell might be her only hope of escaping the MacGregors and returning to her kin, but that didn't mean he could order her around or treat her like a witless bairn.

Unfortunately, it was hard to remain annoyed with him when he was so solicitous and held her arm in a protective gesture as they left the inn. And she certainly wasn't oblivious to the admiring glances slanted his way from more than a few young women. Indeed, by the time they'd collected their horses and were once again heading to the market so he and Symon could purchase the goods for the camp, she had all but forgotten why he had vexed her so.

Maybe she had forgiven him, but that didn't mean he was in the right. And when they were next alone, she would be sure to let him know.

Chapter Fourteen

Aᶠᵗᵉʳ ᵗʰᵉʸ ʳᵉᵗᵘʳⁿᵉᵈ to the camp, the women and bairns crowded around them, eager for the goods they'd brought back. Hugh dismounted, but it appeared Roisin was still irked with him as she swiftly dismounted her mare before he could assist her.

He had no idea how to breach the gulf that had cracked open between them and wasn't sure why she'd taken such offense to his comments. He had only wanted to end the conversation before he said something incriminating in front of Symon. God knew, he almost had. Five years ago, when the MacGregors had seized land and murdered several Campbells in the process, the earl had been left with no choice but to respond.

Any man would have done the same to protect his clan.

Except for a dangerous moment, he'd forgotten Symon was listening to every word. Forgotten that he was living the life of an outcast in a rebel MacGregor camp and that his only tenuous link to survival was maintaining the masquerade of loyalty to Darragh and his clan.

From the corner of his eye, he watched Roisin as she led her mare across the plateau to his tent, where Grear and her wee dog greeted her as though she'd been gone for a month. And then he lost sight of her as Darragh stood in his line of sight, his arms folded, the familiar grim expression on his face.

"Any trouble?" He addressed his comment to Symon.

"No, the market was busy. We won't be remembered."

Darragh transferred his one-eyed gaze to Hugh. "Did the lass behave herself?"

The lack of respect in Darragh's tone when he referred to Roisin irritated him but since defending her would only draw more unwelcome attention her way, he locked it down. Even if it did nearly choke him. "Aye."

Darragh glanced at the women who were transferring the goods they'd bought to the tents. "We'll be moving on at first light."

Taken aback, Hugh forgot caution. "Why?"

Darragh returned his attention to him. "'Tis my decision, that's why."

Hugh clamped his jaw shut, but inside frustration raged. Although his missive to the earl would reassure Roisin's kin that she was alive and well, the carefully coded directions to the town, where he'd hoped to ensure her safe transfer to the earl's men, would be for naught.

"Did something happen while we were gone?" There was no hint of Symon's usual cheerful manner.

"No. I made the decision after Hugh brought the MacDonald lass into the camp. I'm not happy keeping her with us. We'll meet up with our MacGregor brothers in the east, who have more resources to leverage her safe return to her kin."

Outraged, Hugh glared at the older man. "Ye said ye wouldn't use her as a hostage."

Darragh shrugged. "Changed my mind."

"Come, Sergeant." Symon grasped his arm. "We've work to do."

Hugh took a deep breath as Darragh turned away and made his way over to the other men before he glanced at Symon.

"What work?" He sounded disgruntled but couldn't help himself. All he wanted to do was seek out Roisin and clear the air between them.

In answer, Symon took the bridle of his horse and led the way to the far end of the plateau beyond the rocky outcrop where they let the horses drink from the river. As they removed their horses' saddles,

Hugh reluctantly acknowledged the other man had done the right thing in cutting short the conversation with Darragh.

Goddamn it. It was becoming harder by the hour to keep his thoughts to himself whenever Roisin was involved.

"'Twas always Lady Roisin, wasn't it?"

Hugh shot him a sharp look. "What?"

"The bonny lass ye told me about in Eire. She was never yers though, was she?"

Hugh glared at him as denials tumbled through his mind. But before he could push out a credible rebuttal, Symon added, "I can see why ye fell for her, and I don't mean her noble blood or even her face. She looks as sweet as honey, but she'd keep any man on his toes with that quick tongue of hers."

In Eigg, she'd never said a sharp word in his hearing, nor given him a disapproving glance or argued with him the way she had since they had crossed paths again yesterday. She'd been gentle and kind and all his protective instincts had roared to the surface, along with the fantasy of one day calling her his, so he could defend her from the world forever.

Goddamn it. She was still gentle and kind. But he had never imagined she possessed this other side of her, where she didn't agree with everything he said, but questioned his beliefs and rebutted his comments, and he didn't simply find the revelation astonishing.

The discovery made her more irresistible than ever.

Symon shook his head and shrugged. "Don't worry, Sergeant, I'll not say a word to Darragh. No wonder ye never spoke of her again. Ye never had a chance to win a noblewoman like her."

At least Symon was right about that. He'd never had a chance with her, not from the moment the earl had summoned him to Castle Campbell last spring.

There was no point telling Symon he was wrong. It would only make Hugh's denial look suspicious. All he could do was continue with the subterfuge that he was a lowborn Campbell and not the son of a well-respected, if not vastly wealthy, laird. For no peasant could hope to win the hand of a noblewoman who could trace her lineage back for almost a thousand years.

"She must never know." His voice was hoarse, and he tightened his grip around the saddle he held as he thought of the inkwell he'd bought at the market, now secure in his saddlebag. It had been a hasty transaction, without the bartering he usually employed, but he hadn't been able to risk either Roisin or Symon discovering what he was doing. "Give me yer word, Symon."

Symon gave him a strange look. "Ye have it, but are ye blind, man? The lady can scarcely keep her eyes from ye. I'm certain she knows well how ye feel about her."

Christ, he hoped not. The memory of their kiss burned through him, a mocking echo reminding him that was all he'd ever have and curse the heavens, but it wasn't nearly enough. "Lady Roisin was merely playing along, as I asked her to."

"If ye say so." It was obvious Symon thought he'd lost his mind. "Though there was no need for any deception when it was just the three of us in the room at the inn, was there, now?"

Hugh swung away from Symon's curious gaze and began to groom Deagh Fhortan. No, there hadn't been any need for him to hold her hands or become entrapped in her innocent gaze, and yet he had. He couldn't help himself. And now he'd given away the fact he and Roisin had known each other before the bandits had attacked her.

It wasn't that he didn't trust Symon to keep his word. For all that he was a MacGregor, the man had proven himself throughout the time Hugh had known him. It was because Symon had so easily guessed Roisin was the lass Hugh had been thinking of that night so many months ago when reckless secrets had been shared that rattled him.

But no one else knew of that and there was no reason why anyone here should suspect he and Roisin had met before yesterday. Still, he needed to be more careful. Innis had already guessed he was more interested in Roisin than he should be. He couldn't afford to let his guard down, not even for a moment, if he wanted to keep their brief, shared past concealed.

ROISIN PULLED OUT the napkin of food and the apples from the saddlebags and she and Grear took them into the tent. She'd seen how much fresh food Hugh and Symon had brought back and no longer felt guilty about not sharing her small hoard with the women. And even though she had a feeling Innis would ensure she and Grear received their fair share of supper tonight, it was still comforting to have a little spare food in the tent.

"Did anyone bother ye while I was gone?" She gazed anxiously at Grear, who shook her head.

"No, milady. I stayed with the women, as mistress Innis promised, and looked after the bairns."

Although she'd trusted Innis to keep her word, it was a relief to hear Grear confirm it.

As Grear and Ecne tucked into their pasties, she took out her knife and cut up one of the apples to share with her dog. But her mind wasn't on her task. No matter how she tried to stop herself, she couldn't help replaying her last conversation with Hugh. Indeed, she hadn't been able to stop thinking about it throughout the journey back to the camp, and by the time they'd arrived, she had reached the uneasy conclusion that maybe Hugh had shut down their conversation because of Symon.

Not because of her, at all.

She gave an impatient sigh as she gave Ecne a slice of apple. Was that really true, or did she simply hope it was? She was certain she hadn't misinterpreted his interest when he had been on Eigg, or since they'd met again in the Highlands, and he had never spoken to her so abruptly before.

She sat on the edge of her trunk and pulled the kerchief from her head. Before her sisters had wed, they had both had moments where they'd doubted the sincerity of William and Alasdair. Roisin had never quite understood it. To her, it had been as bright as starlight that Isolde and William, and Freyja and Alasdair, had belonged together.

Alas, it was very different when she tried to sort out the tangles between herself and Hugh. Even Amma didn't believe they belonged together and that was before Roisin had discovered Hugh had been banished from his clan. God only knew what her grandmother would think of him now.

There was a muffled tap on the flap of the tent and Grear pulled it open to reveal Hugh standing there. Hastily she straightened her spine, grateful that Ecne distracted his attention by pawing his boot in greeting. It gave her a welcome moment to compose herself. Although, who was she trying to fool? She lost her composure every time she caught sight of the man.

After giving Ecne a good scratch behind his ears, Hugh caught her eye. "I don't mean to intrude, but I'd like a word."

She stood and waved him inside, although it felt ridiculous to invite him to enter his own tent. "Of course." And then she looked at Grear. "Maybe ye can see if Innis and the women need some help?"

It was shocking that she was encouraging Grear to leave her alone with Hugh, but if she needed to apologize to him for jumping to conclusions earlier, she certainly didn't want an audience.

Grear nodded, and left, calling Ecne to accompany her, and the tent flap hung half open, allowing the late afternoon sun to spill into the dim interior.

How magnificent Hugh looked, with his face wreathed in shadows as the light streamed in through the open tent flap behind him. From the first moment she'd seen him at Sgur Castle, he'd taken her breath away, for he was surely the most compelling man she had ever met. But had he always possessed the hint of raw danger that was as much a part of him as his incomparable blue eyes? How had she not felt that wild undertow before, or was it purely a consequence of this rebel life he now led?

When he didn't immediately speak, unease slithered through her. Had he come here expecting an apology from her? While she was half convinced she owed him one, there hadn't been any need for him to sound so condescending in the inn and a small flicker of vexation heated her blood. For all she knew, he had meant every word and the excuses she'd made for him lived entirely in her head.

"I wanted ye to know," he urged. She held her breath in anticipation. "Darragh's decided we are moving on at first light. But don't despair. My pledge to return ye to yer kin remains true."

"Moving on?" she repeated. It was the last thing she'd expected Hugh to say, but she appreciated how he'd made certain she knew what was happening. "Where are we heading?"

"East." Frustration threaded through the word. "To meet up with another branch of the clan." He flexed his jaw, and she had the strangest certainty he was battling the urge to say something else. It appeared caution won when he exhaled a deep sigh and scrubbed his hand over his face. How could such a seemingly exhausted gesture cause her heart to flutter in her breast and her lingering resentment against him to flee?

"Well, we just need to make the best of it." After all, what else could she do? "At least my sisters will soon know I am well."

"Aye, that they will." He still looked tortured, though. What had he decided not to tell her? Maybe it was nothing at all. She had to stop imagining there were unspoken messages everywhere. "Look, Roisin, I didn't mean to offend ye back at the inn. I couldn't risk us saying something that might give Symon an inkling of who we both truly are."

Relief spilled through her. In this, at least, she had been right. "'Tis fine, I understand. It would be a disaster if he saw through our subterfuge."

Something akin to awe transfigured his features, or maybe it was a trick of the light. "Ye were playacting when ye said those things to me?"

It would be so much easier on her pride to agree with him that her retorts in the inn had been part of an admirable strategy. But she couldn't do it. Because, in the end, she didn't need to lie to Hugh to keep herself alive.

"No. Ye irked me greatly, and I couldn't keep my thoughts to myself."

He grinned and the lines of worry that had carved dark shadows on his face vanished. It was a wondrous phenomenon, and she couldn't stop herself from smiling back at him.

"I hope ye never feel the need to keep yer thoughts to yerself when ye're with me." And then he sighed. "Unless we're not alone."

"I shan't make that mistake again. The truth is, and I know it makes no sense, but I had forgotten Symon was in the room with us. I would make a terrible spy, wouldn't I?"

"I'm sorry ye need to think before ye speak. It shouldn't be this way." His callused hand cupped her face, as though he couldn't help himself, and the gentle caress of his thumb over her cheek caused her breath to catch in her throat. "I wish to God we'd had more time together on Eigg."

She threaded her fingers through his, pressing his palm more securely against her face. Her chest was tight, and her heart thundered against her ribs, and all she wanted to do was melt against him and feel his strong arms hold her close. But first she had to know one thing. "Why did ye kiss me, Hugh?"

He swallowed and the sight was more enticing than it had any right to be. "Ye know why."

Thrills skittered over her skin at his implication. But it wasn't enough. She needed to hear him say the words. "Because ye needed anyone who looked our way to believe we were wed?"

"No." His denial vibrated through her body like ripples of flame invading her veins, and fiery need bloomed between her thighs. Her breath hitched as he loomed over her, and even though it was too dark to see the color of his eyes, his intense gaze ensnared her, nonetheless. "I kissed ye because I needed to taste ye the way a man needs air to breathe or bread to live. Ye'll never be mine, Roisin, but for a brief moment I dreamed that ye were."

Thrills cascaded through her, sparks of pleasure but also shards of pain, as the truth of his tortured words sank into her mind. So many times since she had watched him sail away from her eighteen months ago, she'd imagined Hugh declaring undying devotion to her, even though as time had passed, she'd slowly lost hope of ever seeing him again.

But nothing her imagination had conjured came close to the tortured, bittersweet words he whispered nor the unmistakable despair that throbbed in the hot air around them. How certain he was they could never have a future together.

"I can be yers." Her voice was so soft she wondered if he would even hear her, but his fingers tightened against her face and a harsh breath escaped him. Emboldened, she closed the small distance between them, pressing herself against his hard body. The heady aroma of worn leather and wild grasses enveloped her in a sensual cocoon, heightening her senses and a maelstrom of need and desire collided deep in her core. "I'll always be yers, Hugh."

"Don't say that," he responded harshly. Although he kept his voice low, his words were filled with anguish that pierced her heart. He raked his fingers through her hair, and she flattened her hands against his broad chest, where his heart hammered as erratically as her own. "I cannot offer ye anything, Roisin. Don't make this harder than it already is."

"We have this," she breathed, as she trailed her hands up his chest and across his magnificent shoulders. It was hard to find the words she needed, when all she wanted was to lose herself in his arms, but somehow she managed. "'Tis enough for now."

His burning breath fanned her face. "This will never be enough."

He may have fallen in with rebels, but his honor was as intact as it had been in Eigg, where he'd done no more than briefly touch her hand. But they were no longer on the isle of her birth nor constrained by the rules she had lived with all her life. And although he had kissed her in the town, there was a certain safety in such public places that was missing from this tent, pitched so far from all the others.

If she wanted more, it was up to her to take it.

Exhilaration surged through her. Hugh wanted her, and that was all she needed to know. Before she could think better of it, she went onto her toes, linked her hands behind his neck, and pressed her lips to his.

Her eyes fluttered shut as his admirable restraint crumbled and he wrapped his arms around her, crushing her so close she could scarcely breathe. But who needed to breathe when Hugh claimed her mouth as though he were a dying man and she his only hope of salvation?

His tongue teased the seam of her lips and shivers of delight danced across her skin. She opened her mouth, and he pushed inside, and she reveled in the sensation of him possessing her so intimately. An unintentional moan escaped, and his deep-throated growl in response reverberated through every particle of her body.

Feverishly, she speared her fingers through his hair, gripping his head in case he had the mad idea to step back. But he didn't try to break their kiss. Instead, he leisurely withdrew his tongue, caressing the soft flesh inside her mouth with infinite promise, before pushing inside her once again.

It was decadently arousing, and her head fell back in silent submission. He didn't relent, teasing and exploring and when she swirled the tip of her tongue against his, his grasp hovered on the precipice between pleasure and pain.

Without releasing her from his possessive embrace, he caressed her back and cradled her bottom. Sparks of desire ricocheted between her thighs, and she shuddered as she instinctively dug her nails into his head.

Roughly, he broke their kiss, panting in her face, but made no move to release her. "Tell me to stop." It was a harsh demand. "Tell me to go, Roisin, or God help me—" he clamped his jaw shut, and she knew she should end this illicit encounter but couldn't bring herself to.

"No," she breathed and pulled his head down and captured his mouth once again.

His kiss was ravenous as he hiked up her skirts, and she gasped into his mouth as his hand glided over her naked buttock. His fingers stroked and teased, and a tremor of wild delight cascaded through her when his hand cupped her mound.

The tip of his finger caressed her tender folds, circling her swollen clit, and she shuddered as blissful pressure swirled wherever he touched. She shifted, pushing herself more securely against his exploring fingers, needing more, so much more.

He pulled free from their kiss, and she sucked in elusive air as his lips and teeth trailed a burning path along her throat. Skitters of pleasure erupted across her skin and her nipples hardened, straining against her chemise. She wanted to rip off his shirt, to feel his naked chest against her, but she was helpless beneath the magic of his tongue and mouth.

And still he teased her damp slit, dipping inside and caressing her sensitive flesh. She forgot where they were, forgot everything but Hugh as waves of pleasure consumed her, and her senses shattered into a thousand starlit fragments.

Her legs shook but Hugh held her securely and she sagged against him, her heart thundering and breath erratic. Delightful tremors wracked her body as Hugh tenderly stroked her hair. A sense of deep comfort enveloped her.

We do belong together.

It was only when he gave an oddly strangled groan and eased back from her she realized that while she was feeling blissful and as though she could take on the world, Hugh remained unsatisfied.

She grasped the front of his shirt in both hands and gazed anxiously into his eyes. "Ye did not finish."

"'Tis fine." He did not sound fine, although he did attempt to smile. "Roisin, I—"

"No," she said urgently, and her heart melted at how he had been so solicitous of her pleasure at the expense of his own. She might not have any experience of men, but she knew well enough, from overheard whispers among the women on the Small Isles, that such thoughtfulness was rare. "There must be something I can do."

His gaze dropped to her mouth. "There isn't." His voice was hoarse, as though the words were forced from the darkest pit of hell. With apparent reluctance he dragged his gaze back to hers and gave her a pained smile. "Don't fret, mo ghràdh. I'll live."

Mo ghràdh. *My love.* She hadn't thought it possible to fall any harder for Hugh Campbell, and yet with two little words, here she was. And she would have it no other way.

"There is," she whispered, grasping his plaid.

"Roisin." He sounded shocked and gripped her hands. "What are ye doing?"

"I fear we don't have much time." She had completely lost track of how long she had been alone in the tent with Hugh. Grear might return at any moment. But she was determined he would remember this encounter for the rest of his life, just as she would. "I'm not entirely sure what I should do, but I have a general idea."

He snorted, and she cast an anxious glance at the tent flap. No one appeared to be outside, and she ignored his restraining hands, and once again attempted to hike his heavy plaid up his thighs.

"Ye'll be the death of me," he groaned as he plunged his fingers through her hair.

"Oh," she breathed as she finally caught sight of his astonishing manhood. It was thick and long and jutted upwards with proud indifference to her awe, and once again fiery need licked deep within her sheath. "That—that is quite admirable, to be sure."

"I'm gratified with yer approval."

Tentatively, she ran her finger along his rigid flesh, and he shuddered in clear agony. She hesitated, unsure whether she should continue, but her curiosity got the better of her and she swirled her finger around the head of his erection.

"God's bones." He sounded rabid as he grabbed her hand and wrapped her fingers around him in a frighteningly hard embrace. "Aye, that's it." Raw lust throbbed in his voice as he rubbed her hand along his hot length. His fierce gaze never wavered from hers and a thread of alarm spiked through the passion-soaked fog that filled her mind. Surely she was hurting him?

The sound of his harsh breaths filled the tent, and his fingers slid from her hair to cradle her face. She forgot her worry as he captured her mouth in a brutal kiss that sent her senses spinning, and with her free hand she clutched his shirt to stop herself from collapsing to the ground.

"Christ." He ground the word between his teeth and abruptly released her head before grabbing the napkin she'd folded and left on top of her trunk. Bemused, she watched him wrap the napkin about himself, before pressing her hand around him once again and roughly pulling her close. So close, their bodies all but melded, and the exhilarating friction against her palm sent spirals of need tingling between her thighs.

With a desperate groan, he buried his face in her shoulder as his body went rigid, and he pumped his hot seed over her napkin-shielded fist.

For endless moments, they remained locked together. Then she breathed in the elusive scent of arousal and worn leather and reveled in how right it felt to be in Hugh's arms. But slowly, the outside world intruded. A horse's snort outside the tent caused her to lift her head from his chest in vague alarm.

With evident reluctance he eased back from her and gently loosened her grip around him. She stood, swaying a little and feeling oddly cast adrift as he screwed the napkin into a ball and shoved it into one of his leather pouches. Then he caught her gaze and gave a rueful smile, and she didn't feel adrift any longer. "I didn't want to ruin yer bonny gown."

"'Twas thoughtful of ye."

He pressed his forehead against hers. "I didn't mean for this to happen, but God forgive me, I cannot say I regret it."

"There's nothing to forgive," she assured him, tracing her fingers along his day-old, beard-roughened jaw. "I was the one who kissed ye first, remember?"

He grinned and gave her another, way too fleeting, kiss. "I'll remember it always."

"I hope ye do." For she always would.

He straightened. "I all but forgot. I got ye this at the market." From one of his pouches he pulled out the inkwell she had so admired, and she gasped. It was a beautiful piece of art, and she knew well how expensive these imported goods were.

"Ye shouldn't have." She couldn't resist tracing a finger along the delicate lines of Danu's gown. "It is too much, Hugh."

"It's impractical, I know." He sighed. "But I hope ye'll find use for it once ye are back where ye belong."

He was right. It was impractical here, in the camp, and she would never be able to use it. A magnificent sculpture such as this was something to be admired on a grand desk and it was certainly something she'd use every day.

Once she was back home.

But the only home she wanted was one where Hugh was, too.

"I love it," she said softly. "And I shall treasure it always."

"I'm glad." But his smile was sad and tugged at her heart. Then he took a great breath and took a step back. "I'd best be going before either of us are missed."

With an oddly formal nod, he turned and left the tent, and she hugged the inkwell against her breasts. It was obvious Hugh was still convinced he could never return to his home but she wasn't giving up on her dream.

She wasn't sure how she would manage it, but if it was the last thing she did, she was determined he would return to his rightful place in Clan Campbell.

CHAPTER FIFTEEN

THEY HAD BEEN traveling for four days, going deeper into the mountains but although they traveled farther away from Creagdoun with every passing hour, he knew they were heading in the general direction where the earl had one of his manors.

The previous day, Hugh had managed to send another message to the earl from a small town they had bypassed, under the pretext of buying a few essential supplies for the camp. Surprisingly, Darragh hadn't objected nor insisted another man accompany him, but Hugh always worked under the assumption that he was being watched and hadn't taken any chances.

He just hoped the earl had received his first message already and was aware of the situation regarding Roisin. Because until he did, Hugh couldn't expect to receive word from him at any of the towns or villages he managed to visit on the way to wherever the hell it was Darragh was leading them.

As he pitched his tent in Darragh's designated small clearing, he surreptitiously watched Roisin as she helped the women prepare supper. And, as always, whenever he looked at her, a bittersweet ache filled his chest that this was all he would ever have of her.

It had been sheer good luck no one had caught them in the tent the other day when he'd lost his mind and all but made her his. Christ, how close he'd been to taking her. Even now he could scarcely believe he had managed to retain at least a sliver of integrity and resist the temptation.

Every night her face, as she had fallen apart in his arms, haunted his dreams, and every morning he awoke with lust pounding through his veins, frustration hammering at his temples, and an erection so damn hard he could scarcely function.

With grim determination, he tore his besotted gaze from her and concentrated on securing his tent. But his cock thickened, despite his best intentions, and his mind endlessly replayed Roisin's soft gasps and the way her body had responded to his touch as though the fates drew pleasure from his discomfort.

Yet, as surely the devil himself knew, Hugh would have it no other way.

By the time he'd finished, Roisin had taken the bairns to the edge of the campsite where, doubtless, she was spinning them another of her tales of the mythical fae folk from Eire. Ecne lay in front of her, his head on her satchel that she'd placed on the ground, and her writing case was propped against her knees. On the other side of the camp the men had congregated, and by rights that was where he should head, on the off chance that Darragh might let slip more information on where they were going.

Except Hugh knew the other man would never share anything by accident.

To hell with it. There was never any doubt in his mind that he'd make his way to Roisin, the way he had every day this week since they'd left the plateau. His pledge to keep his distance, and maintain the illusion she meant nothing to him, had crumbled before the masquerade had even begun.

But in the end, it didn't matter. No one cared that he couldn't hide his interest in her. The only thing that mattered was no one guessed they'd known each other longer than a few days, and the only reason why Symon knew was because Hugh had shared his secret on that long-ago, drink-fueled night.

He didn't care if the women made good natured jests, so long as they were always aimed at him. Which they were. The women appeared to have welcomed Roisin as one of their own. While he still had no idea what had happened to change their minds about her, he was just relieved they had.

As for the men, they could say what they liked, but in the end they were guided by their womenfolk in such matters, and he didn't give a damn about their mockery. It was a negligible price to pay for the chance to spend a few peaceful moments in Roisin's company.

He strolled over to her and hunkered down outside the circle of entranced bairns, but close enough to Roisin so he could see what she was drawing. It was a sketch of Rhona, wearing a crown of flowers that weaved through her hair as she danced through a forest, and the breath caught in his throat at the detail Roisin had wrought with her quill.

"The magical lights danced over the dark sea, and the fierce Pict queen led her fearless warriors into the waves." Roisin paused in her drawing to send a sweet smile his way that instantly reignited the fire in his blood, before she continued with her tale. "'Tis said the lights were the slain monks' vengeance for the queen and her warriors having slaughtered them, but 'tis my belief the great sea god of the Tuatha De Danann, Manannan mac Lir, rode his mighty horse across the water, calling the queen and her women home to him."

"Did they all die?" one little lad asked in awe.

"Maybe they did," Roisin said. "But as long as we remember them and tell their tales, no one truly dies."

Innis called the bairns to come over to her, and Roisin handed Rhona her drawing, who looked thrilled with it. As the bairns left and Roisin cleaned the nib of her quill, he shifted closer to her.

"Which mythical tale was that? I don't recall it from those ye shared with me before."

She glanced at him, and it took all his willpower not to steal another kiss from her. "I didn't tell ye this one. 'Tis the history of our Pict queen foremother, who refused to give up her land for the Christian monks to build their monastery on our isle."

"So she slaughtered them?"

"That's how the story goes. But she passed down her edict to her eldest daughter, who didn't perish in the sea like all the other women."

"Her edict?" Once again, he was drawn under the spell of her storytelling, just as he had been on the Isle of Eigg. Although, truth be told, she could tell him the most mundane of things and she'd still manage to bewitch him.

"That the daughters of Sgur can never leave our isle."

"That was the command she wanted handed down through countless generations?"

Roisin frowned and dusted the end of her quill across her lips as though she were considering the matter. "'Tis more than a command, and yet—" she hesitated and then shook her head as though trying to dislodge troublesome thoughts. "Her edict has been handed down from mother to daughter for over nine hundred years. 'Tis not something to be taken lightly. But there have never been three daughters of Sgur in the same generation before which, I feel, is a powerful portent."

Despite enjoying her story, he was skeptical. "There is no way ye can possibly know that for sure, Roisin. 'Tis far more likely that many daughters have been born than not."

"Ye may be right," she conceded. "But my mother was the only daughter of Amma, and Amma was the only daughter of my great grandmother. And she, in turn, was the only daughter born of her mother. We can trace our blood kin back for many generations and the single daughter holds true throughout. But although what ye say is possible, 'tis just as possible what we've always been told is true."

He had to admit the truth of what she said. "Maybe. But it seems unlikely it could have happened in an unbroken chain for nine hundred years." And then the obvious occurred to him. "Did yer fierce

Pict queen curse her bloodline, then?"

"Curse?" Roisin seemed confused. "What do ye mean?"

"I mean did she weave a spell or some such that her descendants would never produce a son and only a single daughter every generation?" Not that he believed in such things as spells, of course. But nine hundred years ago, when the Picts, with their pagan beliefs, had still held power across the Highlands, who knew what might have occurred?

"Oh." Now she appeared amused. "No, 'tis not a curse. And for yer information many sons have been born over the centuries. But Sgur passed through the matrilineal line, even before there was a castle built on the land. As the eldest daughter, it was always assumed Isolde would inherit, but Amma betrothed her to William because she was certain Isolde's path did not lay on Eigg."

And then he saw where she was heading with this. "And after Lady Freyja wed Alasdair, the inheritance fell to ye."

Roisin sighed. "'Tis a strange thing when ye believe something is certain all yer life, only to discover..." she paused and bit her lip. "That it isn't."

"Is that what ye mean about this being a powerful portent?" He still couldn't make sense of that comment. "Because of how unlikely it was that ye'd inherit, with two older sisters?"

"No." She dropped her gaze, and her fingers played with the feather of her quill. "I've never spoken of it before, even though it's something that's troubled me since I was a small bairn."

He took her hand and gave her fingers a comforting squeeze, wishing they were alone so he could pull her into his arms and kiss her worries away. "Ye know ye can tell me anything, Roisin."

She shook her head. "My sisters think I'm fanciful. I'll not deny it. But I've always thought it strange how neither of them, nor even Amma, saw the significance."

She'd lost him, but he didn't like to admit it. Yet he couldn't help himself. "What significance?"

"Three is a powerful number, Hugh."

He'd never thought about it before. "I suppose it is," he said, but couldn't hide the doubt in his voice although Roisin didn't seem to notice.

"'Tis always three." Her voice was hushed. An eerie shiver raked along his arms. "Birth, life and death. The maiden, the mother and the crone. Three is woven through so many of the ancient myths and legends, and why do ye think that is?"

She didn't appear to expect him to answer, as she continued with scarcely a pause. "Because it is a sacred number. And I've never been able to shake the feeling that our Pict queen ancestor is somehow reaching through the years to tell us something."

It was a fanciful concept, indeed, but he didn't like to voice his disbelief in case he hurt her feelings. "'Tis an interesting idea for sure."

"And I have always wondered if perhaps we've never fully understood what she meant by—by her edict."

He had the oddest sensation Roisin had been about to say something quite different and had inexplicably changed her mind at the last moment. "About not leaving the isle?"

She shrugged and focused on their clasped hands. "Amma is certain that once I return to Eigg, the edict will continue to be fulfilled. We only need one daughter to remain, after all."

Something in her tone alerted him and he frowned. "Do ye not want to remain on Eigg, Roisin?"

She lifted her head, and their gazes meshed. "'Tis not that." Her voice was soft. "I love Eigg and Sgur Castle. 'Tis the only home I've known. I know, in the end, that is my destiny."

Ecne raised his head from her satchel and gave a little whine. She lay down her quill and stroked him, and he edged onto her lap, heedless of her writing case. With a grin, Hugh released her hand and picked up her writing case so the dog had more room, and a sheet of paper slid out.

"Oh." Roisin sounded mortified and reached for the paper at the same time as he, and their fingers collided. But his gaze was fixed on the exquisitely crafted image on the paper. Was that *him*?

Hastily he released his grip, and Roisin pushed the paper back inside her writing case. For a few awkward moments silence reigned, and he didn't know how to break it. Then Ecne pawed Roisin's arm, and she expelled a ragged breath and finally caught his gaze.

"'Tis merely a sketch I did of ye when ye visited Sgur."

"Do ye have any objection if I have a closer look?"

She scratched Ecne's throat, and he had the feeling she was trying to think of an excuse to say no. Eventually she gave a great sigh and pulled the sketch from her writing case. "If ye must."

He stared at the portrait, since calling this a sketch was scarcely short of slanderous. And while he had always known of her talent and had admired her drawing of Rhona a short while ago, it was completely different to be confronted with something so unexpected. The likeness was frankly uncanny.

"I'm sorry ye don't like it." Roisin attempted to take it from him, but he shook his head and lowered the portrait, so it rested on her knee.

"I do like it." His voice was hushed. "I'm merely stunned into silence at yer brilliance, Roisin. I've never had my portrait done before."

A delightful blush stained her cheeks, and she gave him a shy smile. "Brilliant, am I? Well, I'm gratified ye think so."

He glanced at it again and noticed her signature rosebud in the corner, with her name encircling it. "If things were different, I should commission a portrait in oils from ye, and that's a fact."

She gave a soft laugh. "I've never painted in oils before, although I should very much like to. But ye can have that one, if ye really want it. I have plenty of others. Oh." She slapped her hand across her mouth before shaking her head. "I said that out loud, didn't I?"

He grinned, inordinately pleased by her confession. "Aye, and ye cannot take it back."

"I shouldn't wish to, although I never meant to tell ye."

His mirth faded. Didn't she deserve to hear the truth, now he had indisputable proof that the fleeting time they'd spent together on her isle had meant as much to her as it had to him? "Roisin, I always intended to return to Eigg to see ye. I wasn't simply spinning ye a pretty line to see ye smile. But—" He couldn't tell her the earl had summoned him and sent him into this life, no matter how much he wished he could. "It wasn't to be."

"I should so dearly like to know why ye're living like this." Her voice was scarcely above a whisper. The way she laid her hand on top of his was almost his undoing.

"Maybe ye'll know one day," he lied. Because there wasn't any way she'd learn the truth from him, and who else could tell her? No one. Because, apart from the earl, no one else knew the truth.

CHAPTER SIXTEEN

I T HAD BEEN ten days since the brigands had attacked, and Roisin had ended up in the MacGregor camp. Sometimes it seemed she'd lived this way forever, and her life on Eigg was nothing more than a dream, and then she had to battle the clawing abyss of panic that tried to swamp her.

She wouldn't let anyone see how every now and then she was so close to falling apart it frightened her. Because all she had left was her pride, and when she compared her lot to those of these women and their bairns, at least she knew there was an end to her plight. And not once had she witnessed any of the women come close to cracking.

If they could be brave, then so could she.

They had stopped for the night beside a river and as the men pitched the tents she'd joined the women and was doing some mending with Grear, with Ecne dozing at her side, while Elspeth oversaw the preparations for supper. A couple of times over the last few days, one of the men had detoured to villages or towns and sold a horse, so the camp's supplies were well-stocked.

Which meant the bairns were well-fed.

She stole a glance at Hugh, where he was pitching his tent a short distance from the others and as always whenever she looked at him, her heart melted. It wasn't just the women's stoicism that helped her get through the days. It was Hugh.

Who was she trying to fool? It was mainly Hugh who had man-aged to keep the terror of being ripped from everything she knew at bay. It wasn't only that he was a link to her real life or that she had known him before.

He was the reason she was safe. The alternative of being captured by the brigands would have been infinitely worse, and a shudder inched along her spine at how easily that fate could have been hers and Grear's.

Hugh straightened, wiped his brow with his forearm, and then he glanced her way. She smiled and when he grinned back, the lingering worry of her situation faded, as it always faded when he turned his charm her way.

But it was more than charm. He had told her so himself that he'd always intended to return to her after he had left Sgur. And she believed him. There was no reason for him to lie. And while she couldn't wait to be reunited with her sisters and Amma, part of her didn't want this strange existence to end, if it was the only way she could be with Hugh.

But no. She wasn't going to think about that. Because when she left the camp, so would he.

Innis sat beside her. "Don't be getting any ideas about that one," she said as she began to darn Rhona's wool stockings. "Nothing can come of it."

Roisin's cheeks heated and she tore her besotted gaze from Hugh and concentrated on her mending. Sometimes Innis's blunt remarks reminded her of Freyja, except Innis wasn't her older sister and didn't have the right to reprimand her. "I'm not getting ideas."

Instantly, her mind flew to the breathtaking tryst she and Hugh had shared in his tent a few days ago. She replayed those moments so often, they were branded into her brain, and every morning she awoke with frustration blazing through her blood and fragmented echoes of passion-filled dreams haunting her mind.

Nothing close to that encounter had happened since and although she and Hugh had shared a few furtive kisses when they were sure no one was looking, she got the distinct impression he was deliberately avoiding being alone with her in the tent.

So, no. She wasn't getting ideas. She didn't need to. She already knew how Hugh felt about her.

"Good," Innis said. "When ye return to yer kin, ye'll need to put all this behind ye. There's no future to be had between a lady of the Western Isles and a common Campbell outlaw."

It was just the kind of thing her practical sister Freyja would say. Except Hugh wasn't of common stock, although unfortunately it couldn't be denied he was currently an outlaw. Still, she was optimistic the earl would pardon him for whatever crime he had committed once he learned how Hugh had saved her from ruin.

She should keep her mouth shut and agree with everything Innis said. Except she couldn't. "Stranger things have happened."

"Oh, aye." Innis didn't try to hide her skepticism. "In fae tales for bairns no doubt. But those kinds of miracles don't happen in real life, Roisin. I'm only trying to keep ye from heartache."

She knew Innis was only trying to be kind, but she made her feel like a bairn herself by the way she spoke to her. "Thank ye, but there's no need for concern. I'll be all right."

"At least ye know enough not to go back to yer fine kin with a bellyful."

Roisin shot her a scandalized look, but inside panic flickered to life. Did Innis know what she and Hugh had done? To be sure, there wasn't any danger that she might have fallen pregnant, but it had still been foolish and risky, for anyone might have seen them. But they'd been lucky. Or so she thought.

"I haven't—Hugh would never—" Good Lord, she needed to stop talking before she completely gave herself away, if her burning face hadn't done so already.

"Hugh is a man. If ye give him the slightest chance, he'll take whatever he can get from ye."

Outraged by the slight on Hugh's honor, she couldn't hold her tongue. "He most certainly would not."

Innis shook her head. "'Tis yer life. I'm only reminding ye to beware. Ye may think this is a romantic way to live with yer very own outlaw, away from the responsibilities of yer kin and heritage. But the shine would soon wear off once winter descends."

There was a thread of bitterness in Innis's words, and just like that, Roisin's indignation evaporated. She had always felt badly for how the women and bairns had been forced into this life but none of the women had ever discussed it and she certainly hadn't raised the subject. But there was a pinched look on Innis's face as she concentrated on her darning, and an air of angry resignation emanated from her and Roisin couldn't remain silent.

"I know 'tis not my place." Her voice was hushed, and she questioned the wisdom of continuing. She didn't want to offend Innis or be the recipient of a scathing retort but a stubborn part of her wanted the other woman to know of her regard. "But I do admire yer strength, Innis. And I thank ye for welcoming me when ye have every reason not to."

Innis shook her head and after a few moments of silence she sighed and gave her a weary look. "Before this feud with the Campbells, my uncle Darragh was laird of a grand estate, and my husband owned two manors. We lost everything that had been in our families for generations. That is how easily it can happen, Roisin. Do not take yer good fortune for granted."

"I'm so sorry," she whispered.

Innis gave a mirthless laugh. "Don't be. 'Tis not yer fault. But mark my words. One day Clan MacGregor will rise again. We have the blood of MacAlpin, the first king of Scotland, running through our veins and that is what the Earl of Argyll cannot abide."

She didn't answer and concentrated on her mending, but Innis's words echoed around her head. Was that the real reason why the

MacGregors had raised arms against the Campbells, because, with their bloodline, they resented not being the most powerful clan in the Highlands?

It was possible. The news they received on Eigg came from travelers and merchants, and special messengers employed by Amma. But they only relayed what they had been told, and many of the reports came directly from the earl's circle.

Long ago, the MacDonalds had ruled the Western Isles, until the Campbells, backed by the Crown, had grabbed much of the prestigious land for themselves. It was all in the past now, and MacDonalds and Campbells no longer considered themselves mortal enemies. But despite their alliances, old wounds still ran deep, and Clan MacDonald had never forgotten their formidable seafaring history.

She cast a surreptitious glance at Hugh, who had finished pitching his tent and was now leading his horse to the river. Whatever Innis might think of her, she wasn't so foolish as to imagine living on the run from the Earl of Argyll was in any way romantic. But if it came to a choice between returning to Sgur Castle alone or remaining by Hugh's side with an uncertain future, did she really know what her answer would be?

HUGH HAD JUST finished grooming Deagh Fhortan when one of the men who had been on lookout returned to the camp with a stranger by his side. He and Darragh grasped arms in greeting before walking along the riverbank away from the other men.

Unease prickled along the back of Hugh's neck. Was the man from the MacGregor brothers in the east that Darragh had referred to? If so, what was he doing here?

Inevitably, his thoughts—and glance—returned to Roisin, where she was sitting with the women. It had only been a week since he'd found her on the road but now he could barely recall what his existence had been like before she'd joined the camp. He often rode beside her during the day while they traveled and Grear would ride ahead with one of the lasses she'd become friendly with, leaving them with the illusion of privacy. During those times it was too easy to forget Roisin wasn't here by choice. And that, once he heard from the earl, their time together would end.

In the dead of night, when lust plagued his body and impossible dreams haunted his mind, the despicable hope clawed through him that he might never hear back from the earl.

When supper was ready, he sat beside Roisin, as he had done for the last few nights. There had been no need to share his food with her since the first night, and Ecne had become a firm favorite with the bairns, who plied the wee thing with so many treats it was a wonder his belly didn't touch the ground.

"Who is the visitor?" Roisin's voice was low. "No one speaks of him."

That was interesting. He'd assumed Elspeth and, by extension, Innis would know. But then, maybe they did and simply hadn't passed on the information. Which didn't ease the undertow of apprehension in the pit of his gut that had refused to settle since first seeing the stranger arrive.

"I'll find out." He had to, in case Roisin's safety was impacted. In all the weeks he'd been with the MacGregors, this was the first time a man had strolled into the camp, and as though he had every right to do so, too. But what if he was connected to the bandits who had attacked Roisin a week ago? His suspicion that a group of MacGregors could be behind the ambush had never left him, and if he was right, and this stranger was involved, Hugh doubted things would go well for him once the man learned a Campbell had killed some of his compatriots.

It was imperative he discover the man's identity and whether he posed any threat. For if Hugh was executed in retaliation for foiling the ambush, there would be no one to protect Roisin.

After supper, as Roisin helped the other women to clear away, he sought out Symon, who was sitting on a rock by the river's edge inspecting his sword. "Who is he?"

The other man swept his gaze across the camp and then addressed his sword. "His name is Fergus MacGregor, but I've never met him before. As far as I can tell, Darragh and Fergus grew up together."

Hugh sat on a neighboring rock and proceeded to examine his dagger. "He just so happened to be in the area?"

"He's on his way to the MacGregors in the east, where we're heading. Sheer luck he crossed our path."

Hugh wasn't sure he believed in sheer luck. Although, he had to concede it had certainly been fortuitous when he'd come across Roisin last week. "He'll be traveling with us?"

Symon sheathed his sword and caught Hugh's gaze. "I don't know. But I'll tell ye one thing. There's something about him that makes me uneasy."

It wasn't a welcome admission. Because it meant his own impression that Fergus MacGregor was a threat couldn't be dismissed as purely the fact Hugh was here under false pretenses and needed to be suspicious of everyone.

He could only hope the man had no connection to the attack on Roisin and went his own way at first light.

BEFORE THE FIRST streaks of dawn splashed across the sky, Hugh stealthily made his way to the river and after ensuring no one was yet stirring, except for the two men on the last shift of the night watch, he stripped and plunged into the fast-flowing water.

Even though it was the middle of summer the water was frigid.

But at least it managed to dampen his erection, and he sucked in a sharp breath before completely submerging.

He stayed under, welcoming the biting chill that permeated into his very bones and whipped away the lingering remnants of sleep. When his lungs burned and he had no more breath left to hold, he burst to the surface, sucking in great gulps of air, as he swiped the water from his eyes.

And then he froze as an eldritch shiver scuttled along his spine and he spun about, senses on alert.

No one stood on the riverbank, but his heart still pounded, and he strode from the water as the uncomfortable certainty gnawed through him that just moments before someone had been watching him.

Watching him? Or worse? His gaze dropped to his clothes piled on the ground and something akin to panic gripped him. Had his belt been moved? He crouched and hastily untied one of the pouches attached to his belt and pulled out its contents.

Relief flooded through him. The handkerchief Roisin had given him in Sgur Castle, and the portrait she'd drawn of him the other day, were still safe. Only when he'd replaced them did it occur to him to check that his stash of coins was still intact.

Nothing appeared to be missing. If anyone had rifled through his belongings, they would surely have taken this small fortune. Yet he couldn't shake the feeling that while he had been utterly exposed, danger had lurked.

Goddamn it. He raked his fingers through his wet hair and silently cursed at his carelessness. From the moment the earl had sent him into exile, he'd kept his wits about him. It was the only way to survive. But this wasn't the first time his judgment had failed him since he'd brought Roisin to the camp. What had he been thinking, to stay underwater for so long? It was an indulgence he couldn't afford. He was only thankful his suspicions appeared to be unfounded.

By the time he had dressed, the camp was stirring, preparing for another day of travel. But as he made his way to his tent, from which Roisin and Grear had already emerged, a shred of unease that he hadn't imagined the sensation of being watched wouldn't leave him.

And it didn't take much to assume the surveiller was Fergus Mac-Gregor.

CHAPTER SEVENTEEN

ONCE ALL THE tents had been packed and loaded onto the wagons, Roisin put Ecne in his basket and placed it on the wagon Darragh had commandeered from her the day she'd arrived. Her sweet lad wasn't happy about it, but it was a better way to travel than balancing the basket on her lap for hours. Besides, she rode right behind him so he could keep an eye on her and not fret that she'd abandoned him. As if she ever would.

As they wound their way along the riverbank, the clouds grew darker and the breeze fresher. She shivered and tugged her shawl more tightly about her shoulders and hoped it wasn't about to rain. Still, they'd had almost a week without rain, so one couldn't grumble.

It wasn't long before Hugh ended up beside her and she smiled at him before nodding at Grear, who eagerly rode on ahead to accompany one of the older lasses she'd befriended a few days ago. After a few minutes of light banter, Hugh glanced around to make sure they weren't overheard, before he drew closer to her.

"There's a town half a day's ride away that Darragh wants to visit." His voice was low, and she stared straight ahead, in the hope that would give anyone casting a stray glance their way the impression that their conversation was inconsequential. "I'll find a way to join him. 'Tis possible there may be a message there for us."

Her fingers tightened on her reins as hope surged that soon she and Hugh might return to their former lives. "That would be good news, indeed."

"Aye." He sounded resigned by the prospect, and she disregarded whatever propriety she still retained and reached across the space between them and gently clasped his hand.

"Good news for us both," she clarified. Why wouldn't he share the reason he had been banished? Several times over the last few days she'd tried to encourage him to confide, but he always changed the subject. His stubbornness refused to daunt her. If all else failed, she would ensure Freyja made certain Alasdair spoke to the earl on Hugh's behalf. "Ye'll see."

᛭

THEY HAD BEEN riding for several hours and were traveling through a glen with towering limestone cliffs dotted with caves when the sky darkened and drizzle filled the air. Roisin pulled her shawl over her head, not that it would do a lot of good at keeping her dry if the rain became heavier.

Thunder rumbled and without further warning the heavens opened. The rain pummeled onto the ground and mist rose around them, making it hard to see Ecne in the wagon in front of them, never mind the path they were meant to be taking. Hugh grasped her wrist as she clutched the reins and disembodied voices filtered through the hammering downpour.

"Take refuge in the caves."

Hugh veered a sharp right, guiding her horse along with his own, and her protest was lost in the biting wind that whipped through the glen. She twisted on her saddle and, through the pelting rain, just caught sight of the wagon with her darling lad vanish into a cave up ahead.

"We'll need to dismount." Hugh raised his voice above the cacophony, and she peered at the low entrance to the cave he had led her to. In the shadows cast by the lowering clouds, it looked like a

157

dark, gaping mouth ready to devour unwary travelers and she hastily pushed the fanciful notion to the back of her mind.

She dismounted quickly, and they led their horses into the cave. The entrance was so low she had to bow her head but once inside, the roof was high enough for the horses to stand without any problem.

As she squeezed water from her shawl, she couldn't help voicing her concerns. "I hope they don't leave poor Ecne in his basket. He'll be frantic, thinking I've left him."

"Grear took shelter in that cave, Roisin. She'll be with him. Do not fret."

She released a relieved breath, silently childing herself for not noticing that herself. Ecne would be comforted by Grear's presence, and after all, it was only until this fierce summer storm passed.

Hugh grabbed the rolled-up blanket from her saddle and dropped its leather covering to the ground before handing the blanket to her. "Here. This will help ye dry off."

Gratefully, she wrapped the blanket around herself. "What about ye?"

"Don't worry about me." He appeared to be searching for something on the cave floor, and after a few moments, she realized what he was doing. He had pulled a tinderbox from one of his pouches and was searching for kindling. She crouched and picked up whatever dry twigs and old leaves she could find, and he focused on catching a spark and building a small fire.

"It's not much." He eyed his handiwork before glancing at her. "But maybe it's enough for ye to dry yerself, along with the blanket."

The doubt in his voice was palpable. Since she was drenched to the bone, it was unlikely this wee fire would do much to keep the chill at bay, but his thoughtfulness touched her.

"'Tis more than enough." To prove her point, she kneeled next to him on the stony ground and warmed her hands on the small flames. The fresh scent of rain and worn leather swirled around her, driving back the mustiness of the cave, and the mist that billowed beyond its narrow mouth gave an otherworldly visage, as though they had fallen through a crack in the world into the land of the fae.

She shook her head at her outlandish thoughts, but she couldn't help smiling. He caught her, and grinned, and her heart leaped in her breast, the way it always did when he looked at her so.

"What's so amusing?" He tenderly stroked a wet curl from her cheek and his finger lingered, a warm counterpoint against her chilled skin.

"This." Her voice was husky, but she didn't mind if he knew how he affected her. How could he not know? She'd proven that beyond all doubt in his tent just a few days ago.

The memory scorched her senses, and a fierce longing to feel him hold her once again burned through her. Tenderly, she cradled his jaw, and his sharp intake of breath sent sparks of pleasure dancing through her blood.

"Ye find this amusing?" His finger traced along her cheek, leaving ribbons of fire in his wake. "'Tis pure torture for me."

"Are ye certain?" She leaned closer and brushed a kiss upon his lips. He tasted of raindrops and of unspoken promises, and smoky need coiled tight between her thighs. "Is this torture, Hugh?"

"It is when this is all we can have." He gripped her shoulders, his hot gaze scorching her. "Do not test me, Roisin. A man can only take so much."

"I'm not testing ye."

"Ye do not understand."

"Why wouldn't I? Are ye going to say something insulting now, Hugh?"

He gave a reluctant grin. "I wouldn't dare and that's the truth. But ye don't know—" He clamped his jaw and briefly screwed his eyes shut before stealing whatever shred of decorum she retained with the intensity of his fierce gaze. "Ye don't know how I burn for ye, every hour of every day. How I dream of ye at night and wish there was a way to make ye mine forever. Ye've stolen my good sense and my heart, but nothing can come of it. And it's tearing me apart."

His tortured words spun through her mind and sank deep into her heart, a spellbinding confession the likes of which she had never quite dared to dream. How could he believe there was no future for them, when they were so in accord with the certainty that they belonged together?

"I do know," she whispered. "For I feel the same. How could I not? Ye're my soulmate, Hugh Campbell, and there is nothing ye can do about it."

He cradled her face and even with the thundering backdrop of the rain against the cliffs, the sound of his harsh breath filled the cave with spine-tingling promise.

"I've nothing to offer ye." Raw agony filled his voice, and she clutched desperately at his wet shirt in case he had the mad idea of pulling away from her. "I cannot risk ruining ye, mo ghràdh, when I can't give ye what ye deserve."

She knew what he meant. He wouldn't risk giving her a bairn, when he couldn't offer her marriage. Stubborn man. To be sure, he couldn't know there wasn't a risk of her falling pregnant this day, but why did he need to be so adamant that they were destined to always be apart?

It wasn't something she had ever envisaged saying to a man. Not even to Hugh who, to be fair, was the only man she'd ever wanted anyway. But it seemed it couldn't be helped. She only hoped he understood without her needing to explain the specifics.

"Ye will not ruin me." Her voice was scarcely even a whisper and even though she trusted Hugh with her life, she found she couldn't hold his gaze and instead focused on his mesmerizing chest. "My moon time is due within the next day or two."

Lord, her face was burning. She should have kept quiet. But if she didn't explain things to him, his honor would never allow him to take what she so wished to give him.

The silence hurt her ears but just as she couldn't bear it any longer, he slid his finger beneath her chin and raised her face so once again their gazes locked.

"Moon time?" His voice was hushed and mortification twisted through her. Did she truly need to enlighten him? She wasn't certain she was up for the task.

But she had to try. She dragged in a ragged breath and gathered her courage. "I won't conceive yer bairn, Hugh."

Comprehension slowly dawned in his eyes. "Are ye sure this is what ye want, Roisin?"

"I am. I've only ever wanted ye, from the first moment I saw ye in Sgur Castle."

He cradled her face, his thumbs stroking her cheeks and her breath stalled in her throat. "In a cave?" His voice was rough with desire and shivers of need coursed through her. "'Tis not how I imagined taking ye, Roisin."

"Then it will be something different to remember."

His laugh sounded tortured. "As if I'd ever forget this."

She wound her arms around his neck and the blanket fell to the ground. Her wet clothes clung to her, and she longed to be free of them but even now, alone here with Hugh, she wasn't certain she had the nerve to simply strip in front of him.

He claimed her mouth, and she dug her fingers into his hair, holding him close. His tongue teased her unmercifully as his fingers loosened the ties on her bodice, his touch sending hot spikes of need between her thighs.

With a frustrated groan, she tore blindly at her clothes and felt him smile against her lips.

"'Tis not funny." Her words were slurred, and he kissed her again, as though he wished only for her to lose her mind.

"Wait." His whisper burned her flesh, before he hastily spread the blanket on the ground. She wriggled out of her wet things until she stood before him clad only in her chemise, and he sucked in a harsh breath as his gaze roamed over her. "Ye're more beautiful than any of my dreams of ye."

Heat suffused her, warming her from the inside out. Even her damp chemise seemed to burn her skin. "And so are ye."

Tenderly, he lay her on the blanket before unwinding his plaid and throwing it over them both, enclosing them in a warm, dry cocoon, and she gasped her delight. "'Tis like we have slipped into a forgotten corner of the world of the fae."

"Ye're the only fae I need." Hugh loomed over her, his plaid draped over his head and shoulders and pooling on the ground around them. He nibbled kisses along her face and neck, and his fingers delved beneath her chemise, easing the material up as he caressed her hips and waist. She shuddered, gripping his shoulders as pleasure spun through her. He inexorably inched higher until he cupped her tender breasts.

Roisin breathed shakily as Hugh lowered his head and teased her nipple with his tongue. His warm breath dusted her sensitized flesh and then he sucked her aching peak into his mouth, and she pressed her knuckles against her lips to stifle her groan of need.

He wrapped his hand around her wrist and pushed her arm to the ground. "Don't." His voice was hoarse as he lifted his head just enough so he could gaze into her eyes. "I want to hear ye, Roisin. Don't hold back."

She rasped. When he resumed his torturous teasing, she couldn't have kept silent even if she'd wanted to.

"That's it." His harsh encouragement as he moved down her body was as potent as an aphrodisiac from the mythical gods themselves. She shifted restlessly beneath his exquisite ministrations until his hot breath dusted her mound, and she froze.

"Hugh," she breathed. In answer, he kissed her, stroking her wet slit with the tip of his tongue and teasing her clit until her last shred of reason fled.

Her heart hammered and she could scarcely breathe as he cupped her breasts and played with her nipples, while his mouth and tongue created sweet havoc within her slick sheath. She squirmed mindlessly, and he dragged one hand from her breast and gripped her bottom in his large, calloused hand.

It was too much. Starlight exploded behind her eyes. She bucked helplessly, scarcely aware of how he roughly kneed her legs apart until she felt an unyielding pressure against her sensitive flesh.

She gasped as he pushed inside her, and he stilled, his erratic breath harsh in this magical, twilight world. "Roisin?"

"'Tis fine," she panted, digging her nails into his shoulders and distractedly wishing he'd taken his shirt off so she could admire his naked chest. "I think."

In answer, he glided his hands over her thighs and calves before pulling her legs around him in a decadent embrace. She groaned and her eyes fluttered shut but the brief sensation of discomfort melted as Hugh slowly withdrew, before pushing deep inside her once again.

"My Roisin." His tortured whisper filled their makeshift world, thrilling her to her soul. He filled her so completely she was afraid to move, until he grasped her hips, moving her in time with his ever-increasing thrusts.

Shudders rippled through her, and she forgot about everything but this moment, this man. *My Hugh*. And when his teeth grazed her shoulder, she lost the last remnants of restraint and convulsed around him, and his muffled roar of release was the sweetest sound she had ever heard.

CHAPTER EIGHTEEN

HUGH LED THE horses from the cave, with Roisin by his side. When she smiled at him, his heart twisted in his chest. It took all his willpower not to wrap her in his arms and kiss her. Yet if he did, he wasn't sure he'd be able to stop.

That was a lie. He knew he wouldn't be able to stop. Hadn't he just proven that when it came to Roisin, all his grand ideals of honor fled?

Renewed lust, streaked with despair, burned through his veins as they made their way to the next cave where Grear was emerging with Ecne at her heels. Aye, he'd proven it all right. Proven he'd been unable to resist the temptation of making Roisin his, even though they had no future together.

He was despicable. But, even knowing that, he didn't regret what had happened in the cave. He could only hope, with everything he was, that Roisin never would, either.

As she greeted Grear, before crouching to give her wee dog a cuddle, a dark possibility crawled through his mind like a poisoned fog.

What if he delayed sending the earl another message? He and Roisin could spend more time together until the inevitable end when she would return to her kin.

No. He couldn't do that to her.

But the shining prospect of a few weeks together burned in his brain, a forbidden oasis in a future that otherwise stretched like a bleak panorama of unremitting duty without escape.

She would never know he'd failed to do everything within his power to secure her release. So far, he had. And he hadn't heard back from the earl. The chances of receiving a reply within the next week or so were, at best, remote.

But it was always possible.

He exhaled a long breath and rubbed Fhortan's neck, but the familiar gesture didn't afford him any comfort. Disgust curled through him, but he couldn't push the despicable idea aside. Every day that passed made the possibility of a future with her less likely. But if he could keep her by his side for just a little longer, was that really too much to ask?

Inevitably, his gaze shifted to Roisin, where she stood arm-in-arm with Grear. Christ, what was he thinking? Had he lost all the honor he had once possessed since joining the rebel MacGregors?

He didn't want to face that prospect. And yet still his dark design of delaying her release clawed relentlessly in the back of his mind, a toxic thorn he could not shift.

He was torn from his reverie by the approach of Darragh and instantly his senses went on alert. It couldn't be good news for the chieftain to seek him out with such purpose.

"We'll stay here for the night," Darragh said. Hugh gave a brusque nod. It made sense. They could use the caves as additional shelter, although he couldn't fathom why Darragh had made the effort to tell him personally.

"While they set up camp," Darragh indicated the rest of the Mac-Gregors with a glance over his shoulder, "we'll go to the local town."

Hugh managed to hide his surprise. Although he'd decided not to send the earl another missive just yet, he still needed to go to the town to see if there was a message waiting for him, but he'd expected he would need to persuade Darragh to let him go. The last thing he'd anticipated was being invited to join the chieftain without any preamble.

He sensed a trap and instantly thought of Roisin. *Goddamn it.* What had raised Darragh's suspicions?

"Don't worry about the lass." There was no mistaking the thread of dry amusement in the older man's tone and Hugh silently cursed. Not simply because of Darragh's disrespect whenever he spoke of Roisin. But the fact Darragh apparently knew how she was always at the forefront of his mind. "She'll come to no harm here. We need to leave now. 'Tis a fair trek to the town, or so Fergus tells me."

With that, he swung about and since he didn't have much choice, Hugh followed. As he passed by Roisin, she sent him a sweet smile, and a sharp pain twisted low in his gut at how she trusted him to do the right thing.

And he would. All he wanted was the chance of a few more weeks with her. As for Darragh, whatever trick he might be planning, Hugh would be ready for him.

"We'll take one of the horses to sell." Darragh strode over to where the horses they'd claimed from Roisin's men were being led from one of the larger caves ahead. "Fergus, are ye ready?"

Fergus MacGregor appeared in the mouth of the cave. "Aye."

The chances that he was being led into a trap magnified. But why now? What had changed Darragh's mind about him? Christ, did Fergus recognize him from before he had become a redshank?

It was a possibility he'd always known might happen, from the day he'd set foot in Eire. The Campbells and MacGregors had engaged in several skirmishes during the last five years, and he'd fought alongside both William and Alasdair in a few of them for the earl.

But he didn't recognize Fergus. He could only hope he was wrong and Darragh had no ulterior purpose for the invitation to accompany him to the town.

They set off, Fergus leading since he apparently knew the way. They skirted woodlands, where birdsong filled the air, and despite Hugh keeping a sharp eye on the two men, he didn't notice any stealthy glances between them. Maybe he was being overcautious but that was better than being ambushed.

They'd been riding for a good two hours when Fergus pulled to a halt. "Not far now," he said. "I'll go first."

Darragh gave a sharp nod and Fergus rode ahead, disappearing around a bend in the path. Hugh and Darragh followed, and the town spread across the glen before them. As they approached the gates, the older man threw him a glance.

"I'll go sell the horse and get the provisions. Fergus says there's a tavern by the mercat cross. We'll meet there when our business is done."

This was verging on the surreal. Why the hell had Darragh brought him along when it seemed the chieftain had no use for him?

"What do ye want me to do?"

Darragh shrugged. "Go buy yer lass some pretty ribbons for her hair."

What?

Heat scorched through him. God's bones, surely Darragh hadn't guessed what had occurred between Roisin and himself in the cave? To be sure, it had been reckless. But no one would have ventured out of their shelter during that downpour merely to spy on him.

No. It was true Roisin's reputation may have been harmed by the fact they'd been alone in the cave, but no one could prove anything had happened. He'd cut out his tongue, aye, and anyone else's before allowing a slanderous word against her to be uttered.

"Lady Roisin is not my lass." His tone was barely civil, but he couldn't help that. It was taking all his willpower not to punch the smug look from the older man's face.

"'Tis nothing to me if she is or if she isn't. But a lass likes to know she's appreciated. Buy her something bonny and mark my words, she'll make yer life far easier."

The suspicion that, somehow, Darragh knew Hugh had taken

advantage of Roisin hammered through his head. It was one thing for the entire camp to guess how he felt about her. It was something else entirely for anyone to even obliquely denigrate her honor.

"Lady Roisin is under my protection. That's all. There's no need to buy her trinkets. She knows it's my intention to return her to her kin as soon as possible."

"Oh, aye, and I can see how hard ye're working on that, Hugh. Do whatever ye want with her, but we'll still be demanding a ransom for her return. Unless ye decide to keep her indefinitely in which case on yer head be it."

With that, Darragh urged his horse forward and Hugh was left glaring at his back. He'd promised Roisin she wouldn't be used as a hostage, but Darragh appeared intent on doing so. *Well, let him.* In the end it made no difference. Roisin would return to her kin and that would be the end of it.

But he wasn't going to think about that. Not until he had no choice. He waited until Darragh had disappeared through the town gates before he made his own way there and dismounted. Even though he wasn't sending the earl an update, he still needed to check if the earl's network had delivered anything to this town.

He strolled around the busy market, keeping a sharp lookout for both Darragh and Fergus, although it was unlikely they'd try to assassinate him in the town, when they could have attacked him at any time during the journey here. He still couldn't work out why Darragh had invited him. They hadn't even interrogated him during the ride. What game was the other man playing?

After exploring the town and going into a few likely places where a message might have been waiting for him, he hitched his horse outside the blacksmith's and stepped inside. The heat from the forge filled the workshop and he cast a glance over the range of tools for sale as the blacksmith eyed him from the other side of his anvil.

"Ye looking for something?" The blacksmith wiped his brow with the back of his wrist.

"Browsing." Then he shared one of the many coded phrases used in the earl's extensive network. "'Tis a grand anvil ye have there, and no mistake."

It was a banal remark, meant to be forgettable if overheard by a passerby, or directed at anyone not in the know. A comment that was both justifiable in context but also something that no one would, in fact, actually utter.

The blacksmith glanced at his anvil. Clearly, he considered Hugh to be a half-wit, and he prepared to leave. But then the blacksmith responded.

"Aye. They don't make anvils like this anymore, and that's a fact."

Hugh nodded sagely. "Approbation to yer skilled forefathers."

"And to the forge."

At this point, Hugh usually passed on his message. But since he had no message to send, he inclined his head in farewell. "Until next time, go with God."

"Hold up." The blacksmith, after a swift glance at the door of his workshop, pulled an envelope from his belt and handed it to Hugh. "Delivered just hours ago."

Hugh palmed it and after a brusque nod, left the premises. Once outside, he took Fhortan's reins and surreptitiously scanned the area. He couldn't see either Darragh or Fergus but either of them could appear at any moment. With studied nonchalance, he opened a saddlebag, as though he searched for something, before sliding the letter into the bag to hide it from view.

Swiftly, he read the missive from the earl. It seemed not only had Hugh's first message been received shortly after he'd sent it, but the earl had lost no time in planning for Roisin's return. Decoding the cryptic missive, it transpired the earl and his men were barely half a day's ride from this town, at the very manor Hugh had been thinking of the other day, and merely needed confirmation of a rendezvous to safely deliver her into his charge.

The words burned into his mind and his gut clenched. Roisin could leave the camp tomorrow. And although he had no right to keep her by his side, a despairing rage churned through him at how twisted fate could be. What, after all, were the chances one of the earl's messengers would travel to this town, just hours before Hugh arrived? The truth was, he hadn't expected an answer this quickly, despite knowing how vast the network of spies was spread across the Highlands and beyond.

God knew, the man might still be here, on the slender possibility of having an update by the end of the day to report back to the earl.

Methodically, he ripped the paper to shreds as he did with every message so there was never any chance of one being found and fisted the evidence. While the message had been clear about rescuing Roisin, there had been no mention of Hugh's release from this life.

What more did the earl want from him? The whisper he had heard in Eire of his brother's sighting in the Highlands had come to naught. How could he discover Douglas's whereabouts, if his brother had been murdered and buried a year or more ago, and God only knew where?

"There ye are." The sound of Darragh's voice pulled him sharply back to the present. He straightened, tightening his fist around the incriminating proof that he was working for the Earl of Argyll. "We've time for an ale before Fergus leaves."

So Fergus wasn't returning to camp with them. It was good news, since there was something about the man that caused his flesh to crawl, but it wasn't enough to lift his mood. Nothing could do that. Not now, when he knew his chance of even a fleeting happiness with Roisin was nothing more than the charred remnants of an impossible dream.

The three of them made their way to the tavern in the center of the market and hitched their horses outside the small, whitewashed building that had seen far better days. As they entered, Hugh followed last, and he tossed the destroyed message into the fire that burned low in the hearth.

They ordered ale from the tavernkeeper and sat on a bench in a corner of the room. The two other men clashed tankards and took long swallows of the liquid, ignoring Hugh as if he were part of the wall. Which was fine by him. He just wished he hadn't been roped into this awkward gathering.

Fergus lowered his tankard and finally acknowledged Hugh's presence. "So ye were a redshank."

"Aye." Hugh took a swallow of his ale as he braced himself for an interrogation. But again, why bring him all the way into town to do it?

"Saved Symon's life more than once," Darragh remarked. "Which is why I let him stay with us."

It was true. He had saved Symon's life on a couple of occasions when they'd been in Eire, but they had been comrades in arms, and he'd never turn his back on a man under his command. Even if that man was a MacGregor.

"And then ye rescued Lady Roisin MacDonald from an attack by bandits."

He didn't like the turn the conversation had taken but managed to keep his tone casual. "'Twas fortunate Symon and I came across her when we did."

"Fortunate is a matter of perspective. Exactly how many of my best men did ye slaughter, Hugh?"

Hugh froze, locking his gaze on Fergus. His suspicion that the MacGregors had been behind the attack had been correct. He just hadn't expected them to admit it. Had Darragh been involved in the plot, too?

Darragh gave a dry laugh. "Ye told me they were mercenaries. And lousy ones they were, too, since they botched the job. 'Tis just as well Hugh and Symon found her. At least they brought her back in one piece."

He should likely keep his mouth shut, but he had to know. "What do ye want with Lady Roisin?"

"What do ye think?" Fergus gave him an unpleasant smile and before he could stop himself, Hugh surged to his feet.

"Hold yer fash, lad." Darragh waved a hand at him, sounding faintly amused, and Hugh glowered at Fergus, who appeared supremely unconcerned as he took another mouthful of ale. Inhaling a long breath, Hugh sat back on the bench.

Darragh remarked, "They planned on holding her for ransom, that's all. Ye don't mistreat a valuable hostage." He tossed Fergus a mocking glance. "Isn't that right, then?"

"Aye." Fergus's response didn't sound convincing. "That's right."

"I'd always planned on meeting up with Fergus and his kin later in the summer," Darragh said. "When ye rescued the lass, I brought my plans forward."

It seemed Darragh hadn't been a party to the original threat against Roisin, although he certainly wasn't averse to using any circumstance to his advantage. Hugh recalled the fallen tree Roisin had told him about and eyed Fergus. She had been specifically targeted, and he needed to know why. "Ye went to a lot of trouble. What's so special about Lady Roisin?"

"Don't ye know?" Fergus gave him a calculating look, and ice gripped Hugh's gut. Fergus knew exactly who Roisin was. But maybe he was mistaken. It took every shred of self-control for him not to react. Instead, he shrugged.

"Know what?"

"She's one of the MacDonalds of Sgur Castle. Her sister is wed to William Campbell."

Contempt dripped from every word, but Fergus's response jarred in Hugh's brain. William was a wealthy laird to be sure, but it was Alasdair who had the close connection to the earl. He'd been certain that, had Roisin been targeted because of her relatives, it was because her other sister was married to the earl's half-brother.

It stood to reason that if Fergus knew of William, he had to know Lady Freyja was wed to Alasdair. It didn't make sense. But he would discover the reason.

"And who is William Campbell?"

"William Campbell," Fergus said with undisguised loathing in his voice, "is the pox-ridden turd who murdered my half-brother, Alan MacGregor. I'll see justice done if it's the last thing I do."

Christ, no. Hugh finished his ale to give him a moment's reprieve so he didn't need to hold Fergus's glare, but inside he was reeling.

Alan MacGregor was the man who had infiltrated William's inner circle more than two years ago and had tried to murder him by pushing him overboard during a storm. And then, after William had wed Lady Isolde, Alan had set his sights on her.

His heart thundered in his ears at the realization that the danger against Roisin had magnified a thousandfold. It had never been merely a kidnap attempt by Fergus to exchange a valuable hostage for specific demands.

It was personal.

"Alan," said Darragh, his single eye boring into Hugh as though he were about to impart a great revelation, "was the true laird of Creagdoun Castle."

More than four years ago Torcall MacGregor, Alan's father, had rebelled against the earl and in the battle that followed, the earl had killed him and claimed his castle and lands. He had then bequeathed it all to William in recognition of his loyalty to Clan Campbell.

Hugh needed to say something. The last thing he could afford was to raise their suspicions when, for whatever reason, they seemed to trust him enough to share such information in the first place.

"And Creagdoun should now be yers?" He eyed Fergus.

"No. Torcall wasn't my father. But no way in hell should Creagdoun be infested by Campbells."

"Does Creagdoun not mean anything to ye, then?" Darragh said.

"What?" Hugh shot him a sharp glare, his defenses on full alert. Were the jaws of the trap finally snapping around him and he had failed to notice?

"Never mind." For a bizarre reason, the older man appeared to be dryly amused. What in the name of God was going on? "Ye should be glad to know the lady will continue to be under yer protection when we arrive at Fergus's camp. I'm certain ye'll make the best of it."

Fergus stood. "I'll take my leave and see ye in a week or so. I'll be watching out for ye."

Darragh also stood and the two men grasped arms. After a piercing glance in Hugh's direction, Fergus left the tavern and Darragh turned to him. "We'd best be making our way back to camp if we want to be in time for supper."

They walked outside, and as they unhitched their horses, his head throbbed with what he knew had to be done.

Whatever Darragh might say about Hugh being responsible for Roisin's safety, the truth was that the moment she stepped foot in Fergus's camp, she would be in mortal danger.

There was no choice anymore. As if there ever had been. He needed to send a message to the earl, confirming the time and location where he could ensure Roisin was safely returned to her kin.

CHAPTER NINETEEN

ARM-IN-ARM WITH GREAR, Roisin watched Hugh ride away with Darragh and Fergus and a thread of unease twisted through her.

Be careful.

The warning reverberated around her mind like a distant heart-beat, and she could only hope that, somehow, Hugh would understand the need to be on his guard. Ecne whined and nudged her ankle, and she crouched to give him another hug, as she silently berated herself.

Hugh was a warrior. He knew how to take care of himself without her fretting over his safety. But it didn't stop the knot of unease from tightening in her chest. She didn't trust either Darragh or Fergus. Why had they wanted Hugh to accompany them into town?

Grear crouched next to her. "Ye must get out of these wet things, milady." Anxiety threaded through her voice and Roisin took her hand. To be sure, her clothes were wet through, and even Hugh's spare shirt, that he had insisted she wear beneath her gown, was now damp as it clung to her skin, but Grear was just as soaked as she.

"And so must ye." They stood and she glanced around. The men were unloading the wagons, preparing to set up camp inside the caves. They didn't appear to be interested in the small cave where she and Hugh had sheltered.

Delicious shivers raced through her, pooling between her thighs, as she recalled what they had done. It was scandalous, but she didn't regret it. Not for a moment. Although if she did harbor one regret, it was not knowing when she and Hugh might ever have the chance to be alone like that again.

She shook her head, as though that might help to force such negative notions aside. They might not have the opportunity again while they remained in Darragh's camp, but Hugh was working tirelessly to ensure her safe return to her kin, and there was nothing in Christendom that would stop her from persuading him to join her.

Or, if she was truthful, nothing from the mythical land of the fae, either. Not now when she was sure beyond all doubt that he felt as deeply for her as she did him.

"Come," she said to Grear. "Let's get our chest from the wagon and take it to the last cave."

They made their way to the wagon where her chest was stowed, and between them carried it and Ecne's basket back to the smallest cave, the reins of her and Grear's mares looped around her arm. She brought the mares inside, before pulling off the shawl that had covered her tangled hair and pretended not to notice the startled glance Grear sent her.

Alas, she feared Grear would be further shocked in a few moments when she saw Hugh's shirt.

The fire Hugh had set still glowed, and she quickly fed it with more sticks and leaves that covered the floor of the cave while Grear opened the chest and found their spare clothes. She shook out the blue gown that always reminded Roisin of Hugh's incomparable blue eyes, and Roisin quickly undressed as she kept a wary eye on the low mouth of the cave. Not that she really expected anyone to enter, but one never knew.

Grear carefully placed their dry clothes by the fire, before hastily pulling off her own drenched clothes. And then she stopped dead and gazed at Roisin as though she'd seen a wraith.

"'Tis all right," Roisin whispered, although no one could overhear her. "Hugh gave me his shirt in the kind, but misguided, assumption it would keep me dry."

It wasn't a complete fabrication, but that didn't stop the blood from rushing to her cheeks, and she sighed. She had never been able to hide her feelings and Grear, who knew her almost as well as her own sisters, certainly wasn't fooled. "Do not look so stricken, Grear. Hugh was perfectly honorable and there is no need for any concern."

"Aye, milady." Grear hesitated, and then clearly couldn't help herself. "But are ye certain?"

"I am." Despite her best intentions, she couldn't stop a dreamy smile from escaping. "We are destined to be together, just as Isolde and William, and Freyja and Alasdair. All will be well, ye'll see."

"If ye say so. But do ye truly think we'll ever escape this camp?"

She pushed her daydreams aside. "Of course we will. Very soon, I have no doubt." She cast a glance at the cave entrance, but no shadows lurked of anyone who might be eavesdropping. Nevertheless, she lowered her voice. "Once Isolde receives my letter, she will ensure the earl knows of it."

Grear nodded and without another word, helped pull Hugh's shirt over her head. For a foolish moment, Roisin had the urge to cling onto his shirt, as though it were a talisman against anything going wrong.

But nothing was going to go wrong. She and Hugh were destined to be together, and that was all there was to it. Which meant he wasn't walking into a trap set by Darragh and Fergus. Sometimes her imagination was such a trial.

She dried herself as best she could before she pulled on her dry clothes and then helped Grear deal with their wet garments. Alas, it would take forever for them to dry this way.

Grear had just finished braiding her hair when Innis appeared at the entrance. The other woman bent low and came inside, before she cast a shrewd glance around.

Roisin could feel her cheeks burning. Had Innis guessed what she and Hugh had done during the downpour?

Not that it mattered. It was none of the other woman's business. And yet still she found herself hoping Innis had no idea. She was certain the older woman didn't believe in such things as soulmates or the fact that Roisin had known Hugh was the only one for her from the first day they'd met. And what was more, she didn't want to feel as though she needed to justify her actions.

"Bring out yer wet things," Innis said. Roisin sighed with relief that she wasn't about to be subjected to probing questions. "They'll never dry in here. We've a grand fire outside, and poles where ye can drape yer clothes."

They followed Innis outside and while Grear hung up the clothes, Roisin busied herself with preparing vegetables for the evening meal alongside several of the other women. As they worked, the conversation turned to Fergus and his clan and unlike the previous night, when no one had said a word about him, it seemed the fact he was no longer in the camp had loosened their tongues.

"There was always a dark madness in him," Elspeth remarked. "Even as a lad with Darragh he was not one to cross. But he got worse after his half-brother's murder."

Roisin glanced at the older woman, but it seemed everyone knew what she was talking about, and she didn't elaborate. But it proved one thing. Her unease about Fergus was justified.

Please beware, Hugh.

"I've the greatest respect for Darragh, as ye well know." Innis wagged her knife in Elspeth's direction. "But I'm not happy about joining Fergus's clan."

"There's safety in numbers," another woman said.

"Aye, but 'tis harder to hide, too." Bitterness threaded through Innis's words and Roisin's heart squeezed in sympathy. How she wished there was something she could do to return to these women all they had lost. "I fear it will be a long time before the Highlands are safe for MacGregors."

Roisin couldn't help herself. "Where else can ye go?"

Innis looked at her. "My husband has a cousin in Eire. He's only followed Darragh this far to please me. I know, in his heart, he wants to leave. It wouldn't be an easy life, but at least it would be better than this."

"Darragh wants us all to stay together." There was sad resignation in Elspeth's voice as though she knew a fork in the road was inevitable.

"Then he should make plans to lead us to Eire." Innis glanced around the group of women before once again focusing on Elspeth. "We've followed him for five years, Elspeth. 'Tis long enough to see the cursed Earl of Argyll has no plans to stop hunting us. I want more for my bairns. We all do."

Roisin looked at Rhona, who was sitting beside her, engrossed in copying the sketch she'd done of her the other day. Yesterday, she had given Rhona one of her spare quills and a small inkpot and the young girl had spent every spare moment since then practicing her art.

Back on Eigg, when she'd accompanied her sisters to the village, she'd enjoyed spending time with the bairns, spinning tales and sharing the history of their isles, as well as teaching them their letters and how to write their names. 'Twas only a small thing, to be sure, and it had never been enough, and she had often wished there was a way where she could impart her love of reading to them.

But the children of the village had their lives preordained, just as she and her sisters' lives had been determined before they had been born. Yet even though the village bairns might not be destined to learn all the things she so wanted to share with them, at least they knew where they belonged. On the isle of their birth, where their forebears had lived for generations without number.

Her chest grew tight and her eyes stung. Innis was right. This was no life for a bairn, continually on the run. Not when there was a chance of a stable life, even if it was far from their homeland.

A shiver trickled over her arms. Would she give up everything she had ever known and flee to Eire with Hugh?

AFTER FERGUS LEFT the tavern, Hugh bided his time until he and Darragh reached the town gates, and then he drew to a halt. "Goddamn it. I forgot to purchase ribbons for Lady Roisin. I'll catch up with ye, Darragh."

Darragh grunted and set off, and Hugh swung his horse around and reentered the town. Quickly dismounting, he made his way back to the blacksmith's. He hoped to God the earl's messenger hadn't left yet and would collect his missive before the gates shut for the night.

It didn't take long to write a cryptic note. Once decoded, the earl would know Hugh intended to ensure Roisin arrived safely at his manor the following day, by traveling through a particular glen with a distinctive double waterfall. He'd also understand that Alan MacGregor's half-brother was still alive and posed a deadly threat not only to William, but also to his lady wife's kin.

Hugh knew he wouldn't receive any confirmation from the earl. There wasn't enough time. He had less than one day left with Roisin, and then he would take her to the earl's manor.

Their final goodbye.

And then what? Darragh would surely guess he'd helped her escape. He'd think of something. He couldn't worry about that now.

Grimly, he once again left the town and after following the road for a while, headed to the nearby woods where he'd be less likely to meet any fellow traveler. But as he approached, a shadow emerged from the trees.

Fergus MacGregor.

Hugh pulled up, senses on alert. Was this where he was to be ambushed? Although he kept his gaze on Fergus, he couldn't detect any movement in his peripheral vision that suggested Darragh was waiting to pounce.

But that didn't mean the chieftain wasn't lurking behind a tree.

"Fergus." He kept his voice neutral. "I thought ye would be well on yer way by now."

"I wanted a word." Fergus folded his forearms across the pommel, his gaze never leaving Hugh's. "Darragh trusts ye, but I have my doubts."

He had severe doubts that Darragh trusted him as far as he could throw him, but he wasn't about to tell Fergus that. Although it was strange Fergus had that impression of the chieftain, since Darragh had only ever tolerated Hugh's presence in the camp, and nothing more.

He wasn't going to dignify Fergus's remark with a response, and so he waited. After a tense silence, the other man continued. "I ask myself, how far will a man like ye go to keep a noblewoman such as Lady Roisin safe and by yer side?"

It always came back to Roisin's safety. And he didn't need Fergus to tell him that once they reached his camp, her safety would be a precarious thing, subject to the vindictive will of Fergus himself.

Maybe it was foolhardy to show his hand, but he wouldn't let the other man be under any illusion that Hugh would stand idly by and allow Roisin to be mistreated. "I'll go as far as I need to. Always."

"Aye." There was no surprise in Fergus's tone. "That's what I thought. Darragh thinks ye acted out of a sense of loyalty, but I don't believe that. Ye did what ye did because ye don't want to give up a warm body in yer bed."

Fergus's odd comment was swept to the wayside as rage washed through him at the other man's disrespect regarding Roisin. "Watch yer mouth. Lady Roisin does not share my bed."

That was true enough, but the accusation bit deep. Aye, he desperately wanted Roisin to share his bed every night and the knowledge she never would was a stark reality he couldn't deny. But it was more than that.

It didn't matter how willing she had been in his arms. He had taken her maidenhead when he'd had no right. And while he would live with that bittersweet knowledge for the rest of his life, he couldn't stomach the thought that anyone might speculate and denigrate her honor.

"Sure, she doesn't." Fergus sounded sardonic. "Not through lack of trying on yer part, I'm certain. But 'tis irrelevant. Ye didn't send her letter to her kin for yer own purposes, not because ye have any sense of loyalty to Darragh."

Her letter.

Before he could stop himself, his fingers gripped the pouch where he'd hidden Roisin's letter the other day. *Goddamn it.* He hadn't imagined the feeling of being watched first thing this morning while he'd been in the river.

Fergus had been there and rifled through his belongings.

Why the hell hadn't he checked his things more thoroughly? But he knew why. It was because the only possessions he valued were Roisin's handkerchief and the portrait she had drawn of him. And Fergus hadn't taken them, since they weren't incriminatory.

God's bones, no wonder Darragh had asked him if Creagdoun meant anything to him. It was because Fergus had shared Roisin's letter with him, where she'd written *Lady Isolde MacDonald, Creagdoun Castle* on the envelope.

Heat scorched through him. He had betrayed her trust by not sending her letter. But the thought of these MacGregors reading her private correspondence sickened him to his core. The only shred of light was she'd respected his wish not to reveal specific details or disclose who had saved her from the bandits. If she hadn't, he had no doubt he'd be dead in a ditch by now.

"It wasn't loyalty to Darragh that stayed yer hand," Fergus said, obviously determined to get an admission of guilt from him. "Isn't that right?"

"Aye." There was no point denying it, because one thing had become crystal clear. Fergus was on a mission, and he wouldn't patiently wait for Darragh to arrive in due course. Hugh could see the cold determination to exact vengeance lurking in his eyes, and as soon as Fergus had gathered a band of loyalists, he'd return to Darragh and personally escort Roisin to his camp without delay.

Hugh couldn't allow Fergus to leave these woods. He drew his sword at the exact same moment as Fergus, which merely confirmed his suspicion that the other man had never intended him to leave the woods alive. Steel clashed against steel, startling the woodland birds that abandoned the trees in a flurry of wing beats. Fergus pressed forward, and Hugh parried his attack, as Fhortan skillfully sidestepped the other man's mount despite being surrounded by trees.

Hugh's heart pounded in his ears and lightning charged through his veins, the way it always did when he engaged in battle. There was a wild gleam in Fergus's eyes, and by God, he'd use that to his advantage. If there was one thing he'd learned during his time as a redshank, it was to never lead with anger.

Fergus lunged, and Hugh instinctively ducked, the blade missing his throat by a hairsbreadth. He instantly swung about, catching the other man's sword arm, and Fergus bared his teeth. "I know ye, Hugh Campbell. I couldn't place ye until now. Ye're the earl of Argyll's man. Ye're the damn cousin of William Campbell."

Hugh didn't bother wasting his breath by responding. There was no need. They both knew how this would end. If Fergus left this place alive, Roisin would die.

Fergus transferred his sword to his left hand, his right arm hanging uselessly by his side as blood dripped to the ground, and Hugh gave him no quarter. Before the other man could recalibrate his strategy, he swerved, catching Fergus off guard, and plunged his blade through his enemy's heart.

Chapter Twenty

S UPPER WAS READY, just as Darragh returned to the caves. Anticipation sizzled through Roisin as she watched for Hugh to follow, but he didn't. Alarm prickled along her arms, and she peered into the forest some distance away, willing him to appear, even though she couldn't imagine why he'd be trailing so far behind Darragh.

Nothing stirred at the edge of the forest.

Heart thumping, she watched Elspeth greet Darragh, leading him away from the others. Was she telling him of Innis's wish to leave?

Roisin chewed her lip and once again gazed across the glen at the forest. Where was he? And then something else occurred to her. Where was Fergus?

Panic churned her stomach, and she gripped her hands together. It was far too easy to imagine the worst. Had Darragh murdered both Hugh and Fergus?

She sucked in a shaky breath. No. She wouldn't think it. Hugh was perfectly safe.

So why wasn't he here?

When the women served supper, without anyone remarking on Hugh's absence, her dread magnified, seeping through her veins and twining around her heart like thistles. Darragh and the men took their plates and settled down to eat, and as Elspeth dished up the women's and bairns' portions, she had the terrifying sensation that she might vomit.

It was foolhardy beyond belief to speak to Darragh at any time, unless she had no choice, never mind when he was digging into his food with an expression of thunder on his face. Barely two weeks ago the idea wouldn't even have crossed her mind.

But now she couldn't get it out of her head.

'Twas no good. Placing her plate on the ground, she stood and made her way over to where Darragh sat on a rock. As she approached, he became aware of her, and his eye fixed on her as though he could see her innermost thoughts.

She battled the overwhelming urge to run back to Grear and took another step closer. Her heartbeat echoed in her head and her hands were clammy, but she'd come this far, and she wasn't going to turn back now. It didn't help her wavering courage when the camp fell silent, as though everyone were staring at her.

Who was she trying to fool? Everyone *was* staring at her. She licked her lips and halted in front of Darragh, who didn't say a word as he continued to eat, pinning her to the spot with his one good eye.

He clearly had no intention of making this easy for her. But she had to know Hugh's fate, even if there was nothing she could do about it. "Darragh." Her voice was hoarse with nerves, but she refused to wince, because he would see and mock her for it. "Where's Hugh?"

The silence intensified, as if such a phenomenon was even possible, but she fancied it pressed in on her like a mantle of invisible fog.

If only I were invisible.

No. She could no longer hide behind her sisters. She braced her shoulders and refused to wilt. If Darragh guessed how badly her legs were shaking, he would never deign to answer her.

Finally, he spoke. "He had business in town. He'll be back when he's done."

What business did Hugh have in town? She couldn't imagine. Unless it was something he was doing for Darragh, in which case she wasn't sure she wanted to know. And then another possibility occurred to her. Maybe he was sending another message to his mysterious contact, and she had just put him in peril by drawing attention to it.

"Oh," she said, inadequately, wishing desperately the ground would open and swallow her whole. Since that wasn't going to happen, she gave a small nod, as though Darragh's remark had eased her concerns, instead of increasing them. "I see."

There was no mistaking the grim amusement that flashed across Darragh's face. "Never fear, Lady Roisin. He's not run off and left ye."

She managed a tight smile before retreating. By the time she sat down next to Grear, conversation had resumed but she could still feel how everyone's eyes had bored into her just now.

And what was with Darragh calling her Lady Roisin? He hadn't used her title since the day Hugh had first brought her to the camp, and it made her uneasy although she couldn't quite pinpoint why.

Even though she'd lost her appetite, she forced herself to eat her supper, and Hugh still hadn't returned when she had finished helping the women clear away. Anxiously, she scanned the glen, but there was no sign of him.

Grear came to her side, worry etched on her face. "What will we do if Hugh Campbell doesn't return?"

It was the kind of question Roisin would have asked her sisters, had they been there, and doubtless both Isolde and Freyja would have soothed her with calming words. But her sisters weren't there, and she had no one but herself to ease Grear's distress. So she pushed her own fears aside and smiled, even though it hurt her face. "Of course he'll be back, Grear. There's no need for concern. Ye'll see."

But as twilight fell across the glen, her anxiety coalesced into a hard knot in the middle of her chest. Darragh might well be telling the truth, but suppose the reason Fergus hadn't accompanied Darragh back to the camp was so he could confront Hugh?

She didn't want to think about what might have happened, but she couldn't stop the graphic images from flooding through her mind.

As she and Grear made their way back to the small cave, Ecne suddenly gave three short yaps of welcome, and she followed his gaze to the shadow-strewn forest. Relief tumbled through her, making her lightheaded, as she recognized Hugh riding Deagh Fhortan. And with her relief, she realized he hadn't been so far behind Darragh, after all. It might have felt like hours, but now she considered it, Darragh himself had only arrived back not that long before twilight.

Instead of heading towards the small cave, where she stood with a welcoming smile on her face, it seemed Hugh didn't even see her as he made a beeline for the large cave at the far end of the limestone cliff, which Darragh had claimed for the night.

It was foolish to feel slighted, but she did. Even though she knew the reason was because Hugh didn't want to draw unwelcome attention to them both, which would certainly have happened had he instantly ridden to her side, it didn't make her feel any better. The best thing she could do was get settled for the night with Grear, but she still lingered, as the rest of the women got their bairns into the caves, and she watched Hugh dismount and stride over to Darragh.

Although he was too far away to see the expression on his face, his entire attitude gave the impression he was furious, and unease shivered through her. Had he received bad news in town from his contact? But it didn't make sense he'd share that news with Darragh. She hoped Hugh would come to see her when he'd finished speaking with him, even if it did set tongues wagging. Far better that than to fret all night wondering what new problem faced them.

And then she shook her head at her folly. What was she thinking? Of course, Hugh would come to see her. He had slept outside the tent every night since she'd joined the camp, and there was no reason to suppose he wouldn't sleep outside the cave tonight. Indeed, after the magic they had shared together earlier today, there was no question that he'd seek out her company. She was letting her imagination run away with her. Hugh hadn't ignored her. He simply needed to see

Darragh first.

"Come, Ecne," she said, glancing at her feet, but her dog wasn't there. Alarm streaked through her. Wildly, she glanced around and saw him bypassing the men who sat around the fire and trotting towards Hugh.

Shaking her head, relieved he hadn't simply disappeared, she hurried after him and although he must have heard her call his name again, he merely speeded up. She knew he was fond of Hugh, and Hugh appeared to reciprocate the sentiment, but she'd caught Darragh giving her darling lad dark glances on more than a few occasions. She didn't want to run any risk by having Ecne interrupting the men and Darragh taking the opportunity to give him an impatient kick.

The terrible notion of him hurting her sweet lad had her picking up her skirts and running, just as Hugh and Darragh left the mouth of the cave and walked a short distance beyond, where long ago landslides had left jagged towers of rock.

Ecne paused by the rocks and cocked his head as though he were eavesdropping. She smiled at her foolishness and scooped him into her arms but as she spun about to head back to the cave, Hugh's low voice stopped her in her tracks.

"So ye don't deny it?"

"Why should I?" There was a hard note in Darragh's tone that sent a shiver along her spine. "I've known Fergus all my life and if he felt the need to search yer belongings, that's a good enough reason for me."

"He had no right."

"And ye have no right confronting me like this, Hugh Campbell. I let ye stay because of Symon and ye've proven yer worth, but don't go thinking that gives ye any special privileges."

It was awful overhearing Darragh speak so badly to Hugh and indignation on his behalf burned through her. She needed to leave, but before she could make her feet move, Hugh responded.

"I don't, and I'm thankful ye let me stay, but I want that letter back."

What letter? Nerves churned through her although she wasn't sure why.

"No. I believe I'll keep it to ensure ye don't get any ideas. I doubt yer lady love will look so kindly upon ye if she discovers ye didn't send her message."

Darragh's mocking words echoed in her ears, magnifying with every heavy beat of her heart. No. She wouldn't believe it. He couldn't be talking about the letter she'd written to Isolde the other day. She'd seen Hugh with her own eyes speak to someone in the inn to send the message.

But a terrible thread of doubt assailed her. It was true she'd witnessed him speaking to the innkeeper's wife, before he'd strode with purpose as though he knew exactly where he was heading. But she hadn't seen him actually give anyone her letter, had she? She had simply taken his word for it.

But he wouldn't lie to her. Why would he? He was committed to reuniting her with her kin, just as she was committed to ensuring that when she did, he would join her.

"Lady Roisin is not my *lady love*." Hugh sounded incensed by the notion, and Roisin involuntarily clutched Ecne as a despairing pain lanced through her breast. Did he really mean that? Or was he merely trying to protect her reputation against Darragh's insinuations?

"Then ye're a bigger Campbell bastard than I took ye for."

"I swore to protect her, that's all. There's nothing between us."

Ecne gave a small whimper at how tightly she hugged him, and it was an effort to loosen her arms around him when all she wanted to do was bury her burning face in his familiar fur. But she couldn't afford such an indulgence. It didn't matter how she wished the ground would open and swallow her whole so she could escape this unraveling nightmare. She needed to get back to the small cave and compose herself before she saw Hugh again.

Before she could even take a breath, both Hugh and Darragh emerged from behind the rocks, having clearly heard Ecne's whimper, and the expression of horror on Hugh's face as the realization hit him that she had overheard his conversation caused her heart to squeeze with mortification.

Aye, mortification. That was all this was, and she would recover from it. For she could never recover from a shattered heart.

"Roisin." He sounded as though he'd torn her name through the bowels of hell itself. "Are ye all right?"

She summoned up every shred of pride she retained, straightened her shoulders and gave him a withering glare. At least, she hoped it was withering. "Why shouldn't I be? What a foolish question, Hugh Campbell."

Darragh, damn the man, laughed, even though he didn't sound especially amused. "There goes my leverage over ye, Hugh."

"Lady Roisin." Hugh took a step closer and then froze as though something in her eyes warned him. Did he think by using her title he could somehow soften her up? Make her forget what she had overheard?

Lady Roisin is not my lady love.

"I must speak to ye alone."

"Must ye?" *Is that truly my voice?* She sounded so cold. As though none of this was tearing her apart inside. And thank God for that. It was bad enough she had misjudged him so, without the added humiliation of him seeing how deeply his deception had wounded her.

"Aye, he must, if he wants to win yer favor once more." Darragh cast Hugh an unpleasant glance before returning his attention to her. "But I'll tell ye something else. Fergus wanted to take ye with him so he could return ye to yer kin without any further delay. But Hugh here wouldn't hear of it. Yer self-appointed protector believes only he has the right to decide yer fate."

Something akin to guilt flashed across Hugh's face before he rounded on the other man. "That's not true, and ye know it."

"'Tis true enough."

"Fergus," Hugh sounded as though he were having trouble just saying the name. "Had his own agenda that didn't include taking Lady Roisin to her kin."

"Told ye that, did he?"

"A parting shot in the town. After ye left."

Had Fergus really offered to take her to her kin? She wasn't sure she believed Darragh, except if it was a lie, why had Hugh looked so guilty? But regardless, the prospect of going anywhere with Fergus made her flesh crawl. Whatever Hugh had done, or not done, the truth was she would rather stay by his side than Fergus's, but that wasn't the point. Hugh hadn't given her the choice.

"After I left?" For some reason, Darragh appeared confused by that statement, but Hugh didn't answer. Instead, he turned to her and for a despairing heartbeat, as she gazed into his mesmerizing blue eyes, she wished she had never overheard the damning exchange between the two men. But if she hadn't, she would still be living in a fantastical web she had woven herself from nothing more substantial than foolish daydreams and tales of the fae. For while she had believed their fates were entwined, it seemed Hugh believed only in himself.

Despite the times she'd tried to coax a promise from him, not once had he spoken of leaving with her. And after they had made love, she'd been so sure, in her heart, that he'd do anything to gain the earl's pardon so they could be together.

But none of it had been real outside of her own imagination.

"This is not what it seems."

Was she imagining that note of desperation in his voice? She probably was. Did he think she might disclose that he wasn't an ordinary Campbell at all but Hugh Campbell of Balfour Castle, something she knew Darragh would never forgive?

As if she would. She had promised to say nothing of that, and unlike some people, she kept her promises. "Alas, it seems very clear to me."

"I'll tell ye what's clear." Darragh's eye bored into her before he turned to Hugh. "I'm taking Lady Roisin MacDonald to Fergus's camp, and that's the end of it. Ye can accompany me and continue protecting yer precious noblewoman, or ye can join the others heading to Eire, but either way this discussion is now over."

With that, he marched back to the caves leaving her alone with Hugh.

"Roisin." Urgency throbbed through his voice, but she refused to acknowledge his concern. Why was he concerned, anyway? She was as securely trapped today as she had been on the day he'd first brought her to Darragh's camp. Even if she and Grear escaped, where would they go? She had no idea where they were. They could ride for days without encountering another soul, and what were the chances that if they did meet anyone, they would be inclined to help?

She was, after all, no longer in the Small Isles, where everyone knew of the MacDonald daughters of Sgur Castle and who would no sooner harm them than they would chop off their own arm. Instead, they were trapped in the wild Highlands where, it seemed, enemies lurked in every shadow, and no one could be trusted.

"Roisin," Hugh said again, and she reluctantly caught his gaze. Why, even now when she could no longer believe anything he said, did butterflies collide within her breast and starlight spike through her blood every time she looked at him?

"What?" She wanted to sound indifferent, but instead she just sounded so weary she wished she hadn't said anything at all.

He took a step closer to her, and Ecne wriggled with excitement in her arms.

"I couldn't risk sending yer letter." His voice was low, as though he imparted a great secret, but she didn't know why he bothered. No one was around to hear him. "If it fell into the wrong hands, it could have put ye in danger."

"It did fall into the wrong hands."

He sucked in a jagged breath, and she couldn't fathom why the sound made her heart ache so. Perhaps this was what the death rattle of love felt like.

"That's down to my carelessness." Frustration threaded through his confession but if he expected her to be impressed by his candor, he was sadly mistaken. "But ye're right. I should've destroyed it."

Her lethargy vanished, and she glared at him. "Is that supposed to make me feel better about the fact ye lied to me?"

"I didn't want to run the risk of anyone connecting ye to William Campbell. And I was right to be cautious. Fergus MacGregor knew exactly who William was."

It was just as well she was still holding Ecne, as she had the alarming conviction that otherwise she may have slapped Hugh's face.

"Ye still don't understand, do ye? It's not that ye didn't send the letter to Isolde. Ye could have told me ye thought it too dangerous. But no. Ye let me believe it was possible and that ye had found a messenger to take it to her. Why would ye do that?"

She wasn't sure he could look more taken aback even if she had physically attacked him. "I tried to tell ye it was dangerous. But ye were so set on it. I couldn't take away the hope shining in yer eyes."

Stung, she stared at him as she recalled their conversation on the way to the town that day. And realized that he had, indeed, told her sending a message to her sister was dangerous.

But she'd insisted. And he had capitulated. Or so she thought.

He'd never intended to send her letter. And the reason he'd agreed to, simply so she had hope to cling to, was somehow even worse than him deciding not to for his own purposes. As though she was a fragile creature who needed coddling.

"I see." Ecne continued to struggle in her arms, but she wasn't going to release him because she knew he would greet Hugh. How happy she had always been that her beloved dog was so fond of Hugh Campbell. She had taken it as another sign that she and Hugh were meant to be together, for Ecne had impeccable taste when it came to who he bestowed his affection upon.

It appeared both she and her dog had lost their senses when it came to Hugh.

She settled Ecne more securely in her arms and attempted to find whatever remained of her pride. "How exactly were ye planning on escorting me to Creagdoun? Ye never did tell me. If I couldn't send a letter to Isolde, I imagine it was too dangerous for ye to communicate with yer mysterious contact, too. Was that all another fabrication?"

"What?" He frowned, as though her question made no sense before his brow cleared, and he shook his head. "Of course it wasn't a fabrication. I sent several messages to—" He clamped his jaw shut and shot a furtive glance over her shoulder, as though ensuring no one could overhear them. "Why would ye think I hadn't taken action to reunite ye with yer kin?"

Was he serious? "Why would I think ye had? Ye didn't tell me the truth about my letter to Isolde. Ye've never told me anything about how ye intended to get me to Creagdoun. How can I know ye haven't lied to me about everything?"

"I haven't lied to ye." He exhaled an impatient breath as though he considered she was being unreasonable and then he raked his fingers through his hair in a distracted manner that was entirely too endearing. "Except in the matter of yer letter. But I've explained about that. I did that to protect ye. Why can't ye see that?"

The irksome thing was, she could see it. He *had* warned her before they had gone to the inn that sending the letter could be dangerous. But he'd still let her go through with the farce of writing the cursed thing. Her face burned as she recalled how hard it had been to find the right words and how Hugh had watched her from across the table. At the time she'd been grateful for his patience, but now she knew all he had really been doing was indulging her.

The humiliating memory seared into her mind, and she wanted nothing more than to stalk back to the cave, so she didn't have to face him any longer. But that was the easy way out and would only prove she couldn't face a bitter truth.

She offered him a brittle smile as she recalled the guilt that had flashed across his face when Darragh had been berating him. He was still hiding something, and she was determined to know what it was. "What exactly were yer plans for me, Hugh?"

Except it was starkly obvious. He had made little attempt to hide his interest in her, and the women had gently teased her about it from the day after she'd arrived in their camp. But Innis had seen the truth and tried to warn her, and instead of heeding the more experienced woman's advice, she'd been offended by the slight against Hugh's character.

His charm had got him what he'd wanted, and she had no one but herself to blame. How easily he had won her over, with his recollections of the time they'd spent together on Eigg and his assurances that he'd always intended to return to the Isle for her.

She doubted he'd spared her a second thought once he'd sailed away from her eighteen months ago.

"My plans?" He gave a hollow laugh that sent prickles along her arms. "I never had plans for ye, Roisin. How could I? But I'll tell ye this. When I was in the town today, I came this close to doing all in my power to keep ye with me, whatever the cost to ye."

She gave a soft gasp, transfixed by the savage gleam in his eyes. A fierce, untamed tension swirled in the air between them, and heat suffused her, fiery tendrils that scorched her blood and caused sparks of lightning to collide between her thighs. For countless moments, she was caught in his seductive web, as purple and orange shadows painted the sky and unfurled across the distant mountain peaks.

This was not the courteous Hugh she'd first known in Sgur Castle. Nor yet the menacing outlaw who had saved her from the brigands. This Hugh was a raw, contradictory enigma who radiated a primitive air of lethal authority and bewitching allure, and a chilling fear gripped her that if she didn't retreat, his compelling intensity would consume her utterly.

She took a stumbling step backwards, fighting against the overwhelming compulsion to remain where she was and silently agree with whatever Hugh might command. Because if she allowed herself to fall completely under his spell, she would lose herself forever.

Swiftly, she spun about, but even as she hastened away, her mind was filled with his unforgiving blue eyes, and she could feel his unrelenting gaze boring into her as she made her way back to the far cave.

Since the day he had brought her into the camp, she'd placed her own, Grear's, and Ecne's wellbeing in him, so certain he was formulating a plan to get them safely to Creagdoun Castle. She'd never questioned him. Never pointed out that with each passing day they traveled farther away from William and Isolde.

Because she had trusted him.

His confession hovered in her mind, like an angry wasp intent on retribution, and she shivered. Maybe Darragh's veiled accusations were correct, and the truth was Hugh had never intended taking her to Creagdoun, not from the first moment he'd caught her fleeing in the forest.

She reached the cave and put Ecne on the ground before straightening and catching Grear's anxious gaze. She could no longer rely on Hugh, Darragh couldn't be trusted, and the prospect of arriving at Fergus's camp sent cold dread through her very soul.

It was time she took control of her own destiny.

Chapter Twenty-One

HUGH WATCHED ROISIN turn and walk away from him without a backward glance, and the insane notion hammered through his head that all he had to do was follow her, sweep her into his arms, and refuse to ever let her go.

And everything would be all right.

He huffed and fisted his hands, as though that might quell the raging torrent that flooded his body with the need to do something, to show her, unequivocally, that she belonged with him and that there was nothing in this world that could keep them apart.

Except God knew, everything in this world conspired to keep them apart.

That damn letter. He should have destroyed it, and yet he'd been unable to because Roisin had created it. How dearly they'd been forced to pay for such foolishness on his part. If Fergus hadn't found it and passed it onto Darragh, Roisin would never have discovered how he'd needed to deceive her.

To keep her safe.

But he hadn't managed to keep her safe at all.

At least she was no longer in any danger from Fergus MacGregor. He'd dragged that bastard's body farther into the forest and heaved it into a ditch, before covering it with debris. He doubted it would be long before the body was found, but it would be long enough for him to get Roisin to the earl's manor and that was all that mattered. No one would connect the extra horse he'd tethered outside the inn to

Fergus. And if they did, it would be too late to do anything about it.

"Sergeant."

Symon's voice dragged him brutally back to the present, and he gave the other man an abrupt nod. The last thing he wanted to do was discuss what had just transpired between him and Roisin and he made to march off. But Symon, damn him, stepped in front of him.

"Ye heard what happened?" Symon's voice was low, and Hugh gave him a sharp look. That didn't sound as though Symon referred to Roisin. And it wasn't possible news had reached the camp of Fergus's death. It could take months, if ever, before even his own close kin discovered what had become of him.

"What about?"

"Innis and her kin are leaving for Eire in the morning, and more than half of the others are going with them."

Darragh had said something about that, but Hugh had been too caught up in everything else to give it any attention, but now the chieftain's words came back to him.

"Ye can accompany me, and continue protecting yer precious noblewoman, or ye can join the others heading to Eire."

Tomorrow, he needed to ensure Roisin arrived at the earl's manor. If the clan split, it meant Darragh would have far fewer men on hand to command, but it also meant his absence—along with Roisin and Grear—would be more noticeable.

"Will ye go to Eire or follow Darragh?"

Symon shrugged. "I'll go wherever ye lead, Sergeant. Ye know that."

A thread of guilt twisted through him. If Symon knew the truth about him, he'd plunge a sword through his heart, and that was a fact. He sucked in a great breath and pushed the notion to the back of his mind. There was nothing he could do about it, even if he wanted to. He and Symon would always be on opposing sides. All he could do was hope they never met on a battlefield, should the earl one day call him home.

"I'll go with Darragh for now," he said. "I've pledged to protect Lady Roisin, and I'll see her safe if it's the last thing I do. But afterwards—" He paused, as the prospect of a bleak future without her unfolded in his mind. He wouldn't be able to return to Darragh, once he'd ensured Roisin was safe. The chieftain would never allow him to return after such a betrayal. If he didn't receive instructions from the earl to the contrary, there was nothing keeping him in the Highlands. "I'll go back to Eire."

Symon gave a nod. "Aye. Sounds like a plan." He glanced over his shoulder at the caves, and Hugh's gaze lingered on the one where Roisin had disappeared, and a dull ache filled his chest. All day he had harbored impossible dreams of sharing one last night with her, or at the very least, holding her again in his arms.

But now he would be lucky to receive one last smile from her.

Symon looked back at him. "'Tis a pity about Lady Roisin. But ye always knew nothing could come of it, Hugh."

"Aye." His voice was hollow, and he had no more words to say, but Symon seemed to understand as he gripped his shoulder and gave a quick nod before striding away.

Hugh went over the fire, where supper had been put aside for him, and he sat on a rock, methodically eating the food although he scarcely tasted a thing. He still needed to tell Roisin about the plan for escaping on the following day, although as yet he wasn't sure how he was going to split away from Darragh without the chieftain charging after him. But compared to the prospect of facing Roisin again, after witnessing the disdain that had glimmered in her eyes before she had turned away from him without another word, Darragh was a minor hurdle to overcome.

He'd speak to her first thing in the morning.

☩

BACK IN THE cave, as Grear made a fuss of Ecne, Roisin tried to push Hugh from her mind, but his last feral words to her echoed around her head in an endless refrain.

"I came this close to doing all in my power to keep ye with me, whatever the cost to ye."

How many times had she dreamed of hearing him confess that he believed they should be together? That he'd do anything to ensure they would never be parted?

Too many times to count. But in her fae-inspired fantasies, his words had been as sweet as honey, his eyes had glowed with love, and he had never threatened she would be expected to suffer for it.

Shivers trickled along her arms, and she hunched her shoulders in a futile attempt to throw off the despairing sense of catastrophe that wrapped spectral fingers around her. She should have known better than to think there could have been a way for them to find lasting happiness together. The ancient gods in her beloved tales had always demanded a high sacrifice for any wish they granted, and she'd no reason to believe God Himself was any different in that regard.

Hugh, it seemed, would keep her by his side if she said the word. But the price was too high. She had seen honor when there had been only lies and mistaken lust for love.

She had been nothing but a foolish, reckless lass. The only small relief on the bleak horizon was the knowledge that at least there would be no lifelong consequence of the magical hour they'd spent together in this cave.

Alas, it didn't make her feel any better.

"Milady." Grear's voice was hushed, and Roisin forced a smile on her face and took the younger woman's hands. Even if everything had been different, the stark truth was she could never have stayed with Hugh in this life. Not unless Grear could have been safely returned to Eigg.

But then, that had never been what she really wanted. Right from the start, she'd dreamed of Hugh escaping the life of an outcast to be with her.

"We must pack as much as we can from the casket into the saddlebags." They needed to travel as light as they could and while she could carry Ecne's basket while riding, the casket was too unwieldy. "Tomorrow, we shall begin our journey back to Oban."

"Shall we?" Grear sounded dubious, but Roisin didn't want to consider all the things that could go wrong with her plan, especially as she hadn't finalized it yet.

"Aye." She opened the casket and from the glow from the small fire began to sort out its contents. As she packed the saddlebags, her fingers brushed against the inkwell Hugh had bought her, and pain squeezed her heart. She'd been so sure it was proof he felt the same for her as she did for him, but now she wasn't certain of anything.

The best thing she could do was leave the inkwell here in the cave, so she could pack more supplies from the casket in the saddlebag. But she couldn't do it. Maybe it didn't represent everlasting love, but it would serve to remind her to never let her foolish feelings rule her actions in the future.

When she and Grear had finished, she couldn't delay any longer. "I won't be long, Grear. Ecne, stay," she said, before ducking out of the cave. Although the sun had set long ago, twilight still bathed the land, giving her plenty of light to see how Hugh still sat morosely by the fire. As though he were aware of her presence, he turned and caught her gaze and she despised how, even now, she wanted nothing more than to go to him and have him tell her everything was not the way it seemed.

No. Roisin wouldn't make a fool of herself with him again. She clearly had little pride when it came to Hugh, but she had managed to salvage a shred, and she was determined to cling onto that tattered remnant until the bitter end.

Innis and a couple of the other women were also around, folding blankets that had been drying beside the fire all afternoon. She took a deep breath to boost her courage and approached them.

"Innis, might I have a word?"

Innis stretched her back and came over to her. Since they were still uncomfortably close to Hugh, and the last thing she wanted was for him to overhear what she had to say, she took Innis closer to the small cave.

"I can't go to Fergus's camp." Her voice was low, but she didn't quite manage to hide the quaver of fear. "I'm certain if I do, I shall never see my kin again."

Innis glanced over her shoulder, perhaps to ensure no one could overhear them, and then she sighed and shook her head. "He's Darragh's oldest friend, although I've never had much to do with him. I want to tell ye he'll abide by Darragh's word to ye to see ye safely reunited with yer kin but," she hesitated as though she battled against familial loyalties. Finally, she took a great breath as though she had reached a decision. "I cannot. And it grieves me to admit for if Clan MacGregor loses its honor, what do we have left?"

"Innis, we need to accompany ye to Oban. I can book passage back to Eigg from there."

Innis looked troubled. "We're not sailing from Oban, Roisin. We're traveling farther south before we cross the sea."

She gripped her fingers together. She'd been worried about that. "Ye'd be traveling in the general direction though. I must get home." There was a thread of desperation in her voice, but she couldn't help it. Innis was, quite literally, her last hope.

Innis squeezed her hand, a quick, unexpected gesture, before she tugged her shawl more securely around her shoulders. "We're avoiding Oban. There are too many Campbells who use that port. But there are other ports along the way, and I'm certain we can divert to one of them for ye. Don't worry about that. The bigger problem is Darragh, but we'll deal with him in the morning."

Roisin released a relieved breath. "Thank ye, Innis, truly. And if there is anything I can ever do for ye in the future, send word to the Small Isles, and I'll do all I can."

Innis smiled, but it was a sad smile, and deep in her heart Roisin knew that once they parted ways, she would never hear from the other woman again.

She turned and made her way to the small cave, but just as she ducked her head to enter it, Hugh appeared by her side and grasped her wrist. She gasped and spun about, trying to pull free. With obvious reluctance, he released her.

If he thought, for even one moment, she was going to invite him inside to stay the night with her, he was even more deluded than she was a fool.

"What were ye discussing with Innis?"

It took a full heartbeat before his question penetrated her turbulent thoughts, and it was so far from anything she had imagined him saying, she covered her confusion by glaring at him. "What business is that of yers?"

He released a jagged sigh. *Damn the man.* Why couldn't he be rude and obnoxious so she could feel justified in telling him she had no intention of ever speaking with him again? But no, he had to gaze at her with those cursed eyes of his and make her feel as though she was the one in the wrong.

Well, I'm not. She folded her arms and pressed her lips together before she did something unforgivable. Such as pulling him close and kissing him until this bottomless ache in her soul eased.

Finally, he broke the silence. "It's my business because I pledged to keep ye safe, and I don't break my pledges."

She managed to make a scoffing sound, even though it broke her heart a little more. "What a noble sentiment. Will it help if I release ye from this pledge, Hugh Campbell, so ye might once more go on yer way unburdened by such a troublesome promise?"

His gaze raked over her face in a far too intimate manner, and her cheeks heated in reaction. And then he spoke. "No."

She blinked, momentarily unsure what he was talking about. "Oh, well that is unfortunate, indeed, since I'm not only releasing ye from this pledge ye made without even consulting me, but Grear, Ecne and I shall be leaving with Innis in the morning and returning to Eigg."

With that, she marched into the cave since her eyes stung, and she would rather die than let a single tear fall in front of him. But she didn't even have time to draw a breath before he followed her inside, and she sucked in an indignant gasp at his presumption.

"Ye can't leave with Innis." His voice was low and filled with urgency. Despite herself, she was intrigued. What on earth did he imagine he could say that would induce her to change her mind?

"I think ye'll find I can. 'Tis already arranged."

Hugh still appeared staggered that she had taken matters into her own hands. Had he honestly expected her to continue to do nothing, now she knew he'd never had any intention of taking her to Creagdoun?

"Roisin, ye can't. The earl and his men are expecting ye."

"What?" The *earl*?

"One of his manors is but half a day's ride from here. I received word from him in the town today, and I'm taking ye there tomorrow."

Distress twisted deep inside her chest at how silver-tongued lies fell so easily from Hugh's lips. Did he truly think her so gullible that she'd still believe anything he told her? Then again, why wouldn't he? She'd believed him when he had said he was working with a mysterious contact, hadn't she?

"How convenient. So ye've been happily exchanging correspondence with the earl the whole time, have ye? And it didn't occur to ye to tell me before now?"

Of course, it hadn't occurred to him. Because until now, she hadn't threatened to leave him, so he hadn't needed to fabricate such a ridiculous tale.

"I couldn't tell ye. 'Tis complicated, Roisin, but ye must believe me. I told ye I was in contact with someone to return ye to yer kin, didn't I? This is what I was doing. Communicating with the earl to find a safe place to deliver ye."

Deliver her? She wasn't sure why that remark stung so badly, considering everything else she'd discovered about Hugh this day, but it did. "Well, ye can deliver yerself to the earl, Hugh Campbell, because I'm still leaving with Innis in the morning."

Incredulity crawled across his face, as though her refusal to fall in with his farcical plans genuinely stunned him. "Is there nothing I can say to make ye change yer mind?"

"Not a thing." And even if he did tell her everything she had so wanted to hear him say for the last eighteen months, it wasn't as though she would believe him. Not now when she knew Hugh would say anything to get his way.

He expelled a harsh breath. "In that case, I shall join ye and see ye safely aboard a ship bound for Eigg."

"Ye'll do no such thing. I'm perfectly capable of boarding a ship by myself."

"It wasn't a suggestion."

There was no menace in his words. He sounded simply weary, and her anger at his high-handedness faded.

No. She couldn't afford to let down her guard for even an instant. For all she knew, this could just be another one of his tactics to make her fall in with his plans. Wildly, she scrabbled through her mind for something that would show him she wasn't to be so callously trifled with.

She couldn't think of a thing.

Ecne, who had been sitting patiently at her feet throughout the exchange, gave a small whine and pawed Hugh's boot. He crouched and scratched her lad behind his ears, and Ecne all but wrapped himself around Hugh's hand in undisguised bliss. It was an act of mutual affection between them she'd witnessed many times, both on Eigg and since she'd been forced into this camp, but this was the first time it caused her stomach to clench with anguish.

Was this show of fondness even real on Hugh's part? It made everything so much worse if he had stooped so low as to deceiving her sweet lad that he cared for him.

As he straightened, she had the wretched conviction that if he left the cave after having had the last word, it would put her at a disadvantage. She had the fleeting notion of returning the inkwell to him with a cutting remark, but it was buried deep in one of the saddlebags, and the thought of having to dig through her possessions to find it was a humiliating prospect. It certainly had nothing to do with the pitiful truth that she simply didn't want to give it back.

And then it came to her. Perfect in its simplicity and heartbreaking because of the hours of misplaced devotion she had spent upon it.

"Before ye go, I will have the portrait back."

Shock flashed over his face. At least, she told herself it was shock, for why would he be devastated by such a request? The portrait would only mean something to him if he truly cared about her.

"Certainly." His voice was devoid of any warmth and a shiver coursed over her arms. That dashed any lingering hope she may have harbored that he really cared. For if he had, surely he would have asked to keep it?

In silence, she watched him pull the folded paper from one of his leather pouches and as he handed it to her, something dropped to the ground. Ecne instantly pounced on it and Hugh cursed before he gingerly freed it from Ecne's enthusiastic possession and hastily stuffed it back into the pouch.

Stunned, she watched him bow his head in farewell, refusing to meet her eye, before he smartly turned and left the cave.

It was obvious he hoped she hadn't seen what he'd picked up. But

she had. She would have recognized it anywhere. It was the embroidered handkerchief she had given to him, with so many dreams and
hopes woven through every stitch, the day he had sailed away from
Eigg.

Chapter Twenty-Two

HUGH DIDN'T BOTHER pitching his tent. Grimly, he built a small fire near the entrance of Roisin's cave, concentrating on the familiar actions so his mind didn't replay the final moments he'd spent with her.

When the fire burned to his satisfaction, he sat back on his heels and released a heavy sigh, and inevitably, Roisin invaded his thoughts. It was too late to send a message to the earl to let him know of the change of plans, but he wasn't concerned about that. It would be easy enough to send one on their way back to Oban and more to the point, he wouldn't need to send it through the spy network.

Hell, since neither of them would no longer be in the camp, Roisin herself could send a letter to Isolde to let her know what was happening.

He was certain she'd find that irony satisfying.

But there was a darker side to this turn of events, one he didn't want to face since it was entirely selfish, yet it crawled across his mind, regardless. For if they journeyed back to Oban, he wouldn't be saying farewell to her on the morrow.

He retreated from the fire and sat with his back against the limestone wall, and finally he could no longer hide from the humiliating spectacle he'd made of himself. As if it weren't bad enough that Roisin had demanded her portrait back, but far worse than that, her handkerchief had dropped to the ground.

He wasn't certain she had seen it, and he hoped to God she hadn't, but it didn't ease the relentless gnaw consuming his chest. Her handkerchief was all he'd had of her for this last year and a half, and it was all he would have in his future. If she had demanded its return, he wasn't sure he would have complied.

He propped his elbows on his knees and dug his fingers through his hair, gripping his scalp, as though that might somehow alleviate the throb that tormented his brain. During daylight hours, it was easier to keep the demons that lived in the darkest corners of his mind at bay. To ignore the uncertainty of his future and the growing inevitability that he would never see his sisters or father again.

And above all, the searing knowledge that he had long ago lost any possibility of securing Roisin as his bride.

He yanked his hair, and he welcomed the pain as his bitter thoughts turned to his brother. What the devil had Douglas done to the earl, to warrant having Hugh's entire future ripped away without a second thought? He had obeyed without question, for the sake of his sisters' futures, and he would never regret that. But God knew, he regretted being put in the position where he needed to restore his kin's tattered reputation.

A shadow emerged and hunkered down next to him, and he forced his fingers to relax before he tore out great chunks of his own hair. His hands fell to his knees as Symon sat beside him and after several heartbeats of silence, the other man spoke.

"Do ye want to be alone?"

What he wanted was as impossible to capture as a star itself and being alone or not would never alter that. And so he shrugged, and Symon took that as a sign to lean back against the rockface. A part of him wanted to tell the other man of the change of plans. Symon had, after all, already said he would follow Hugh whichever path he took. But there was also a chance he'd tell Darragh, and Hugh didn't want the chieftain to be made aware of it until the last moment.

On balance, leaving with Innis was a better idea. He and Roisin wouldn't need to steal away. This way, they could do it openly and considering how few men were remaining by the chieftain's side, it was unlikely he'd be willing to shed blood over the matter.

"Sergeant."

"Aye."

"I trust Darragh with my life."

"I know that." And that was why he wasn't sharing his revised traveling plan with Symon.

"I don't trust Fergus."

Hugh grunted. Fergus was no longer a problem.

"What I'm saying," Symon kept his voice low, "is I don't think Lady Roisin will be safe once we reach Fergus's camp."

Hugh didn't respond. Although it was interesting that Symon had reached that conclusion.

"I know ye're hatching something. Just want ye to know I'll have yer back. We saved Lady Roisin and Grear from the bandits, and I'm willing to save them from Fergus, if it comes to that."

There was an odd constriction in Hugh's throat, and he turned his head to look at the man who had been by his side from the first day they'd met. He couldn't tell Symon the truth, but he could acknowledge what Symon was offering.

"I'll remember that." His voice was hoarse. Clearing it didn't help dislodge the blockage. "Good man."

"Christ, don't go weeping on me now, Sergeant." Symon grinned, and Hugh cracked a reluctant smile. "It'll work out, ye'll see."

Aye, it would work out. Roisin would return to her protected life on her isle where she would never be in danger again and that would need to be enough for him.

⟁

WRAPPED UP IN a blanket next to Grear on the floor of the cave, Roisin watched the shadows shift and fade across the ceiling as dawn broke. And she was still no closer to a decision.

The same doubts plagued her now as they had last night when Hugh had dropped her handkerchief.

Why would he have kept it all this time, if she meant nothing to him?

Ecne, bundled under the blanket between her and Grear, licked her nose, and she wound her arm around him, but her mind would not still, and just as it had for most of the night, it replayed all the conversations she and Hugh had ever shared.

"I always intended to return to Eigg to see ye. I wasn't simply spinning ye a pretty line to see ye smile. But it wasn't to be."

He'd said that to her the day she'd given him the portrait. She had hugged that confession deep inside her heart, so sure that nothing could stand between them. How could it when he was as committed to her as she was to him?

But when she discovered he hadn't sent her letter and, worse, had let her believe he had, everything she'd imagined and dreamed and built around him had shattered. There could never be a future of any kind with someone she couldn't trust. With someone who, most certainly, had forgotten about her the moment he'd left Eigg and only recalled her existence when they had met once again in the forest.

She hadn't believed his ludicrous tale of being in contact with the earl. How could she? The earl had banished him.

Had he, though? Hugh had never told her that. She'd simply assumed it because why else would he have chosen to live as an outlaw?

She sighed and scratched Ecne behind his ear. If Hugh had wanted to gain her favor, after she'd overheard the damning conversation between him and Darragh, all he needed to do was show her the handkerchief. To prove he had never forgotten her, and his promises to return to her had been more than pretty lies.

But he hadn't. And when it had dropped to the ground, he'd appeared appalled and fisted the delicate lace as though he wanted to make it vanish before she remarked upon it.

Were those the actions of a man who would say anything, do anything, to get his way?

All night the question had haunted her. And she could only think of one answer.

No, they were not.

But if that were true, it meant he hadn't simply flung another outrageous lie in her face last night when she'd told him she was leaving with Innis. Only a man coldly determined to have his will obeyed would have cited the earl's involvement in his schemes.

Or a man who was telling the truth.

She squeezed her eyes shut, but it didn't help ease the incessant thumping in her head. If she accepted the truth that Hugh had always intended to return to Eigg for her, she had to accept the truth that he'd been in communication with the earl. And if she accepted that, then she had the choice of later today arriving at the earl's manor and doubtless within days being with her sisters or leaving with Innis and returning to Eigg.

'Twas no good. She could scarcely think straight with all the tangled threads and conflicting notions that filled her mind, and she sat up, careful not to disturb Grear, who still slept soundly. Stealthily, she pulled on her boots and wrapped her shawl around her shoulders before she ventured outside.

No one was stirring yet, but it wouldn't be long before they broke camp, and she wanted to get this confrontation out of the way before there was any chance of an audience. Hugh sat next to the cave entrance, leaning against the rockface, and her heart stuttered in her chest as she caught his unblinking gaze.

"Hugh." Her whisper sounded unnaturally loud in the still morning air. She glanced at Symon, but he appeared to be fast asleep next to Hugh, but she wasn't about to take any chances. "May I have a word?"

If he was surprised by her request, he didn't show it. He stood, rolling his shoulders and straightening his spine, and her mouth dried as she watched the magnificent play of his muscles beneath his white shirt.

Somehow she managed to drag her mesmerized gaze away before he noticed and moved to the other side of the cave entrance. He followed her and stood before her, not close enough to touch, but close enough that he sent every sense she possessed into freefall.

She gripped the ends of her shawl in the vain hope that that might focus her unruly thoughts. She could speculate all she liked, but there was only one way to know for sure.

"Hugh, why did ye keep my handkerchief all this time?"

An expression of unfettered alarm flashed over his face, as though she had trapped him in a field of giant thistles with no way out. For a surreal moment, she even had the certainty he was about to swing on his heel and march back to Symon, but then he suddenly sucked in a deep breath and squared his shoulders as if he were about to enter a battle without a weapon.

"Ye know why. Because ye gave it to me."

He said it almost like an accusation. But the intense glow in his eyes told another tale, one she knew so well from the stories she cherished of the fae and ancient gods, where hearts and souls entwined, and where she had always rewritten the bittersweet endings so love prevailed.

Suppose I'm wrong?

She had been wrong about so many things since Hugh had caught her in the forest. Or had she? It was so hard to fathom her own thoughts when he gazed at her so. Everything she believed she knew about him tumbled in her mind like uprooted saplings in a winter's storm.

From the corner of her eye, she saw the camp begin to stir. Grear emerged from the cave; Symon stood and stretched. Her heart thundered and her pulse raced, but there was no longer any time to ponder and contemplate all the possible reasons as to why Hugh had done all that he had since the day they had met.

She needed to make a choice right now. Keeping her voice low, she put her trust in Hugh. "I'll come with ye and rendezvous with the earl today."

Chapter Twenty-Three

SPEECHLESS, HUGH WATCHED Roisin hurry back to the cave as his mind reeled. He had half expected an inquisition after his confession, not have the air taken from his lungs by her sudden decision to change her plans.

Once, he had thought her so easy to understand. A genteel lady, soft-spoken and one who cast light wherever she went. A noblewoman who would, God willing and if luck were on his side, make him the perfect, agreeable wife.

That he would protect and cherish her had gone without saying. And when he'd rescued her from the bandits, his pledge to protect her had consumed him, for how could she hope to survive a brutal life like this, no matter how brief it might be, without him?

But she wasn't easy to understand. Looking back, he realized she never had been. He had simply never seen it. Even on Eigg she hadn't been the conventional lady for while she loved her embroidery, she had also pursued her love of writing and illuminating stories of the fae. And while royal courts were likely full of noblewomen who spent their time with their quills, he imagined their writings were somewhat more religious in nature.

She did not wield a sword, the way her sister, Lady Isolde did, nor share forthright views with strangers, like her other sister, Lady Freyja, had when he had met her at Sgur Castle. But in her quiet way, Roisin stood up for what she believed in and forged her own path as surely as anyone he had met.

Yesterday, he had reluctantly understood why she refused to believe a word he said and why she'd insisted on traveling with Innis. He didn't have to like it. All he had to do was ensure she reached Eigg without incident.

But now, she had changed her mind. And unless he'd completely lost his own mind, which was certainly a possibility, it appeared she changed it because he'd been cornered into admitting that he'd kept her precious handkerchief. The one thing he'd been determined to keep from her at all costs, because it would expose a part of him he couldn't afford to lay bare, had been the catalyst in restoring her trust in him.

He wasn't sure what to make of it. Once, it would have given him hope. But while hope had been the one glimmer of light during those dark months in Eire, the reality was once he left Roisin with the earl, it was doubtful he would ever see her again.

Grimly, he set to saddling Fhortan as around him the camp prepared to split. It appeared Innis was taking possession of the wagons, and he paused as he sized up the situation. Symon had said half the camp was leaving, but by the looks of things only a couple of men, besides himself and Symon, were remaining with Darragh.

Without a wagon, Roisin wouldn't be able to take her casket. Then again, they wouldn't be able to take a wagon with them even if one had been available when they broke away from Darragh later this morning since speed and dexterity would be paramount. He'd need to speak with her about transferring as many of her possessions as she could into their saddlebags.

Roisin emerged from the cave, carrying her casket. Hugh watched, fascinated, as she walked over to Innis and Elspeth. He could tell by the way Innis shook her head and gesticulated that she clearly disapproved of Roisin's decision to stay with him, and his suspicion was confirmed when Innis shot him a dark glance.

He didn't worry that Roisin would let slip that he was secretly taking her to the Earl of Argyll. She hadn't betrayed him by telling Darragh yesterday who he really was after she'd overheard that conversation between them, and truth be told, he'd had a terrible moment when he feared she might. And he wouldn't even have blamed her.

But she'd kept her word, even when she thought he had broken his.

He'd never break his word to her. And yet an uneasy thorn dug into his mind. For sure, he hadn't broken his word, but Roisin hadn't known about his connection with the earl. All she knew was he hadn't sent her letter to her sister when he had told her he would.

Goddamn it. His grip tightened on Fhortan's reins. He'd explained his reasoning. But had he told her he regretted not being clear with her from the start?

He wasn't sure he had.

She handed over her casket to Innis, who passed it to Elspeth, and then did a very un-Innis-like thing. She hugged Roisin, a quick, hard-looking hug, before swiftly pushing her back and taking back the casket from Elspeth.

Frowning, he watched Roisin return to the cave where she led out her mare. Had she just given Innis all her possessions that were in the casket? Or had she already packed them into her saddlebags? Considering how they bulged, he was inclined to believe the latter.

It seemed she had already planned ahead for a streamlined escape.

It wasn't long before those who were heading for Eire were ready, and Hugh eyed the farewells with Darragh, who only showed a crack in his stoic façade when Elspeth gave him a hug. He had to admit he was surprised about Elspeth. She was so staunchly loyal to her brother he'd expected her to remain behind. But she was equally devoted to the bairns, and he guessed she couldn't bear to be parted from them.

Innis gave him a nod of farewell. "Be sure ye keep yer word to Roisin," she said, her voice low. "Get her back to her kin before ye reach Fergus's camp, ye hear me?"

"I hear ye."

She sighed as she hitched her bairn more securely on her hip. "'Tis is a pity there are not more Campbells like yerself, Hugh. Maybe then we MacGregors would not need to flee our land simply to find peace."

There was nothing he could say to that. Because the truth was, he was one of the Campbells who had fought against the MacGregors from the first day the earl had called for arms against the other clan. He had done it without hesitation for that was what one did when one's earl commanded it.

It didn't mean he had to like how so many of the women and bairns had lost everything.

"God go with ye," he said. "I hope ye find what ye're searching for."

As Innis and her group left, he went over to Roisin. Ecne was in his basket at her feet and the wee dog let out a mournful whimper at his imprisonment as Hugh approached. "I'll carry his basket with me, if ye like."

As he made the offer, he recalled how horror-struck she had been when he'd tried to help her with Ecne on the day she'd been attacked by the bandits. This time, she didn't gaze at him as if he were a demon from hell. She gave him a small smile.

"Thank ye, but maybe I should carry it. In case ye need to be... vigilant."

He instantly understood what she meant and silently berated himself that he hadn't thought of the possible consequences of being hampered by the ungainly basket should he need to defend Roisin. Not that he believed Darragh would order his men to attack him, should he realize Hugh's plans to take her to safety, but 'twas best to be prepared.

Within moments, they were on their way with Darragh up front with one of his men, while a second man rode ahead to scout the area, then Symon, and he and Roisin with Grear on her other side bringing up the rear. It was still early as they left the glen behind them and if they kept on their current course, Hugh calculated they were four hours out from the earl's manor.

They had been riding for some time, and he had resigned himself to the fact that it seemed Roisin never wanted to speak with him again when she gave a shuddering breath.

"Hugh." Her voice was barely above a whisper, and he leaned closer and tried not to breathe in her scent of crushed rose petals. An impossible task. How did she always smell so fresh, as though she had just emerged from a steamy bathtub?

"Aye." Unobtrusively, he attempted to shift position on the saddle, but it didn't ease his discomfort, and he silently acknowledged nothing but Roisin herself could achieve that end.

"What is yer plan?"

He forced his mind back to the current situation. No good would come from wishing for the impossible. "If we stay on this path, in an hour or so we should reach a waterfall in a wooded glen, with an ancient cairn. Darragh's bearing east, but we'll turn west. Another two hours ride, and the earl will have men waiting for ye."

She was silent for a moment, before she gave him a sideways glance. "I'm finding it hard to fathom that ye didn't tell me any of this, Hugh. I thought ye were planning on taking me to Creagdoun."

"We were too far from Creagdoun and after the bandits' attack, I couldn't risk taking ye without adequate protection in case our suspicions were right, and it had been a targeted attack." He sighed. "Which it was, as it turned out."

"But I still don't understand how ye could be in contact with the earl."

She had put her faith in him, and he didn't want to keep anything from her, but he couldn't share his connection with the earl without revealing he was a part of the underground spy network. Although,

God help him, it was hard to hold back.

"I sent him a message." It wasn't a lie, but he still felt bad that it wasn't the whole truth.

She gave him another sideways glance, and it was obvious she knew he was hiding something. He could only hope she wouldn't press him for further details.

They continued in silence for a while before she turned to him once again.

"What did ye mean when ye said Fergus knew exactly who William was? Did he have something to do with the ambush that killed my men?"

"He did. When we were in the town, he all but bragged about it." Anger surged at how despicably Fergus had intended to use Roisin and he took a harsh breath. That danger, at least, was over. "Fergus was the half-brother of Alan MacGregor, who tried to bring down William last year. I doubt he would ever have released ye, once ye were in his clutches."

At least, not alive. His stomach clenched at what torture Fergus would have inflicted on Roisin, given half a chance.

"And Darragh agreed with this?" There was a quiver in Roisin's voice, but she seemed more sad than terrified at the prospect.

He shook his head. "I don't think so. They were friends from long ago and I feel Darragh followed wherever Fergus led. Darragh may have decided to exchange ye for a ransom, but he wouldn't have used ye to inflict retribution on William or the earl. He's not a fundamentally cruel man."

It was only as he spoke the words that he realized the truth of them. To be sure, Darragh had never fully trusted him, but when Symon had brought him into the camp, the chieftain had allowed him to stay because he had saved Symon's life in Eire. He could just as easily have killed Hugh on the spot.

"So, we must be on guard against Fergus in case he tries to exact vengeance again on one of us." Roisin shivered and before he could stop himself he reached for her and gently squeezed her hand where she held onto Ecne's basket.

"Ye do not need to worry about Fergus. He'll never harm another soul."

She bit her lip before her gaze caught his. It was clear she understood his meaning. "Did he attack ye in the town?"

"Outside the town. After Darragh had already left." He could leave it at that. But she deserved to know the full truth. "But whether he attacked me or not, there wasn't any way on God's earth he was leaving that place. Ye'd never be safe so long as he was alive and that was something I couldn't allow."

"I understand." Her voice was hushed. "I'm grieved I put ye in that position, Hugh."

"Don't be. I'd do it again in a heartbeat. I know what men of his ilk are like. There's no reasoning with them." And it had nothing to do with Fergus being a MacGregor. There had simply been something rotten in his core.

He realized he still held her hand, and she hadn't pushed him away. Their gazes meshed, and he had the insane notion to kiss her and, that somehow by doing so, he could wipe out the last year and once more be worthy of seeking her hand.

"Hugh." Her whisper was as soft as a summer breeze, and he imagined he saw the promise of something more than an imminent farewell in her eyes. He forgot where they were, forgot everything he had done, and only knew if he didn't tell her how desperately he needed her in his life he would regret it forever.

"Roisin." Her name was like sunlight, filling his dark existence with hope. "I—"

A commotion up ahead as the scout returned whipped the words from him, and Symon wheeled his horse around and came to his side. "Ambush ahead."

What the hell? He narrowed his eyes as Darragh swiftly led them farther into the forest, in the opposite direction from where they'd been heading to the glen with the waterfall.

Goddamn it. He couldn't afford to take whatever detour Darragh had in mind. At some point between the glen and the manor the earl's men would be waiting, and he needed to get Roisin and Grear there without delay.

"Symon." His voice was urgent, and Symon gave him a shrewd glance. "Will ye cover for me? I must ensure Lady Roisin and her maid find safety."

"Aye, Sergeant. Ye have my word."

Hugh gripped the other man's arm. "I'll return and find ye."

Symon gave a sharp nod before turning to follow the other men, and Hugh caught Roisin's gaze. "This way."

They swung around, and he led them away from Darragh, skirting the path they had previously been following, but heading in the direction where the waterfall was. From that glen, it was a straightforward journey to the manor. But first they had to reach the glen.

As he led them deeper into the forest, the notion of the ambush played on his mind. Was it the earl's men? Or bandits?

He couldn't worry about that now. The chances were high that if the scout had been spotted, those engaged in the ambush would follow Darragh and his small band of men. Certainly, he hadn't seen or heard anything that suggested they were being followed, but he wasn't taking any chances, and he continuously scanned the forest for a sign of movement.

They forged onwards as the forest gradually descended into another glen. Even Ecne remained silent, as though he understood the need for stealth. And finally, beyond the birdsong and snuffle of the horses, he heard the sound of cascading water.

The trees thinned, and he caught sight of a double waterfall tumbling into a rock-strewn river. And on the far bank was the earl and two dozen of his men.

CHAPTER TWENTY-FOUR

ROISIN GASPED AS she caught sight of Freyja on the other side of the river and relief surged through her that they had made it to safety. She turned to Hugh, who had an oddly guarded expression on his face, and gently touched his arm.

"Thank ye," she said. She didn't understand how he had been in communication with the earl. Yet surely it had to be a good sign that, whatever the reason was for him having lived like an outlaw for God knew how long, the earl must surely pardon him now.

"'Tis my pleasure." He sounded both strangely formal, considering all they had been through together, and despairingly resigned.

"Hugh," she said, frowning, but before she could continue, he nodded back at the river.

"Yer escort awaits, my lady."

Why was he suddenly using her title? They were still too far away for anyone to hear them, and it made her uneasy. But when she looked back, she saw four of the earl's men were fording the river, and the water was not much higher than their horses' fetlocks.

She glanced at Grear and gave her an encouraging smile before she urged her mare forward, and they crossed the river with the men flanking them.

Freyja instantly rode to her side and grasped her hand. "Thank Eir ye are alive," her sister said, before she gave a loud sniff and blinked rapidly. "What a terrible ordeal for ye, Roisin, ye poor wee lass. But do not fear, ye're coming home with us and will be coddled until this dreadful nightmare is nothing but a distant memory."

She squeezed her sister's fingers, which was all she could manage around Ecne's basket. "'Tis so good to see ye again, Frey. But my ordeal was not nearly as terrible as it might have been, had Hugh Campbell not been by my side."

"Aye, we owe a debt of gratitude to Hugh, and that's a fact," Freyja agreed. "If we hadn't heard from him so swiftly after ye vanished that he had rescued ye from the despicable brigands, I fear Isolde herself would have gone out searching for ye like an avenging shieldmaiden." Freyja glanced at Grear who was next to her. "'Tis very good to see ye are safe, Grear."

"How is Isolde?" Anxiety gnawed through her. But Freyja dispersed the worry that had plagued her for the last two weeks with a wave of her hand.

"Strong and healthy. As I've said, we had to convince her to put down her claymore and let the earl and Hugh arrange for yer escape. Alasdair—" she turned to her husband, "Can ye take sweet Ecne's basket? I'm certain Roisin's arms must be aching."

Her arms *were* aching. Indeed, she could scarcely feel them at all. They had gone numb, but she wasn't certain she liked how Freyja had just announced it to the entire company. But she didn't object when Alasdair, with a kind, welcoming, smile, took the basket, especially when he placed it with Grear, whom Ecne adored.

Something Freyja had said snagged in her mind. "How soon did ye hear from Hugh?"

"The earl got his message two days after ye were due at Isolde's, which is astounding when ye think of it. So we knew very soon that Hugh was protecting ye."

Two days. He must have sent his message the day they went to the town when she had written a letter to Isolde. He hadn't sent her letter. But he had notified the earl. Why had he been more concerned that her letter might be intercepted than he had been about his own missive?

There was something she couldn't quite put her finger on, but it scratched below the surface, like a burr caught beneath her skin. She looked over her shoulder for Hugh, who had been very quiet since they'd crossed the river—

He wasn't there.

Panic gnawed through her as she searched the tree line, but there was no sign of him. Why hadn't he crossed the river with her? Why in the name of God had he returned to Darragh?

"Roisin," Freyja said and by her tone, it was apparent she was repeating herself. "The earl is eager to make yer acquaintance before we leave. Do not be distressed, ye only need to greet him. He doesn't expect ye to converse." Her sister smiled and gave her hand a comforting squeeze, but Roisin wasn't concerned about greeting the earl.

"Before we leave?"

"Aye. We shall return home to Dunochty. It's closer than Creagdoun, and when ye are fully recovered, we shall visit Isolde. I shall send a message to Amma, and she'll meet us there. She stayed at Sgur on the slender chance ye might turn up there."

Roisin glanced at the earl, who sat astride his stallion and had the proud bearing of a man used to giving orders and having them obeyed without question. Once she'd imagined asking Freyja to request that Alasdair intercede with the earl on Hugh's behalf, but how could Alasdair do that when he had no idea what Hugh had been through?

She didn't know everything he had endured since she had last seen him on Eigg, but at least she knew enough to let the earl know that whatever Hugh had done, he had more than atoned for it.

Alasdair came to her side, and the three of them approached the earl where Alasdair made the introductions. The earl smiled kindly at her, and the obscure notion crossed her mind that he looked at her as though she were a bashful bairn.

"We are all greatly relieved ye are safe and well, my lady," he said after he'd gallantly kissed her hand. "Ye may rest assured all involved in this matter will be brought to justice."

The man behind it had already been brought to justice, but she knew her manners. "Thank ye, my lord. I trust the brave men that accompanied me from Eigg have been discovered?"

The earl gave a grave nod. "Indeed they have, and they have been given all due respect as befits their sacrifice."

Freyja was by her side, and she passed a few words with the earl before she turned her mare around, clearly expecting Roisin to follow her lead.

She remained where she was. "My lord," she said, and even though her heart thundered in her chest and she felt lightheaded with nerves, her voice was steady. "If not for Hugh Campbell, my maid and I would have been taken by mercenaries hired by Fergus MacGregor. He was full of vengeance for the death of his half-brother, Alan, and if Hugh hadn't been there, I fear I would now be dead."

Freyja gasped, although whether she was shocked that Roisin had spoken more than the bare minimum protocol required to the earl or by her assertation that she knew quite well Fergus intended to kill her, Roisin wasn't sure. The earl, on the other hand, after raising his eyebrows in clear surprise, appeared intrigued rather than irked by her remark.

"I fear that also," he said. At least he hadn't tried to tell her she was being hysterical and despite her low opinion of him, she had to give him credit for that. "We owe Hugh a great debt, and that's a fact."

Encouraged by that admission, Roisin pressed her advantage. "Indeed, and Hugh didn't just keep me safe. He ensured Fergus MacGregor would no longer be a danger to any MacDonald or Campbell."

"Did he, now?" The earl's eyes bored into her, as if she had just disclosed something he hadn't known. "Ye are well informed, my lady."

Something in his tone alerted her that, perhaps, she was treading on dangerous ground, although she wasn't sure why. Nevertheless, she picked her words with care. "Only because Fergus was a danger to me, my lord. Hugh wanted to reassure me I was safe."

"What else did he tell ye?"

"That he had been a redshank in Eire. My lord, I don't know why he is living as an outcast, but I beseech ye to look favorably upon him, so he might return to his rightful place in Clan Campbell."

The tension that had suddenly spiked between them faded. What had the earl suspected she was going to say?

"Lady Roisin, ye may rest assured Hugh has my favor, as he always has. Frankly, I don't know why he didn't cross the river with ye. No matter. My scouts are out there, and we shall find him when we hunt down the remainder of Fergus MacGregor's misbegotten kin."

With that, he bowed his head in farewell before wheeling around and speaking with his men, while she stared after him in confusion.

Hugh had always had the earl's favor?

"Come, Roisin." Freyja gave her a piercing look. "We must leave."

She tore her gaze from the earl and focused on her sister. "No. I'm going to find Hugh."

There was no mistaking the alarm that flashed over Freyja's face. "Indeed, ye are not. What has come over ye, Roisin? Ye are behaving most unlike yerself."

"Take Grear back to Dunochty. I'm certain the earl will see I'm safely escorted to ye once Hugh is found."

"I'll do no such thing." Freyja seemed outraged by the very idea. "If I cannot persuade ye to see sense, then I shall join ye in this foolish quest. Grear can remain here with guards to protect her until we return."

The earl and his men were preparing to leave, apart from half a dozen who remained in the glen, doubtless with the intention to escort her and Freyja to Dunochty, but who now could protect Grear.

She urged her mare forward and joined the back of the contingent, and Freyja and Alasdair flanked her.

She was thankful to be reunited with her sister, but she couldn't leave things like this with Hugh. If she went to Dunochty without speaking to him, who knew if she would ever see him again?

Chapter Twenty-Five

HUGH WAITED UNTIL Roisin was halfway across the river before he left the glen. The earl had seen him and looked straight through him without acknowledgement. It was plain enough that his presence was unwanted. Better to disappear unobtrusively than risk Roisin witnessing the earl's slight.

He would find Symon and keep his promise to return to Eire. If the earl wanted him, he knew how to find him through his spiderweb network. But his heart was heavy as he retraced his steps as the inevitability of a lifetime without Roisin by his side wrapped dank claws about his shoulders.

He made good time, and when he reached the point where he'd parted ways with Symon, it wasn't hard to track Darragh's progress through the forest. Up ahead, light streamed through the canopy, revealing a small clearing. His years of training kicked in and even though he couldn't see anything untoward, his senses went onto alert.

And then he heard it. The unmistakable sound of steel clashing against steel, and the familiar blazing energy that always preceded a battle surged through his veins. He sucked in a long breath to calm his mind and pulled up at the edge of the clearing. Two of Darragh's men lay lifeless on the ground, arrows protruding from their throats, and Darragh and Symon both fought on foot with two, he surmised, of the earl's scouts.

Goddamn it. If they were the earl's men, he should turn and leave. But suppose they were not? He'd never run from a fight in his life, and he wasn't about to start now. He leapt from Fhortan and drew his sword and then, as though he were trapped in a nightmare and his limbs had turned to stone, he saw one of the strangers plunge his sword through Symon's chest.

Symon dropped to the ground as his assailant whirled about to attack Darragh, who had thrown off the other man. Heart thundering, and denial pounding in his head, Hugh charged into the clearing and fell to his knees beside Symon.

Blood soaked his shirt. Hugh pressed his hand against the wound, but he knew, in his heart, it would do no good.

Symon opened his eyes. "Sergeant," he rasped. "Knew ye'd come back."

"I said I would." Hugh attempted to grin, but it hurt too much. If he hadn't left, he might have saved Symon. But if he had stayed, Roisin wouldn't have escaped. And his priority had always, would always, be her.

But it didn't help to ease the savage pain tearing through his heart.

"Caught us by surprise. Felled two before they charged us." Blood seeped from Symon's mouth and his eyes closed as though it was too much effort to keep them open. Hugh shot a glance at Darragh and the earl's man—or was he a bandit? Hugh didn't care. Either way, the man wouldn't be leaving this forest.

"Save yer strength." His throat ached as Symon once again looked at him. His eyes were glazed, and his fingers clutched at Hugh's plaid. Hugh swallowed and forced a positive note in his voice. "I'll soon get ye out of here, never fear."

"I won't... won't be leaving here, Sergeant. But 'tis been an honor to serve with ye. 'Twas a good day when we met in Eire."

He remembered that day. Remembered too, all the days he and Symon had ridden into battle together; the evenings when they'd drunk ale and he'd listened to Symon's tales; and the winter nights when they'd huddled over a fire to keep the chill at bay.

Symon had been by his side for over a year. A staunch ally who had always had his back and had never questioned Hugh's reasons for why he was a redshank, fighting for survival.

All he'd done was offer friendship. And Hugh had never fully accepted it because Symon was a MacGregor, and Clans Campbell and MacGregor were enemies.

Hugh gripped Symon's limp hand as he faced the bitter truth too late.

Symon had always been more than a friend. He had been a fellow brother-in-arms, a trusted compatriot for all they swore fealty to different clans, and the reason Hugh had shied away from acknowledging the friendship wasn't because Symon was a MacGregor.

It was because Hugh couldn't reveal the truth about himself. And because he couldn't face witnessing the certain contempt on Symon's face, should he learn Hugh was working for the Earl of Argyll.

He leaned close, hoping it wasn't too late for Symon to hear. "The honor was mine. And aye, 'twas a good day indeed when we met in Eire. Ye are among the best of men, Symon, and that's God's own truth."

Symon gave the faintest smile. "Don't let the bastards get ye, Hugh." He exhaled a rattling breath and went silent.

Hugh clamped his teeth together and carefully crossed Symon's hands on his chest. Then he grasped his sword and stood, his eyes fixed on the man who had killed Symon. He stepped over his body, just as Darragh hit the ground, his lifeblood soaking the sodden earth, and his assailant swung around as though he knew of Hugh's approach.

Shock punched through Hugh's chest and a red mist filled his vision as his brother Douglas faced him. For an endless heartbeat, nothing stirred. Then, scalding rage burned through him, obliterating everything but the knowledge Douglas had not only ruined any chance Hugh might have had with Roisin, but he had murdered one of the most loyal friends he'd ever had.

His fingers tightened around the hilt, and he took a menacing step forward. "Ye drunken, misbegotten bastard."

A muscle flexed in Douglas's jaw, the only indication Hugh's insult had touched him. "'Tis good to see ye too, brother."

"Where have ye been hiding this last year? What the hell did ye do to make the earl so goddamn mad at ye?"

Douglas's gaze didn't waver, even though Hugh angled the tip of his sword at his brother's throat. "I work for the earl, Hugh. I always have. And for his father before him."

"Ye lie." Douglas, eight years older than him, had been a genial, lying drunkard for as long as Hugh could recall. The earl barely even acknowledged his existence.

"I've been in the network since I was sixteen." There was no trace of the usual slur that accompanied Douglas's words, and a chill inched along Hugh's arms. This Douglas was one he scarcely even recognized. A man who had been living a double life for seventeen years. Had he ever been drunk in his life? Or was that all part of his act? "I didn't want ye dragged into this world, Hugh, but the earl was certain loose threads could be found in Eire that would lead us back to Torcall MacGregor's remaining kin." He paused for a heartbeat. "And so it did."

No matter how he burned to avenge Symon's death, he couldn't kill his own brother. But the rage and grief, and the gut-wrenching sense of betrayal, ate through him like a canker. Before he could stop himself, he transferred his sword to his left hand and sent a thunderous punch to Douglas's jaw.

His brother reeled back, and Hugh placed his sword on the ground before taking another step closer. He couldn't run a blade through his brother's heart but by God, he'd gain some small satisfaction by cracking a multitude of bones, both his and Douglas's alike.

The sound of horses entering the clearing had him swinging about to see the earl and his men, and he glowered at the earl, daring him to comment on the scene. But before he could say anything, Roisin appeared on her mare.

Christ, no. What the hell was she doing here? He was in no fit state to pretend all was well in front of her, when murder throbbed with every beat of his heart. Yet more than that, she risked her reputation by coming here to see him. It was already in peril by the very fact she'd spent almost two weeks in Darragh's camp without anyone casting aspersions on what may have occurred between him and her. But as she dismounted and hurried towards him, a stricken expression on her face, he could no sooner turn his back on her than he could bring Symon back to life.

It might be the last time he ever saw her.

HORROR STREAKED THROUGH Roisin at the blood that smeared Hugh's shirt and plaid and coated his hands. Her only thought was to ensure he was all right, and she scarcely even realized she had raced across the clearing until she came to an ungainly halt in front of him.

There was no smile of welcome on his face. He simply stared at her, his blue eyes filled with weary resignation, as though she were little more than a stranger. And she was suddenly, excruciatingly, aware that every eye was upon her.

Her face heated, but she refused to slink back to her sister and hide. "Are ye hurt?"

It was a foolish question to ask a man covered in blood and yet he didn't appear wounded. And neither did he mock her. He merely sighed heavily and shook his head. "No."

She saw the furtive way he glanced to the side and the barely perceptible shudder that inched through him. With a foreboding of dread, she followed his glance, and a pained breath caught in her throat at the sight of Symon.

"I'm so sorry, Hugh," she whispered. He briefly closed his eyes before focusing on something over her shoulder. She wouldn't be deterred by his remote attitude. He was grieving Symon and just because he had been a MacGregor didn't mean they hadn't been good friends. After all, she had only known Innis for two short weeks and yet by the time they parted ways, she considered her a friend, too.

"Ye shouldn't be here, Lady Roisin." He kept his voice low but the note of finality in his words as his gaze caught hers struck her more forcefully than if he had snarled in her face. "'Tis no place for a noblewoman. I'm thankful ye are returned to yer kin, and I wish ye well."

With that, he bowed his head, dismissing her as if she were no more than a passing acquaintance. A wild rushing sound filled her head as the trees spun around her, and she sucked in a sharp breath, agonizingly aware of how silent the clearing was and how everyone had just witnessed her humiliating snub.

Freyja appeared by her side and wrapped her arm around her shoulders, guiding her back to their mares. The earl was speaking to Hugh, perhaps, but she couldn't make out the words and didn't object when Freyja and Alasdair, along with several warriors, surrounded her as they left the clearing.

They returned to the glen where Grear and Ecne waited, and she nodded dutifully when Freyja told her they were staying at the earl's manor until the morning. She didn't care where they stayed. All she wanted was to hide away where no one would talk to her.

But most of all, she wanted Hugh's final words to stop echoing around her head in an endless, pitiless, refrain.

LATER THAT AFTERNOON, after Freyja's insistence that she bathe and change into one of her sister's gowns, Roisin sat on the bed in the small chamber the earl had allocated for her, with Ecne asleep on her lap. It felt strange and oddly wrong to be resting on a bed in the middle of the day, and whenever she wasn't picking apart Hugh's last comment, she was worrying about Innis and the rest of the women and bairns.

But at least they'd had the foresight to leave Darragh, before the earl's men had come upon them. She shivered at what their fate might have been otherwise. If only she could be certain that they would one day arrive safely in Eire and be able to build a new life.

She kissed the top of Ecne's head and tried to quell the restlessness that wouldn't leave her. How she longed to escape this chamber and take Ecne for a walk in the grounds. But Hugh had accompanied the earl and his men back here and the last thing she wanted was to accidentally come face to face with him.

Not yet. Not until his polite, distant, dismissal stopped haunting her mind with every beat of her heart.

And maybe not even then.

There was a knock on the door and instantly her foolish thoughts flew to Hugh. Had he come to her to explain he hadn't meant his cold farewell? Instinctively, she straightened her shawl and patted her hair as Grear, who had been dozing on the other side of the bed, jumped up and opened the door.

Freyja came inside and Roisin told herself she was relieved it wasn't Hugh. Unfortunately, she didn't quite believe herself.

Her sister smiled at Grear. "Could ye allow me some privacy with Lady Roisin, Grear?"

Grear bobbed a curtsey and after a quick glance at Roisin, left the chamber.

"Ye're looking better already." Freyja nodded in approval before settling herself beside Roisin on the bed and scratching Ecne behind his ears. His entire body rippled with pleasure. "How are ye feeling?"

Heartsore.

"I'm fine, Frey. Truly."

"That's good." Freyja appeared inordinately focused on Ecne. "Now then, I hope ye know ye can tell me anything. There's nothing ye can say that will shock me, ye understand?"

Roisin understood only too well what her sister was saying. She was only surprised Freyja was being so coy about things. Frey always said what she thought and damn the consequences.

That didn't mean she had any intention of telling her sister what she and Hugh had shared in that cave. Distress churned through her, but she refused to let her feelings show on her face. She didn't regret what had happened between them. But how she wished Hugh hadn't mortified her so when she'd gone to him in the clearing.

"The MacGregor men did not abuse me if that's what ye're asking."

Freyja finally stopped petting Ecne and patted Roisin's arm, instead. "That is good to know, indeed. But if anything did happen, 'twas not yer fault."

Roisin sighed. "The men were rough, but who wouldn't be after a life on the run for five years?"

"Hmm." Freyja gave her a doubtful look, but Roisin hadn't finished yet.

"And the women and bairns. Ye have no idea how they live, Frey. 'Tis heartbreaking."

"There were women and bairns?"

"Aye. Thank God they left the camp before the earl found Darragh."

Freyja patted her arm again and Roisin wasn't sure whether her sister was trying to comfort her or herself.

"Ye know the earl would treat the women and bairns kindly, don't ye? He is a fair man, Roisin."

"He's yer half-brother through marriage, Frey. Of course ye must see the good in him."

Freyja cocked her head and frowned. "Ye know me better than that, surely? If I thought he was a monster, I'd tell ye so."

Roisin had to concede her sister was right. But regardless, Alasdair was related to the earl through blood, and Freyja hadn't seen how the women and bairns had scrabbled to survive.

She shook her head. This was likely something they would never agree upon, but she wasn't going to fight her sister over it. "I glimpsed a life I'd never imagined before, and it's not something I'll ever forget. But I'll tell ye this. There is not so much difference between MacDonalds and MacGregors."

Freyja's hand dropped to her lap, and she gazed at Roisin as though she had never seen her before. "Ye've changed." There was a note of awe in her voice. "'Tis not a criticism," she added hastily. "Truly, Isolde and I were terrified that ye wouldn't survive such a dreadful ordeal, but it seems ye didn't merely survive. Ye thrived."

"Ye are giving me far too much credit. 'Twas Hugh Campbell who rescued me from the brigands, remember, and he took his oath to protect me most seriously, I can assure ye."

"I'm relieved to hear it." Freyja's gaze turned curious, and Roisin silently sighed. Why had she brought Hugh's name into the conversation? Yet she'd had no choice because without Hugh the brigands would have taken her to Fergus, and she didn't want to think about her fate had that happened. "At least we know why none of us heard from Hugh after he left Eigg. Although it doesn't explain why he became an outlaw."

"'Tis no good asking me. I don't know why he did, either."

Freyja looked thoughtful. "Ye know I don't believe in such fanciful things as destiny and soulmates. But I cannot help thinking that, if I did, there seems to be a strange connection between ye and Hugh, after all. 'Tis quite something that he was the one to find ye after the brigands attacked ye, don't ye think?"

She had once been so certain Hugh was her soulmate. And after they had made love, she was convinced of it. But after his dismissal earlier today, she didn't know what to think.

"It could all be pure coincidence and nothing more."

Freyja looked pensive. "I cannot believe I'm seeing a connection when ye are not. Did something happen between ye and Hugh, Roisin?"

She wasn't ready to talk about what had happened between them. Maybe she never would. "Ye know I always wanted Hugh. And I still do. But I don't think it's ever meant to be. Even Amma, who arranged for Isolde to wed William because of dreams she had and who knew Alasdair was yer destiny from the moment she saw him, never believed Hugh Campbell was the man for me. Even when she shared my dream of the Highlands, she never saw me with him. So what do ye make of that?"

"I don't believe in dreams foretelling the future." Despite her words, Freyja sounded a little shaken by Roisin's revelations. "I believe in what I can see and what I can understand. And whatever ye may think, Hugh did not want ye to leave when we were in the forest earlier."

Roisin stared at her sister in disbelief. Freyja was the practical one, and yet here she was, imagining things that, if their positions were reversed, she would be chiding Roisin for harboring.

"I think I know what I heard him say, Freyja."

Freyja made a dismissive gesture with her hand. "Aye. And when people are sick, they say all kinds of things. But it's the way they hold their body, the look in their eyes, even how they breathe—that's what tells ye the truth of the matter. And the last thing Hugh Campbell wants is to never see ye again."

Hugh wasn't sick. They both knew that. And Roisin knew that wasn't the point her sister was making.

She desperately wanted Freyja to be right. But with all that had happened during the last two weeks, she couldn't help fearing that

Amma not having a vision of her and Hugh sharing a future together was an omen.

And then one of her grandmother's favorite sayings whispered in her mind.

One must keep perspective in all matters to be a fair judge of the truth.

How many times had she heard Amma tell Isolde that, and Freyja, too? But although Amma had never said it to her, it seemed her memory was replaying the message with purpose.

She had never been able to keep her perspective when it came to Hugh. From the day she'd met him in Eigg, and then when he had caught her fleeing in the forest, she had been blinded by her feelings for him.

To see the truth, she needed to let go of her wounded sensibilities. Yet what of Amma's visions?

"But the dreams," she began, but Freyja interrupted her.

"Ye speak of dreams I know nothing about. But what if the reason Amma didn't see ye and Hugh in the Highlands isn't because ye aren't meant to be with him, but because his destiny is with ye at Sgur Castle?"

Dumbstruck, Roisin gazed at Freyja as the revelation spun around her mind. It had never occurred to her before, although Freyja could certainly be right. But that wasn't why eerie shivers scuttled along her arms.

It was the uncanny certainty that her future did not lie on the isle of her foremothers.

Chapter Twenty-Six

AFTER ROISIN LEFT, the earl merely nodded at Douglas before giving Hugh a thoughtful look. Hugh ignored it. He had the damning certainty that if he opened his mouth, the words that came out would condemn him for all time.

Instead, he hauled Symon's body to his horse. He'd ensure the man had a proper burial and to hell with what the earl might think. Without a word, Douglas grabbed Symon's legs, and they placed him over his horse, as the rest of the men gathered the bodies of Darragh and his two men.

The journey back to the glen was interminable, and when they arrived, Hugh didn't ask for permission to halt. He simply did, before dismounting and kneeling by the river to scrub his hands clean.

Symon's blood stained the water but no matter how hard he rubbed his hands over sharp stones, it seemed there was no way for him to scour the evidence of his guilt from his skin.

Finally, he stood, and only his own blood streaked his knuckles and fingers. In silence he mounted Fhortan, aware that everyone's eyes bored into him. Let them. None of them knew how he had survived for more than a year, or what he'd done, and therefore they couldn't understand and were not fit to judge him.

None of them. Except maybe Douglas.

The fortified manor was set some way back from the banks of a substantial river, overlooking a local village and sizable forest. When they entered the forecourt through an arched gatehouse, the earl gave orders to his men, before addressing Douglas. "Take Hugh and get him cleaned up. I'll speak to him in my private chamber."

To hell with that. He would trust no one with Fhortan and grimly grasped his horse's reins and ensured Symon's body was taken into safekeeping before he led Fhortan to the stables where he gave him a thorough grooming. Douglas tended to his own horse, and the silence between them hurt his head.

When they were finished, he followed Douglas into the manor. Roisin was here, somewhere. Half of him hoped they wouldn't cross paths. But the other half, the half that, even now, clung onto the foolish wish they had a future together, desperately hoped they would.

Douglas took him into a small, well-appointed bedchamber and pulled out a fresh shirt from a chest. He tossed it on the bed before pouring water from a pitcher into a bowl on a small table and placing a lump of soap next to it. Any other time Hugh would have found the performance amusing, but he doubted he'd ever find anything Douglas did amusing again.

His brother stood back from his handiwork and folded his arms. They stared at each other in silence before Douglas took a deep breath. "'Twas a fair fight, Hugh. I'm grieved he was yer friend and that's the truth, but I wasn't to know that."

Hugh acknowledged the truth of what Douglas said, but it didn't mean he had to accept it. "All right."

"I chose this life. I craved the excitement when I was sixteen. Knowing I was living a double existence that no one else knew about gave me something I cannot explain. But I've given up a lot, Hugh. And that's why I didn't want ye getting involved. The earl will give ye the choice, and for Christ's sake, walk away. Wed yer pretty noblewoman and have the family I never will, and one day Balfour Castle will go to yer son."

"Lady Roisin is not my noblewoman." For God's sake, hadn't he made that plain enough the last time he'd spoken to her? It had all but destroyed him, but he had to make sure no one guessed what had happened between them. He wouldn't risk besmirching her reputation by giving anyone a reason to question his damn integrity. Or, rather, his lack of it.

"Whatever ye say." Douglas shrugged. "Just remember, this last year ye were under orders from the Earl of Argyll himself. There's nothing ye've done that reflects badly on the Campbells of Balfour Castle."

He didn't want to talk about it. But the words poured from him, nonetheless. "How can ye say that? I lied and schemed for a year, pretending to be someone I wasn't for a reason I didn't even know. I thought I was searching for ye, Douglas, not for the elusive kin of Torcall and Alan MacGregor."

"Maybe so. But ye were still following orders, and whatever ye believed, the outcome was the same. Clan Campbell is safer now because of what ye and I have done and ye should not forget that."

Through the red mist of his rage, a fragment of uncertainty glimmered. Douglas was right. He had killed Fergus to ensure Roisin remained safe, but if the earl hadn't sent him undercover in the first place, Fergus's plan might have succeeded. And while it was Roisin's life he cared about, he knew full well Fergus's thirst for vengeance wouldn't have stopped until everyone connected with William had been destroyed.

The truth unraveled in his head. The earl hadn't banished him to punish him for something Douglas had done. There was no tarnish attached to the Campbells of Balfour Castle that might transfer to a noble born bride.

He was a second son, and whatever his brother said, it was Douglas who would inherit Balfour Castle in due course. But while Hugh might not have a castle to offer Roisin, at least he could offer her an alliance unsullied by conflict with the earl, and with the coin he'd amassed from his time as a redshank, he could afford a small stronghold.

It wasn't enough for a noblewoman who could trace her lineage back nine hundred years through fearless Norse ancestors to a fierce Pict queen. But now he no longer had a cloud over his head that Douglas had committed an unforgivable act that would taint their lives forever, a thread of hope glinted in the dark.

Both he and Douglas were bound to the earl, through blood ties and alliances that went back centuries, and his brother was right. Hugh had been following orders for this last year and although his time in Darragh's camp had warped his outlook, if the earl welcomed him back into his circle, no one would ever dare question his loyalty.

In the end, that loyalty was all that mattered. And if it helped him to win Roisin, who meant more to him than any twisted allegiances the earl might command, then by God he'd play by whatever rules he needed to.

He just hoped Roisin would give him a second chance. And from the depths of his memory, he recalled the conversation they'd had where she had told him her destiny was to remain on the Isle of Eigg. He hadn't thought much of it at the time, but now it played on his mind, an elusive whisper of something just out of reach.

And then it struck him.

He had no grand castle or estates to oversee in the Highlands. Certainly, he'd always ensure Balfour was maintained and his father and his sisters were looked after. But the ultimate responsibility lay with Douglas, whatever his brother might think of the matter.

Which meant there was nothing to stop Hugh from making his home at Sgur Castle. It might even be the deciding factor for Roisin to accept his suit, knowing she need never leave her beloved isle again.

Douglas left the chamber and Hugh stripped and used the soap as though it could scrub away the last twelve months and all the dubious decisions he'd made. It wouldn't. Nothing could do that but at least he no longer stank of blood and sweat. He pulled on the fresh shirt and secured his plaid. Now all he needed to do was find Roisin and hope to

God he hadn't ruined his chances with her.

He pulled open the door and all but collided into Douglas. And remembered the earl had summoned him. *Goddamn it.* Frustration simmered through his veins as he fell into step beside his brother, and they went to a chamber that led off from the great hall.

"Enter," the earl said in response to his knock, and he went inside. The earl stood by a desk, his back to Hugh, looking out of a window where a well sat in the middle of a small courtyard.

"My lord," Hugh said, although the words all but stuck in his throat.

The earl turned. "Well done."

"Aye." He knew damn well protocol demanded he should thank the earl for his praise, but he wasn't feeling thankful, and he was sure the earl could see it.

The earl considered him in silence for a few moments, before he walked around his desk and stood in front of him. "Speak freely, Hugh. Ye've earned that, at least."

"I don't think ye want to hear what I have to say."

The earl gave a faint smile. "We've known each other for years. Ye have my word I won't hold anything ye say against ye."

Hugh shook his head, but in the end he couldn't hold his tongue. "Why did ye let me believe Douglas had betrayed ye and that was why I had to join yer network and find him? Why not tell me the truth?"

"It was the truth. I'd not heard from Douglas for weeks, not since he'd gone to Eire. And aye, maybe I gave the impression Douglas had displeased me, but it's a tactic we've always employed, one I continued from my father, to obscure the truth and keep him safe." The earl paused and gave Hugh a calculating look. "Do ye recall when Alan MacGregor tossed William overboard and I excluded ye from information I'd received?"

Aye, he remembered all right. It still stung that the earl had considered he might have been the one who had betrayed his own cousin,

William. He gave a brusque nod, and the earl continued.

"'Twas Douglas who discovered Alan hadn't died alongside his father. I kept ye out of my confidence, Hugh, in case I needed to send ye undercover, and the excuse that we were estranged could help save yer life if ye were recognized."

"I see." And he did understand the earl's reasoning, even if he didn't agree with it.

"'Twas only months after ye'd been in Eire that Douglas got in contact to let me know he'd tracked down the last splinter group of Torcall and Alan MacGregor's kin and was back in the Highlands."

"Douglas was in Fergus's camp?"

"No. He was searching for him and heard rumors of a plot against William. Then ye sent word that ye had rescued Lady Roisin, so I guessed what Fergus's plan had been. I knew she was safe while ye were there. 'Twas only days later Douglas discovered Fergus's camp. Except the bastard wasn't there."

"I believe he'd been searching for his mercenaries when they didn't deliver Lady Roisin." He barely managed to suppress a shudder at how narrowly she had escaped that fate. It was galling to acknowledge the earl's part in that by sending him undercover in the first place, but it didn't make it any less the truth.

"Aye. But when Douglas sent us the location of Fergus's camp, we were able to deduce where Darragh was heading, based on yer communications. Between ye and Douglas, we've managed to eradicate that particular threat against William, but I don't have to tell ye the threat extended far beyond William himself."

"I know." Only too well.

"Douglas is concerned I want to permanently add ye to the network. I don't."

Hugh grunted. The earl didn't take offense.

"I've other plans for ye." The earl eyed him. "Douglas is adamant he will not wed, but I'm not prepared to let the Campbells of Balfour

Castle fade into obscurity. Ye and Douglas may never be able to share the great service ye've done for our clan, but by God I'll ensure ye'll receive recompense."

The only recompense he wanted was Roisin. And the earl was the last person he'd share that wish with.

"Come with me." The earl abruptly strode out of the chamber and with a frustrated sigh, Hugh followed. All he wanted was to find Roisin and ask her—hell, beg her, if need be—to consent to be his wife. If she didn't want him, what else mattered?

As they left the manor, Hugh fell into step beside the earl as they marched across the forecourt and beyond the stables to a neglected orchard, where they came to a halt.

"With closer oversight, this manor and its landholdings would be most profitable."

Hugh didn't doubt it. If the earl was concerned, he should install a more proficient steward, but he didn't see that it had anything to do with *him*.

"A man," the earl added, oblivious to Hugh's growing irritation at being kept from finding Roisin, "needs a worthy estate if he intends to take a noblewoman for a wife."

His irritation vanished, and he shot the earl a guarded look. Had he not been able to hide his feelings for Roisin from anyone?

The earl exhaled an impatient sigh. "God's teeth, Hugh. Ye're as hard to please as Douglas. I'm bequeathing the manor and all its chattels to ye. To be sure, ye'll have Balfour if Douglas continues to be stubborn, but this estate will be yers notwithstanding. 'Tis a small recompense for what we stood to lose if Fergus hadn't been stopped. And now ye have something of worth to tempt a lady's hand."

Hugh cast his bemused gaze over the orchard, then slowly turned and took in the three empty buildings with the stables beyond them. Aye, this was certainly something that could tempt a lady for the potential to expand was considerable, but Roisin wasn't just any lady.

And he hadn't changed his mind about moving to Eigg, if that was what she wanted.

The earl waited for his reply and there was only one thing to be said. "Thank ye, my lord."

It was ironic. Had the earl bequeathed him the manor a year ago, Hugh would have believed it solved all his problems, for he would have something of worth to offer Roisin. But now, it was simply a fine estate, and he knew it wouldn't sway Roisin's mind one way or another.

As the earl strolled back to the manor, Hugh took a deep breath. It was time to face Roisin.

Chapter Twenty-Seven

A FTER FREYJA LEFT her, with instructions she should rest until supper, Roisin went to the window, with Ecne in her arms. It was foolish beyond measure that she was hoping to see Hugh in the courtyard, since for all she knew he could be anywhere in the manor or beyond, and yet she couldn't help herself.

The more her sister's words echoed around her head, the more she doubted that Hugh had meant his final comment to her in the way she had imagined.

He'd always been so mindful of her reputation. Was it possible he had been so formal and dismissive because he didn't want any of the earl's men, let alone Freyja and Alasdair, to suspect how close they had become?

Ecne stiffened in her arms and gave an excited little yap and there, walking across the courtyard to the stables, was Hugh with the earl. Her heart skittered in her chest, and she put Ecne on the floor and hastily pulled on her boots and found her shawl before she took her place by the window again.

She didn't want to interrupt whatever Hugh and the earl were doing, but when she saw them return, she would hasten downstairs and pretend to accidentally cross Hugh's path. Surely it wouldn't be too difficult to request a few private moments with him? And if he brushed her off again, at least she'd know the truth.

It seemed they were gone for an interminable length of time. Maybe they'd decided to go riding? But surely they'd need to cross the forecourt first, and leave through the gatehouse? She nibbled her lower lip and pressed her cheek against the glass, hoping for a better view of the stables.

Finally, she saw the earl striding back. But Hugh wasn't with him, and panic churned through her. Where was he?

She hurried to the door, Ecne at her heels, and made her way downstairs. The earl entered through the double doors and strode across the great hall and as soon as he was out of sight, she ran out of the manor. It was most unseemly, but she didn't care. If Hugh was preparing to leave, she had only moments before he would ride out of her life forever.

Unheeding of the few servants who were around and gave her curious glances, she rushed to the stables and looked inside. Deagh Fhortan was still there, and she spun about, to catch sight of Ecne trotting happily away from the manor, his tail wagging, to where Hugh had come to a halt, his gaze fixed on her.

There was no sign of the blood that had drenched him the last time she'd seen him. A terrible vision that would haunt her for the rest of her life, even if it hadn't been his blood. But even worse than the blood had been the dead expression in his eyes, and it took more nerve than she'd anticipated to meet his gaze.

Relief flooded through her. Although weariness filled them, his eyes no longer sent chills skating through her, and their incomparable blue reminded her of the first time she had ever seen him as he'd strode across the forecourt of Sgur Castle.

"Lady Roisin." He bowed his head, and her relief turned to alarm at how formal he was being. "How are ye?"

She took a few steps closer as Ecne pawed Hugh's boot, and he crouched to give her wee lad a scratch behind his ears. Was she wrong? Or was Hugh still trying to protect her reputation behind a masquerade?

A furtive glance over her shoulder reassured her that they were alone, and so she took another step closer. He straightened, and although he didn't move towards her, he gave a faint smile that turned her insides to warm honey.

"I'm perfectly fine," she said. "Thanks to ye."

An awkward silence fell, and she dropped her gaze to Ecne, who suffered from no such frustrating constraints, as he flopped on the ground, his muzzle resting on Hugh's boot.

This was foolish. There was so much she wanted to say to Hugh, so much she dearly wished to hear him say to her. But she didn't even know how to begin.

"I'm sorry I couldn't tell ye the truth." The words burst from him, and he exhaled a harsh sigh. "I know I can trust ye, Roisin and whatever happens, I want ye to know, although I must ask ye to never breathe a word of what I'm about to share with ye."

"Ye have my word." And because Hugh couldn't move with Ecne using his foot as a pillow, she took yet another step nearer to him, until they were almost close enough to kiss.

"'Tis likely ye've already guessed," he said in a voice so low she could scarcely hear him. "I was spying for the earl this past year, and that's why no one knew where I was."

She hadn't guessed, and she tried not to look shocked by his revelation, since he clearly thought she should already have drawn that conclusion. But if she pretended, wasn't she simply making things more complicated between them?

And so she shook her head. It felt better than pretending she had known something she hadn't. "I had no idea," she confessed. "Even at the end, when ye suddenly tossed his name at me."

Although she had wondered what the earl meant, when he'd told her Hugh was always in his favor, the truth had never occurred to her.

"It's the reason why I couldn't send yer letter to Lady Isolde. I was using the earl's network to communicate with him, and there are safeguards if anything's intercepted. But I couldn't send yer letter through his channels, and I couldn't risk sending it by normal means."

Ah, her letter. She had all but forgotten about it with everything that had happened since, and now it seemed such a small thing to have been so upset over.

"I understand, Hugh. Please don't concern yerself with it for another moment."

"But ye were right. I shouldn't have let ye think I'd sent it. I thought I was doing the right thing, but I see now I misjudged ye. Ye're not a fragile flower, Roisin, and maybe ye never were."

Unaccountably touched by his insight of her character, she smiled. "Well, thank ye. I'm gratified ye think so."

He released a ragged sigh and before she could think better of it, she reached out. He met her halfway and threaded his fingers through hers, a simple touch that warmed her to the core of her being.

"When I took ye to the camp, I thought I'd need to protect ye there at every moment. But ye forged yer own way with the women, and I cannot tell ye how deeply I admired that. I'm glad they left before the earl found them. But by God, I wish Symon had gone with them. He only stayed because of me."

Sorrow twisted deep in her heart. "Ye cannot blame yerself for that, Hugh. It wasn't yer fault. Symon was a good man, from the little I knew of him, and he made his own choices. If ye don't accept that, it will drive ye mad."

"When I was in Eire, 'twas only the thought of ye that kept me from going mad." He sounded hoarse, and her heart squeezed at the pain in his voice. "But the longer I remained in that twilight existence, the less likely it became that I could ever offer ye the life ye deserved."

"But ye're not in that twilight existence anymore," she whispered. "I never stopped hoping ye'd come back to Eigg, ye know. Even when ye disappeared, I couldn't let the dreams of what might have been go completely."

His fingers tightened around hers, and his intense gaze seared her soul. "I love ye, Roisin. I always have. But the way I felt about ye on Eigg is nothing to how I love ye now. Hell itself cannot be worse than the thought of a future without ye by my side."

For so long she had dreamed of Hugh telling her how he loved her and how wonderful it would be. But now that he had, her daydreams turned to dust because even her fertile imagination had failed when compared to reality.

"Ye need not think of hell again." Her voice was husky, and her heart was overflowing with the knowledge she and Hugh, despite everything, had always meant to be together. "For I will never leave ye, Hugh. How could I? I've loved ye since the day I met ye."

"I never had much to my name, but I've more to offer ye now, as befits yer noble status. But I know how ye are tied to Eigg. Ye are the third sister, and ye cannot leave. But if ye'll have me, I'll be honored to remain by yer side in Sgur Castle, when the time comes for ye to fulfill yer destiny."

Awe shivered through her. Neither William nor Alasdair had offered her sisters this choice. But then, they both had grand estates in the Highlands, whereas Hugh was a second son, and Douglas would inherit Balfour Castle. But it was still a noble gesture, to be willing to leave the heartland of his clan for her, for it was not as though Hugh were destitute. He had connections and she knew that, along with her dowry, they could acquire a small stronghold of their own.

"My destiny," she said softly, and he pressed his lips against her fingers in a gentle kiss, his gaze never leaving hers. "Hugh, my destiny lies with ye."

"And I will never leave ye." There was a fierce note in his voice that melted her heart. "Ye told me once yer Pict queen ancestor gave an edict that the daughters of Sgur cannot ever leave their isle. I'll never ask ye to break the promise that yer foremothers have honored for nine hundred years."

An ethereal rustle brushed through her senses, and she shivered as a thread of discordance hovered at the edges of her mind. She had known of the edict all her life but not for the first time she questioned its true meaning.

She gazed into Hugh's eyes, and the words came as though she had always meant to share them with him. "The bloodline of the Isle must prevail beyond quietus."

He cocked his head. "What?"

"That is the edict, Hugh. The Deep Knowing that has been passed down from mother to daughter from our Pict queen ancestor. We were taught that it means we can never leave our beloved isle, or the bloodline of the MacDonalds of Sgur will die. But that isn't what it says, is it?"

"I know nothing of mystical prophecies, Roisin, but it seems yer ancient queen wanted yer bloodline to survive death. I don't know how such a thing is possible whether ye stay on Eigg or leave."

"I don't know either."

His smile was gentle, and he tenderly traced a finger along her face. "Does it matter?"

It shouldn't matter, when Hugh had pledged to remain by her side wherever she chose to live, and yet the feeling that they had misunderstood the Deep Knowing would not abate. "Do ye remember when I told ye there had never been three daughters of Sgur in the same generation before?"

"I remember everything ye've said to me."

She smiled at that, for how could she not? But then she took a deep breath because what she had to say was of a serious nature. "Well, it's always haunted me. It was a warning that the true meaning of the Deep Knowing would soon reveal itself. I'm not sure that it's simply about my sisters and me, Hugh. I just cannot shift the certainty that it means more than we have always believed."

"What are ye saying, mo ghràdh? That ye do not wish to live at Sgur Castle?"

"It's not that I don't want to. It's that I believe I am not meant to."

"Roisin, we shall live wherever ye wish. I can oversee my estates with the assistance of a good steward, so don't let that concern ye."

That caught her attention. "Has yer brother Douglas made ye custodian of Balfour Castle?"

He smiled and shook his head, almost in wonder. "I forgot, ye do not know. And yet ye were willing to take me on, regardless. The earl has bequeathed me this manor for my services to Clan Campbell. But aye, in a sense I'm also custodian of Balfour, unless Douglas changes his mind and takes up his responsibilities."

She tore her besotted gaze from Hugh and glanced around. 'Twas a fine estate, indeed, and the manor itself was, she had to admit, in a far better state of repair than Sgur itself. "Are ye happy with it?"

He pulled her close, wrapping his arms around her. "I'm happy because it gives me something to offer ye. The real question is are *ye* happy with it, Roisin? Would it please ye to be the lady of this manor?"

She couldn't resist teasing him. "Is that yer way of asking me to marry ye, Hugh?"

He groaned and pressed his forehead against hers. "I haven't asked ye, have I?"

"Indeed, ye have not. It's quite an oversight, I must confess."

"I'll make it up to ye, and no mistake."

"And I will ensure ye do."

His big body shook with silent laughter that ended with a soul-deep sigh. "Lady Roisin of Sgur Castle, keeper of the mystical Deep Knowing from yer fierce Pict queen ancestor, I love ye more than life itself. Will ye honor me with yer hand and make me the luckiest man in Christendom by consenting to be my bride?"

Sometimes, on Eigg, especially after Freyja had wed Alasdair, she had imagined how it might be, should Hugh ever propose to her. His simple, heartfelt words surpassed anything her mind had conjured, and she tenderly cradled his beloved face.

There were so many things she wanted to say to him. And she had all the time in the world to say them. But for now, only one thing needed to be said. "I will."

Epilogue

The bloodline of the Isle must prevail beyond quietus.

Ten Years Later, Winter 1577, Balfour Castle

'TWAS THE PERFECT winter afternoon, bright and fresh with the crisp promise of snow in the air, and Roisin breathed in deeply as she and her sisters strolled in the courtyard while the bairns screamed in delight and the dogs barked with excitement as they chased each other.

She smiled as she watched her six-year-old son, Symon, haul his two-year-old sister Innis to her feet before, hand in hand, they raced after their cousins. As if wanting to join in, her babe kicked strongly, and she stroked her swollen belly.

Not long now, my wee yin.

Just another two months until she and Hugh welcomed their longed-for third bairn. Although they spent most of the year at their manor, they often visited Balfour Castle to see Hugh's father, and each of their bairns had been born in his childhood home. And, as much as she loved the home they'd made together in the manor, she was always happy at Balfour, not least because the castle was closer to both Isolde and Freyja.

"Are ye all right?" Freyja, always the healer, sounded concerned. "Do ye wish to return inside and sit with Amma?"

"I'm fine," she assured her sister. Amma had arrived at Balfour a week ago for her usual winter stay with them when they all gathered together to welcome the new year, and she and Hugh's father, who was now quite frail, enjoyed each other's company.

"Ye're doing better than me then." Isolde pressed her hand to the small of her back and sighed. "This rascal is giving me more grief than all of my first three put together. Thank God I told William from the start that four bairns was my limit."

"Maybe *ye* should go inside, then." Freyja gave her an anxious glance, and Isolde laughed.

"'Tis nothing, Frey. Without fail, this babe wakes when I want to sleep so I'm constantly exhausted, and I never had that with any of the others. But 'tis scarcely a cause for alarm. Even if I do have another three months of it."

"I think I should examine ye again, just to make sure all is well."

Isolde sighed. "I'm quite certain I am not expecting twins."

"Aye, well, that notion never crossed my mind either when I was pregnant, did it?" Freyja looked across the courtyard, where her boisterous twins, Ranulph and Archie, were goading each other to climb up the wall of the castle. "Oh, great Eir preserve us."

Freyja marched across the court to her offspring, and Isolde took Roisin's arm. "Do ye think Frey is quite well? She's been quite agitated ever since she arrived a couple of days ago."

Roisin considered her sister, as she wagged her finger at her sons and gesticulated at the castle wall. "Ye do not suppose she might be with child?"

Isolde sniffed. "Are ye brave enough to ask her?"

"I am not," Roisin confirmed. After the shock of the twins' birth eight years ago, Freyja had been adamant her family was complete. "Doubtless she'll tell us if she is."

Little Helga collided into Isolde's legs, and with an indulgent smile, she scooped her three-year-old daughter into her arms. "What is it, my wee bairn?"

"Ingrid won't let me play." Indignation quivered through her voice as she sent a tear-filled look at her seven-year-old sister. "She says I'm a babe."

Roisin retied her niece's hood and dropped a kiss on the tip of her nose. "Why don't ye play with Innis, then?"

Helga gave her a solemn look. "Innis is a wee babe, Auntie."

Roisin and Isolde exchanged glances over Helga's head, both trying not to laugh, before Isolde placed Helga back on the ground. "Supper won't be long. Go tell Ingrid to behave herself and as for ye, be kind to wee Innis."

Helga gave a loud, long-suffering sigh before she trotted off and Freyja returned. "Those lads have no sense of danger. I swear to God they must lay awake at night thinking up new ways to terrify me. Why can't they be more like yer Will, Izzie?"

Isolde scoffed. "Will has his moments, let me tell ye." She sent an affectionate glance at her eldest, where he was on the ground with the dogs sprawled on top of him and a bittersweet pang squeezed Roisin's heart. Sweet Eene, like his littermates, had lived to a great age but even now, six years after he had joined his brothers, she still missed him. Although she had to admit she dearly loved the hound littermates she and her sisters had been given four years ago by their paternal grandfather's greatest friend and steward, Miles. Not least because the pups were descendants of their beloved Afi's favorite dog, Ban.

"'Tis a pity Laoise could not join us this year." Freyja sighed, before she sent a fond smile in the direction of her wayward sons. "Her lasses always bring out the best in Ranulph and Archie."

"How is married life treating her?" Roisin well remembered Laoise's late brute of a first husband, back on the Isle of Eigg. But five years ago, after the death of her mother, she'd accepted Freyja's invitation to move to Dunochty Castle where she'd continued her education in the medical arts under the keen eye of both Freyja and her dear friend, Jane. And six months ago, Laoise had wed Alasdair's steward.

"Very well, indeed. Did I tell ye her sisters who came over from Eigg for the wedding decided to stay in the Highlands? Laoise had been teaching them all those years on the Isle, and their skills are most admirable."

"That is good for her. Who needs that fancy royal college in London when they can train under ye and Jane?" Isolde looked at Roisin. "And Grear is arriving tomorrow? It's been so long since I last saw her."

"Aye, she's accompanying Mary and Agnes. They should be here before supper tomorrow."

She was looking forward to seeing Hugh's sisters again, who were both wed with wee ones of their own. But most of all she couldn't wait to see Grear, who had married a trusted confidant of Agnes's husband four years ago. She and Grear would always share a special bond, not only because they'd known each other since they were bairns, but because of those weeks they'd shared in the camp.

With a clatter of hooves, Hugh and the rest of the men who had gone hunting entered the courtyard and as the bairns and dogs went wild—except for Will, who at ten and a half considered himself far too old for such displays—she and her sisters strolled over to them. Servants hurried over to take the catch to the kitchen, and Hugh enveloped Roisin in a hug that warmed her to the tips of her toes.

Even after ten years, he had the power to steal the breath from her lungs with merely a glance. As they parted, she saw both William and Alasdair with their arms around their wives' shoulders, and happiness overflowed her heart. How fortunate they had all been to find each other, and even though sometimes the strangeness of how all three of them had ended up leaving Eigg with their soulmates gnawed in the back of her mind, she tried not to worry about it.

Even Amma had confessed, years ago, that she no longer understood what the Deep Knowing had truly meant. Roisin doubted that they ever would. And although she and her sisters all agreed they would tell their daughters about it, so far she and Isolde hadn't. It seemed vaguely specious, when the three of them had left the Isle that their foremother had been so determined her descendants should remain on forever.

"Look who I found in the forest, on his way to Balfour." Hugh stepped back, and Douglas bowed his head at her in greeting.

"Douglas, how wonderful to see ye." She went to him, and they exchanged a formal hug. For years after she and Hugh had wed, Douglas had kept his distance, and Hugh had struggled with the guilt he harbored for Symon's death. But after the birth of their own sweet son, the brothers had slowly forged a bridge between each other and now Douglas turned up at odd times during the year, either here or at the manor.

She was always mindful that Balfour would one day go to Douglas, however many times he assured her he did not want it. He had his own castle, although they had never been invited there, but nevertheless, she always kept the hope alive that one day Douglas would throw off the dark shackles of his past and find a woman worthy of him.

They all went inside for supper, and the great hall filled with the happy sound of kin and friends who had known each other forever. Patric, who had left Eigg with Isolde when she had wed William, regaled them with tales of how committed the young village lasses he and Isolde trained in defensive tactics were in honing their skills.

It was something her sister had become passionate about after she had been attacked by Alan MacGregor and so she ensured they could protect themselves against an unwary assault.

Clyde, who had accompanied Freyja from Eigg to Dunochty, was deep in conversation with Amma. He had surprised everyone two years ago by marrying a widow, a gracious gentlewoman, and Clyde was beside himself that, at his advanced time of life, he was to be a father next summer.

After supper they retired to the solar, where a fire burned brightly in the hearth, and many chairs were scattered around. Roisin settled beside the fire and the bairns sat at her feet, even Will, waiting for her to tell them a fine tale of the mystical fae, perhaps.

She never tired of sharing those fantastical stories, and just as she had wished when she'd entertained the bairns in the camp all those years ago, she had managed to persuade the villagers both here, and at the manor, to allow their bairns to spend a couple of hours a week learning their letters under her guidance.

"Which one do ye want?" She cuddled Innis on her lap as Helga snuggled with Amma, her namesake.

"Our fierce Pict queen ancestor," shouted Archie. The others cheered in agreement. She laughed and glanced at her sisters who were both shaking their heads.

"Do they never get tired of that one?" Freyja ruffled Archie's hair.

"It doesn't matter how many times I share that story with them, they always say no one tells it as well as Auntie Roisin." Isolde rolled her eyes and sent her sister a smile.

Roisin looked at Hugh, who sat beside her, gently stroking Innis's hair. "I'm always happy to hear that tale," he said. "I might not understand what she meant by her edict, but at least I know for sure she wasn't cursing yer bloodline."

Even the rest of the men, Clyde and Patric and the faithful warriors who had served Amma for so many years, fell silent, although they had all heard the tale many times.

And so she began the familiar story, the one both Amma and her own mother, Ingrid, had shared with her and her sisters so many times when they'd been young. How the fierce Pict queen and her women warriors had slaughtered the monks who wanted to take her Isle's history from her, and how she had ended up following the mystical lights on the sea to a future they could only speculate upon.

And as always, she finished the tale the same way she had since the first time Hugh had listened to it, that day in the camp.

"But as long as we remember them and tell their tales, no one truly dies."

Innis had fallen asleep, and Hugh tenderly lifted her in his arms to take her to bed. He often joined her when she tucked them into their beds and his open devotion to their bairns melted her heart every time. So many men appeared to want little to do with their offspring, and yet both William and Alasdair were as involved as Hugh.

She and her sisters had been lucky indeed in their husbands.

Later, when all the bairns were safely asleep, the servants brought in hot drinks, and they had scarcely settled around the fire when the door burst open and Miles stood there, frost glittering on his thick hat and surcoat. A servant hovered behind, clearly appalled that Miles had stormed into the castle without proper introduction, but Hugh assured him all was well as Freyja ran to Miles and took his hands.

"Great Eir, 'tis good indeed to see ye, Miles, but at this hour? We were not expecting ye for another few days. Is all well with ye?"

Miles pressed Freyja's hands against his chest, but there was a wild gleam in his eyes as he cast his gaze around them all.

"No." His voice was hoarse, and along with Isolde and Amma, Roisin hastened over to him. What on earth had happened?

Hugh thrust a tankard of warm mead in his hands, and Miles gulped it down, but his hands were shaking and alarm streaked through Roisin as she exchanged glances with her sisters.

"Come, sit by the fire." Alasdair guided Miles across the solar before he and William tugged the surcoat from his shoulders. "What's wrong?"

Miles thrust his tankard at Hugh, who refilled it, and Miles ripped his gloves off before wrapping his hands around the steaming mug. "Sgur Castle has fallen and the village razed."

Horrified, Roisin stared at him as she and her sisters clutched each other's hands. But before they could say anything, Amma rose from her chair.

"What?" Her voice was low, but it seemed to echo around the solar. "Miles, explain."

He drew in a shuddering breath. "We saw the fires spreading across the isle from Kilvenie, but by the time we arrived, there was nothing we could do."

"Who the hell would attack Eigg in such a manner?" Hugh sounded shaken.

Miles shook his head. "We can only surmise 'twas the MacLeods and their cursed feud."

"Christ, Miles." Alasdair gripped his shoulder. "We'll ensure supplies are taken to Eigg first thing in the morning for the villagers."

"Aye," William said. "And we'll rebuild the village, whatever it takes. What of the castle? Was it badly damaged?"

A fearsome frown slashed Miles's brow. "Do ye not understand? The villagers have gone. There is no one left."

Silence throbbed in the air, and Roisin pressed her fingers to her lips as the full horror of what Miles was telling them sank into her soul.

"God help us." Amma stood before Miles, her fingers clasped over her heart. "No, surely that cannot be."

"Amma." Isolde wrapped her arm around her shoulders. "Sit down. We will deal with this. Do not distress yerself."

Amma pulled free and swept her glance over the three of them, and an eerie shiver chased over Roisin's arms. "My bairns," she said but although sorrow filled each word, her voice was strong. "We have been so wrong."

"What do ye mean?" Roisin's voice was hushed, but somewhere in the back of her mind, an inkling of understanding glimmered. If only she could bring it further into the light.

And then Amma spoke. *"The bloodline of the Isle must prevail beyond quietus."*

Roisin gasped softly and beside her Isolde hitched in a sharp breath as Freyja pressed her hand against her chest. The Deep Knowing was not something that could ever be said out loud. It was whispered between mother and daughter, a secret edict from the Pict queen that had been held sacred for over nine hundred years.

To be sure, she had shared it with Hugh. And she knew both Isolde and Freyja had confided in their husbands, too. Yet Amma had just stated the revered Deep Knowing in front of a multitude of people and no matter how dearly they were loved, they were not supposed to know of the Pict queen's final decree to her daughter.

Amma held out her arms and Isolde and Freyja took her hands, and Roisin held her sisters' hands so the four of them stood in a circle in the middle of the solar. "The Deep Knowing was never about the MacDonalds of Sgur remaining on the Isle of Eigg." Amma's voice was hushed. "'Twas about ensuring the bloodline of the isle herself would not perish."

"Are ye saying the Deep Knowing was telling us we *should* leave the Isle?" Isolde sounded unnerved by the possibility.

"That cannot be." Freyja glanced at her sisters, skepticism clear in her eyes. "How could anyone, even our formidable Pict queen foremother, know this terrible devastation would unfold?"

"Do ye not recall, Frey, the tales that she was a druid from ancient times?" Isolde gave a shiver. "Maybe she did see something, after all."

"The power of three," whispered Roisin, and her sisters and Amma gazed at her, uncomprehending. "Don't ye see? We were the first generation in nine hundred years when three daughters of Sgur were born. 'Twas a portent that the Deep Knowing was coming to pass."

"I think yer imagination might be running away with ye." But Freyja didn't sound so sure of herself now, and ancient comprehension dawned in Amma's eyes.

"After my beloved Ingrid and yer dear father died," Amma said, "I was, as ye know, plagued with the conviction that Isolde should wed William Campbell. I knew it meant ye would leave the Isle, and yet it did not feel wrong. After all, two daughters of the isle would remain at Sgur."

"But then Alasdair arrived." Freyja's smile was sad as she looked at her husband.

"Aye. And again, I knew ye had to leave, even though it went against everything I'd believed in my entire life. Because, after all, Roisin was still there to fulfill the Deep Knowing."

"But ye never did see Hugh in my future." She had always wondered about that, but when she'd asked her, nearly ten years ago now, her grandmother had no answer for her.

But now she gave a slow nod. "I did not," she confirmed. "And over the years I have pondered this. And I've come to believe it's because ye and Hugh were not on Eigg when ye needed to decide which path yer fate lay."

She caught Hugh's unwavering gaze, and she understood. Both Isolde and Freyja had wed on the Small Isles and although they loved their husbands, at the time their marriages had been something they could not avoid. But she and Hugh had been bound by no such constraints. Their future had hung in the balance until the very end, and even then, it hadn't been certain whether they would return to Eigg or remain in the Highlands.

A shiver inched through her as she realized her uneasy suspicions had always been right. For while Hugh had offered to return to her beloved isle, it was she who had decided they belonged in Argyll.

"'Tis terrible." Freyja's lip trembled, and Amma nodded.

"Aye. It is. But if I'd had only one granddaughter, I would never have sought that alliance for Isolde, no matter how many dreams or visions plagued me. And many in this solar would have perished alongside us today."

Shock slithered through Roisin and as one she, Isolde, and Freyja slowly looked around the solar. It was true. Patric and Clyde would never have left Eigg, and nor would Amma's loyal warriors.

Grear would have perished, too.

"Blessed Eir." Freyja's voice was hushed. "Laoise and her lasses. And her sisters and their bairns, too."

"And none of our bairns would be here." Roisin's voice shook, and Hugh came to her and wrapped his arms around her. As if in response her babe kicked, reminding her of the bairns who had not yet been born, but whose heritage also came from Eigg.

"I always thought the Deep Knowing meant our bloodline could not leave the Isle." Isolde released a deep sigh, and William took her in his arms.

"I thought our bloodline would die if we left the Isle." Freyja groaned and pressed her hand against her stomach. Alasdair was instantly by her side, and she rested her head against his shoulder. "What a foolish notion. I cannot fathom how I kept believing it, even after all the babes were born."

Roisin had never believed in the Deep Knowing the way Amma and her sisters had but now was hardly the time to share that. It wasn't as if it could change anything.

"*The bloodline of the Isle must prevail beyond quietus.*" Amma quietly repeated the Deep Knowing, and it took on an entirely different meaning from the one they had always been taught. "If the daughters of the Isle hadn't left, the bloodline of Eigg herself would have perished. But her bloodline will prevail because the three of ye forged a new life here and took many from the Isle with ye."

"And our Pict queen foremother will never be forgotten for as long as we share her story." Roisin threaded her fingers through Hugh's. "And one day her bloodline will return to her Isle."

Only the comforting crackle of the fire broke the silence that fell, and Roisin leaned back against Hugh, suddenly feeling exhausted.

And then Freyja cleared her throat. "Well, I wasn't going to say anything yet, but I think maybe I should. It appears there will be yet another bairn born next year who will carry the bloodline of the isle in their veins."

Roisin's exhaustion vanished and she and Isolde hugged their sister.

"We suspected as much," Isolde said.

"'Tis happy news to take into the new year," Roisin added.

"As long as this babe does not turn out to be another set of twins." Freyja gave a weak smile, and Alasdair gently lifted her chin and kissed her. She leaned against him and eyed her sisters. "I confess it would be nice to have a daughter to share the Deep Knowing with. Even though," she hesitated. "It's not a secret anymore. It didn't even mean what we thought it did."

"We must always remember the Deep Knowing." Roisin took Freyja's hand. "But now we can share it with our sons as well as our daughters. It is their legacy, too."

"Even if we did misunderstand her edict for nine hundred years." Isolde shook her head. "But Roisin's right. We can't let her memory fade into the past."

After a few moments Roisin released her sister's hand and turned to Hugh. He smiled at her, his blue eyes as mesmeric as the day they'd first met and pulled her close.

"Are ye all right, mo ghràdh?" His voice was low, for her ears only, and warmth flooded through her. She could not imagine her life without this man by her side and thanked God and the ancient immortals every day that Amma had sent her to Argyll so unexpectedly.

"I am," she whispered. "And I always will be, with ye in my life."

The End

Author's Note

The Isle of Eigg

There is a legend that, in the seventh century, a pagan Pict Queen and her women warriors massacred monks who attempted to establish a monastery on her isle. It is perhaps the reason that historically the Isle of Eigg was known as Eilean Nam Ban Mora—the island of the big women.

I love myths and legends, and the story of this ancient Pict queen warrior fascinated me. And so, I imagined that this queen also possessed ancient Druid blood that gave her a glimpse of a catastrophe that would befall her beloved isle and its people far in her future and wove this thread into my series *Daughters of the Isle*.

After a long-running feud, in the winter of 1577, Clan MacLeod massacred the MacDonalds of Eigg leaving, it is said, only one family alive to continue the bloodline.

Acknowledgements

For my husband Mark and our family, thank you for your support during all the ups and downs of this crazy ride and for keeping me grounded! I'm also sending big hugs to my author buddies: Amanda Ashby, Sally Rigby, Cathleen Ross and Mel Teshco. It wouldn't be half as much fun without you all.

Thanks also to Kathryn Le Veque and the fabulous Dragonblade team for making this journey so enjoyable, to my wonderful editor, Stephanie Marrie for your invaluable insights, and Kim Killion for the gorgeous cover!

And finally, a special shout out to Natalie Sowa for your patience with the glitches in the matrix over the last few months. We got there in the end 😊

About the Author

Christina grew up in England and spent her childhood visiting ruined castles and Roman remains and daydreaming about Medieval princesses and gallant knights. When she wasn't lost in the past, she was searching for magical worlds in the backs of wardrobes and watching old Hammer Horrors from the safety of behind the sofa. She now lives in sunny Western Australia with her high school sweetheart and their two cats who are convinced the universe revolves around their needs. They are not wrong.

Christina's Website:
christinaphillips.com

Christina's Newsletter:
christinaphillips.com/christinas-newsletter

Christina's Facebook:
facebook.com/christinaphillips.author

Bluesky:
bsky.app/profile/christinaphillips.bsky.social

Printed in Dunstable, United Kingdom